DEATH
TAKES
NO
BRIBES

AN ENDURANCE MYSTERY

SUSAN VAN KIRK

PRAIRIE LIGHTS PUBLISHING

ISBN (paperback): 978-0-692-85028-2
ISBN (e-book): 978-0-692-85029-9

Cover image by Phillips Covers
Author Photo by Lori A. Seals Photography & Boutique
Formatting by Cypress Editing
Editing by Comma Sense Editing, LLC

DEATH TAKES NO BRIBES
Susan Van Kirk—1st ed.

*This novel is for all the loyal readers who have made
The Endurance Mysteries possible.*

Prologue

DEL NOVAK CHUCKLED to himself as he listened to "Dancin' Away with My Heart," a country song playing softly on his radio while he dusted the outer office suite at Endurance High School. Humming along with the tune, he thought of his lady friend, Lettie Kimball. She had danced away with his heart all right ever since he met her on a kitchen renovation job at the home of her sister-in-law, Grace. He ambled into the small supply room and emptied the wastebaskets and recycling bin, all the while smiling to himself as he remembered Lettie winning all his money, as well as their friends' stakes, at their poker game last week. And man, could she cook! When he moved to Endurance and met this firebrand of a woman, he struck a pot of gold. Neither of them were spring chickens, but they seemed to scrape along just fine.

Walking back into the outer office, he wiped the wooden counter with antiseptic spray. He liked working by himself on the weekends with nothing but his country tunes for company. Sunday afternoon and everyone was gone, even Marilyn Atkins, the social studies teacher. She had been grading papers in her room down on the lower level when he first got here, but she'd left at least two hours ago, trudging down the snowy walk to the school parking lot, bundled up against the cold wind, carrying home still more papers. He had watched her through one of the first-floor windows, shaking his head. She sure was a worker.

By the time he reached the end of the oak counter, he found a note with his name on it. The secretary, Ann Cummings, wrote that she had left a piece of birthday cake with buttercream frosting for him in the teacher's lounge refrigerator. My, my. He would eat it on his break, along with the thick turkey sandwich Lettie had packed for him. Picking up the wastebasket from behind the main desk, he shuffled over to dump it into the cart he moved from room to room.

People here in Endurance are kind to me, he thought. Everybody smiles and speaks to me, whether they know me or not. Even now, in the winter, the snowy Endurance streets are plowed, and people check on their neighbors.

His girlfriend, Lettie, wasn't real pleased about his decision to take this moonlighting job at the high school. But it brought in a little more money so he could stash some away in case they needed it down the road. Listen to me, he thought. Making assumptions. He put his arthritic fingers on the secretary's chair and leaned over to replace some pencils in a holder on her desk. The music switched to another song, one he didn't know, so he sat down to look at the *Endurance Register*, which lay on the desk next to Ann's attendance pads.

Ten minutes went by and he rose again, carefully pushed in the chair, dusted the other end of the countertop, and straightened the stack of papers into a neat pile. Glancing at the top of the paper pile, he realized the forms were blank copies of teacher evaluations. Now why were those still lying around? Mr. Hardy, the principal, had fussed about the issue all fall with the teachers, and even now this dispute wasn't settled. Del shook his head. Sure was a lot for teachers to do these days. He looked up as a strong gust of wind blew snow against the office windows. Hmm. Must be another storm coming tonight. The weeks in January had been brutal; now it was the start of

February, and he sensed no sign of nature slowing down with the white stuff.

Next, he went into the assistant principal's office, where he wiped down the cold, metal windowsills and the desktop. Glancing out a front window, he saw a dark sedan in the parking lot, its engine running. It was there earlier, too, when he came into work. How long had that car been sitting there? He didn't recognize the car or its owner, and he could barely make out the first three letters in the license plate. He wrote them down on a piece of scratch paper on Alex Reid's desk. It seemed odd to see an unfamiliar car sitting in the front parking lot.

Another gust of wind slapped against the windows, causing the old man to look up and feel the uneasiness a huge winter storm brings to a small town. Sometimes it was a little creepy being alone in the whole building. He swore he could feel eyes watching him; after all, the high school had multiple doors, and it would be easy for someone to enter with a key or pick a lock. At times, he swore he heard footsteps but didn't see anyone coming down the hallway.

In the basement were dark nooks and crannies left over from the original structure in the early 1900s. When he was working on the basement floor, he was always looking over his shoulder, and occasionally he either broke into a sweat at some unusual sound or felt the hairs on the back of his neck stand up.

The elevator was another story. Talk about spooky! On any of the three floors, Del would be cleaning the hallway and suddenly he'd hear a whirring sound. No one else was in the building, but the elevator was stealthily moving between floors. Then the sound would stop, as if ghostly fingers were dancing across the control buttons. Sometimes it paused on the floor he was cleaning, and the whirring sound would cause Del to hold his breath. A bell would ring, signaling a stop on his floor. A pause would follow and Del would stare at the door, waiting to see what happened. The elevator doors quietly slid open, but no one was there. The first time this occurred, Del almost fainted. Even now, the sound of those doors in the silent hallway gave him goose bumps and an uneasy feeling in the pit of his stomach. Then the doors closed, taking the invisible riders to another stop.

He walked back into the outer office, shaking some dust into the cart. His radio shifted to Hunter Hayes' "Storm Warning." Golly, that seems appropriate, he thought. Again, he heard the wind gusts sweep around the corner of the old building. It was still light outside, but the gray February sky and lack of sunshine gave it a feel of dusk instead of four o'clock. He walked over to the windows and noticed the dark car was gone. Del grabbed a clean dustcloth and some antiseptic spray, all the while looking over at John Hardy's office where the door was slightly open. That was strange. He turned, pushing his cart out of his way, and shuffled softly to Hardy's door. Knocking in case the guy was in, Del heard nothing, so he pushed the door open. The first thing he saw was a broken coffee cup on the floor next to Hardy's wooden desk sign with the engraved brass plate saying, "John A. Hardy, Principal." For some reason, both were on the floor under the desk. A pen and pencil holder plus a few papers were also scattered on the floor near the legs of a chair.

"What the heck?" he said out loud.

Looking up, he noticed Hardy's tall leather desk chair was turned around toward the window, a sweat-shirted arm hanging over the side.

"I can come back later, Mr. Hardy, sir," Del said. "Do you want I should come back later?"

Nothing. No answer. Del felt the hairs on the back of his neck stand up. He moved backward a few steps. Then he swallowed hard and said, "Mr. Hardy?" He paused. "Sir?"

Silence.

Del took several deep breaths. What should he do? It was shadowy in the room, so he flipped on the light switch by the door. Taking a step back, he pressed his hand to his heart. The room was in shambles. He moved slowly toward the side of the desk, glancing out the window where it appeared Mr. Hardy was staring. Only snow, wind, gray skies. Nothing special. Coming slowly around the corner of the desk, he held his breath and sensed a bad feeling in the pit of his stomach.

In the chair sat John Hardy—well, maybe it was John Hardy. It was impossible to see his face because a silly, polka-dotted orange lampshade covered his head with orange tassels hanging down from the bottom edge.

"Mr. Hardy, sir?" Del said again. No answer.

He reached over, gingerly touching the bottom of the lampshade, his body ready to move back, every nerve on edge. Holding his breath, he slowly lifted the lampshade up from the person's head. What he saw made him jump, drop the lampshade, and take several steps backward, feeling queasy and light-headed. It was John Hardy, but his eyes were open in a rigid stare, and his mouth was stretched into a terrible, twisted, unnatural grin.

"Well, I never—"

He swallowed several times, backed away from the principal, the chair, the desk, the bookshelves, almost stumbling over scattered ceramic pieces from the broken cup, his shoe smashing several bits into powder. Backing out of the office, he dropped the dustcloth and spray, put his hands behind him to feel for the corner of the counter, and labored to get his breath back.

Sweaty and ashen-faced, Del tried to reach for his phone, but his hands shook so hard he struggled to pull it out of his pocket. His fingers wouldn't hit the right spots on the screen. He stopped and took several deep breaths. Then he wobbled over to the secretary's desk, found her phone with punch keys on it, and grimaced. Suddenly, he was dizzy and had to sit down, his head shaking from side to side as if dismissing what he had just seen in that office. Then he remembered the small refrigerator under Ann's desk. He opened it and grabbed a bottle of water. Twisting off the cap, he took several swallows and dumped some on his shaking hands, using them to splash still more water on his face and neck.

Staring down at the telephone, he remembered what he was doing, picked up the phone receiver, and punched 9-1-1 with careful deliberation.

Chapter One

"GIN!" SHOUTED GRACE Kimball, laying her cards on the coffee table and laughing with glee.

"What? Again? You must be the luckiest person on the face of the planet. Either that or somehow you have these cards marked," said TJ Sweeney. She picked up the cards, examining them for bent edges. "All right. Again. Double or nothing." She pushed six toothpicks into the middle of the table and began shuffling the cards, a disgusted look on her face.

"Me? Cheat? On a Sunday, even? Seriously, TJ?"

"Grace, even schoolteachers cheat."

"Never on Sunday."

"Oh, please."

"Besides, I'm retired, remember?"

"Even more reason to cheat. You have nothing to lose through a moral turpitude clause."

"Spoken like a police detective."

The fire crackled as logs shifted in the fireplace and sparks went up the chimney. Grace glanced out the window while TJ shuffled the cards. She pondered the snow falling, coating the branches of the trees, sticking to the window, and cascading down to heavily snow-burdened sticker bushes. Early February in Illinois—this isn't going away soon, she thought. Then she looked at TJ.

"So how did work go this week at the Endurance Police Department? Any cats to rescue from trees?"

"I'll have you know it was an exceptional week of service to the fair city of Endurance as we protected its citizenry. In fact, the EPD was right here on Sweetbriar Court yesterday morning."

"You were? Where was I? Oh, I was slaving away at the *Register* office."

"You missed a fire engine, ambulance, and Officer Zach Gray, all racing down Sweetbriar Court with hardly room to park one vehicle, let alone a fire engine."

"Really? I didn't hear anything about this."

"And you're working at a local newspaper? You need to get your sister-in-law, Lettie, over to the *Register.* Her jungle telegraph can sniff out any scuttlebutt in town."

"Fine, fine," said Grace, irritably. "What happened?"

"Ardis Brantley happened."

"Down at the end of the court?"

"The very person. She has one of those things she wears around her neck that alerts a security company if she has an emergency or she falls or something."

"Oh, yes. Deb O'Hara got her mom one of those last Christmas. Did she fall? Ardis?"

"Not exactly." TJ spread out her cards in her hand, a smug look on her face. "She was in her kitchen trying to pry a lid off a large pickle jar. Although she finally managed to loosen it, she had to turn it so hard that she put it up against her chest, hitting the doohickey she wears around her neck. The alarm went off, and the security company called both her and her daughter who lives across town."

"Doohickey?"

"Oh, you know what I mean . . . one of those thing-ies people wear for alarms."

"To think I taught you English. I must have failed you miserably with vocabulary."

TJ gave her a pained expression.

"So, it wasn't an emergency, right?"

"Started out that way. While Ardis was on the phone to the security people, her smoke alarm went off, and the operator asked her if something was burning. She couldn't remember cooking anything and seemed a bit vague, which prompted the operator to alert everyone. Meanwhile, the smoke alarm continued to screech—geez, those suckers are loud—and when Zach got there, Ardis was wandering around on the front porch, shivering in the cold. He said she offered him a pickle."

"A pickle?" Grace laughed, rocking back and forth. "What about the fire?"

"Wasn't one. The alarm was defective. By the time the firetruck, ambulance, squad car, and Ardis's daughter's car were all parked hood-to-trunk on the cul-de-sac, no one could get out or in." She threw a card down on the discard pile. "Good thing they didn't have a real alarm somewhere else."

Grace paused, considering the implications. "This is a good town in which to be a detective."

"Oh, you mean because of the various dead bodies which have turned up over the last year or so?"

"I wasn't thinking of that. No. I mean very little ever happens here . . . outside of a murder or two no one expected. Those were unusual. Exceptions. Beyond that we have some petty crime and an occasional false alarm, but otherwise, all in all, Endurance is quiet, wouldn't you say?"

"Yes."

"That's all you're going to say?"

"I entrust all the flowery descriptions to you, Former Teacher. You've already impugned my vocabulary, obviously, the product of an inferior high school English education."

"Gin!" Grace stood up and ran a little victory lap in a circle.

"Seriously?" TJ threw her cards down. "I give up. Take all the toothpicks." She moved everything to Grace's side of the table.

Grace smiled broadly and began picking up cards and toothpicks. "How about one lovely glass of wine?"

TJ looked at her watch. "Well, I'm off call in about fifteen minutes so I could do that. Speaking of wine, I know you've saved a bottle you got at Christmas for Jeff Maitlin's return. Any news on that front?"

Grace shook her head, pushing the deck of cards into a box. "He promised he'd be back this week, but it's now Sunday, the start of a new week. So much for that thought. I could call him—I have—but his phone simply goes to voice mail." She ended this pronouncement with a heavy sigh.

"What's he doing? Where is he?"

"I have no idea. When he left, he said he had to deal with some incident having something to do with his past."

TJ shook her head slowly. "Well, vague enough, isn't it?"

"Lettie's right." Grace put her hand over her mouth in mock horror and said, "You didn't hear me say that. Don't repeat it to her." She hated to admit her sister-in-law was right. Ever.

"Right about what?"

"He is a mystery man. I don't know much at all about his past, but he worked for quite a few newspapers all over the country, ending up at a big one in New York. At least he told me that. Oh, and he isn't married and never has been. Why he moved from New York to this particular small town beats me. He said he heard about the part-time job at the *Register* from some friend who was also a journalist. Thinks this might be a great place to retire. Period." She looked up at her friend. "That's all he said."

TJ looked thoughtfully at Grace's normally placid brown eyes, which now appeared a bit unsure. "I'll get the wine." She walked out to the kitchen, returning with two glasses and a bottle of sauvignon blanc. She poured a couple of inches into Grace's glass and then into hers. She handed Grace her glass, and they clicked them together and each took a sip. "Grace, are you sure you don't want me to do a little background investigation on him?"

"No."

"No, you don't, or no you're not sure?"

"No, as in I'm not sure so maybe I don't. Maybe I don't want you to—"

"I am not as trusting as you, Grace. You know, the world has plenty of people running around who smile and are lovely to look at—like Jeff—but you shouldn't trust them. Maybe he's really a latter-day Jack the Ripper who goes around eviscerating people when he's not being charming."

Grace Kimball laughed and took a long sip of her wine. She folded her arms in front of her. "No, don't see him as Jack the Ripper. He'll tell me when he comes back. I'm sure of it." She nodded her head. "Besides, he just bought a four thousand-plus-square-foot house he is renovating here in town. You haven't forgotten that, right?"

TJ swirled the wine around in her glass and glanced up at Grace. "What if he doesn't come back?"

"Oh, he will. I know he will. I don't know what shape he'll be in. Whatever this mysterious mission is, I'm worried that it may be something upsetting to him."

"That's why you have me here. To pick up the pieces."

"I know, TJ. You're the realist, I'm the daydream believer." She gave her a wistful smile and looked in the fireplace. Suddenly, TJ's phone played "Glory Days," and she pulled it out of her pocket, looking at Grace. "Myers. This is my day off. I hope he's not after me because someone called in sick . . . ." She pushed the accept button on her cell. "Yeah, Myers." Grace watched while the expression on TJ's face darkened as she listened to the desk officer from the Endurance Police Department. "And when do they think this happened?" She listened for another minute. Then, "Okay. I'll be there in the next ten minutes. Tell Jake to hold the fort." She tapped the button off. "John Hardy."

"The principal at the high school?"

"Yeah. What kind of guy is he? You worked for him."

"He was at the high school for my last three years. A decent guy, well-organized, treated me fine. Quite definite about what he wanted done and how he believed the school should be run. Highly disciplined. Always fair. He was a good administrator. Why?"

"Have you ever heard anything shady about him? Does he chase skirts or drink too much or gamble?"

Grace giggled. "Please, TJ. You know me. I'd be the last to know."

TJ shook her head, smiling. "True. Why would I ask you?"

"That was my question. Why?"

"It appears Del Novak was cleaning up at the high school building when he found John Hardy in his office, dead." She cleared her throat, picked up her wine glass, and stood up.

"What? Do they think it was a heart attack or a stroke?"

"Don't know. Myers said they want me in ASAP. Doesn't sound good."

Grace eyed TJ's wine glass. "Good thing you didn't drink the whole glass."

TJ nodded her head. "I may wish I had." She turned and carried the half-empty glass to the kitchen, returning and checking for her badge on her belt.

Grace rose. "Should I call Lettie? Didn't you say Del Novak found him?"

"Yeah, Myers said that. Knowing Lettie, she's probably with him and intends to answer all the interrogation questions for him. Actually, Grace, it's a crime scene, so she can't be there."

"Makes sense. I'll grab your coat and scarf. You need to go." She followed TJ out to the front hallway and pulled her clothing out of the closet.

As TJ stuck her arms in her coat she said, "Think about what I said, Grace . . . about the background check." She opened the door, staring across the street at her own house on the other side of Sweetbriar Court. Then she turned. "I'll let you know what happens with Hardy's death."

"Thanks, TJ. Be careful." Grace closed the door behind her, and wandered back to the living room to pick up the cards. While she loaded the dishwasher, she thought about their conversation.

How awful for Liz Hardy and their children. She had met them socially over the years, but didn't really know Liz. The two children were always well behaved and usually in the newspaper with their names on the honor rolls at their schools. What could have happened? He was way too young to die. How old would he be? Maybe late thirties, early forties? It had to be a heart attack or a stroke. Maybe it was genetic; perhaps his father had died young. In any case, because it was an "unattended death," TJ had to investigate since she was the lead detective.

Her mind wandered to TJ's offer on a background check. Jeff was amazingly good at what he did, and people liked him because he was so personable. Grace couldn't believe he had anything dark or sinister about him. He had moved to Endurance last summer to become the editor of the small town's newspaper. Grace, who had just retired from teaching English at the high school, accepted a part-time job at the newspaper, a job that had morphed into practically a full-time occupation. Then, they'd started dating last fall, just after she turned fifty-seven to his sixty-two.

She remembered his kiss. She had to stand on her tiptoes to return that kiss because he was six feet tall and she just came up to his chin. The warm, soft feel of his lips pressing on hers, his enthusiasm as he'd grabbed her hand to walk up the huge front staircase at the house he was restoring—of course, he'd return. Why wouldn't he?

She thought about her husband, Roger, dead from a heart attack these twenty-seven years. It had been a long time since someone had held her in his arms, kissed her, or made her feel loved and needed. Maybe that was part of the problem, TJ would say. But Grace was sure Roger would have approved of Jeff Maitlin. Grace knew him to be an honest and kind person, intelligent, well-read, professional, traveled, and a great kisser. The last asset was so important, she thought, laughing to herself.

What if TJ were right? What if he had a dark past and somehow it had come back, causing him to change his plans? What if he didn't return?

Grace knew TJ. Something about the detective's face told her that her friend would totally ignore her "no" when it came to checking on Jeff's past. Then Grace would have to decide if she wanted to know.

Chapter Two

TJ PARKED HER unmarked car in front of the main entrance to Endurance High School. Leaving her own pickup at the police station, she had driven with Jake Williams, her partner. The initial crime scene information came from Alex Durdle, a young cop relatively new to the police force. TJ knew Alex was a competent patrol officer; now he was at the school guarding the crime scene, undoubtedly trying to console Del Novak.

Poor Del, TJ thought. He must wonder what kind of town he's moved to. After early January, he probably thinks he should keep an eye on his girlfriend, Lettie, who almost became a crime statistic. Now here he is—the first person to discover a murder. What was happening to her town? TJ had come back after graduating with a law enforcement major and moved up to lead detective. It had always been a relatively quiet, sleepy town. But recently she'd had more than she'd bargained for in murder scenes.

She turned toward Jake, shaking her head. "Well, here we go, partner. Dispatch says it's a 'suspicious death.' Murder stats rise again."

Jake double-checked his pocket for his cell phone and notepad, then nodded to her. "Never had so much excitement until you started work, TJ. How do you know this Del Novak? What's he to you again?"

"Boyfriend to Lettisha Kimball, Grace's sister-in-law. Met him because he renovated Grace's kitchen, an experience where he discovered the terror of the countryside, Lettie. Man, if I had her contacts in town I wouldn't have any need to pay informants. I swear she has my office bugged."

Jake laughed. "Yeah, I know. I ran into her at The Bread Box Bakery where she was holding court with three or four of the workers on break." He shook his head. "And this John Hardy? Do you know him?"

"No. Just know who he is. I haven't been to the school in quite some time—well, except for basketball games, but Hardy was here the last three years of Grace Kimball's career. She thinks he's a standup guy, but then Grace has been fooled before. I've watched him at basketball games, been impressed with his crowd control. He obviously knows his students. I always see him talking to them."

"Last principal I knew here was old Sutter, but he stayed in his office. The building could have collapsed around him. Never knew what went on."

"All right. Let's go. May as well get this over with." They trudged through the snow, their breath flowing out into mini-clouds in the cold air. Two squad cars were parked in front of the school on the circle drive, while a local funeral home hearse waited, its engine running.

Endurance High School was a massive old brick building designed in the early 1900s. It rose two stories above a basement floor, boasting the ornate columns of the time period surrounding the main entrance. But like all old buildings, it had seen various additions, multiple doors, replaced windows, all providing easy access to anyone who wanted to get in unseen. In more recent years, the security was somewhat better since stories of school shootings led the evening news on television. The school had been renovated, maybe thirty years ago, but it still had the look of a twentieth-century school with high ceilings, lots of neutral paint on the inside walls, and one end rising above the main roof because of a gymnasium. It hadn't changed much since TJ's days.

When they approached the front door, they found Zach Gray inside, waiting to open the door for the rest of them. Since 9/11, all the schools had security locks which could only be opened from the outside by keys, or if the secretary pushed a button in response to someone at the door asking for entrance. Made sense, TJ thought, especially with all the school shootings or kidnappings by noncustodial parents. Tiny Endurance was too poor, however, for metal detectors.

"Hi, Zach. Been up there yet?" asked TJ.

"Yeah, TJ. Not bad." He smiled. "Not like last summer with all the blood. Much less excitement."

"I keep telling you, kid, excitement is not good." She chuckled. "We'll send Alex down to keep you company."

"Oh, Zach, call the PD—have them send Martinez and CSI," added Jake.

Up, up the front staircase TJ remembered so well. Before she retired last year, Grace's classroom was at the end of a long hallway on the main floor. She smiled as she remembered how, at first, she had given Grace a run for her money, challenging her to teach this teenager literature and writing. TJ was quite the rebel in her early high school years with a real chip on her shoulder, but after Grace moved her into the honors class, (much against TJ's will), the teenager flourished. Grace mentored her through high school and college, but she guided much more than her education. She touched her soul. Ever since, the two of them had been friends, watching each other's backs. It was a good thing, thought the detective, because Grace didn't realize the darkness TJ saw in her job. Endurance might not be a huge city or urban area, but the darkness was here too. Reaching the landing on the main floor, TJ pointed Jake to the office door, now held open by a rubber doorstop.

Del Novak slumped in a chair in the outer office, drinking a cup of coffee with Alex Durdle seated next to him.

TJ studied Del Novak. The old man looked like he had aged ten years, his body sagging, his hands on his lap to keep them from shaking. He was hunched over, taking deep, studied breaths. His glasses, with thick lenses, lay on the table. Then he lifted one hand to rub his eyes as if trying to dismiss what he had seen.

TJ said, "You doing okay, Del?"

"I will be shortly, TJ. Whiskey'd be better to calm my nerves, but, you know, I'm in a school. Never seen a dead body like this before. Missed all the various wars. Never had to go. My ticker isn't in the greatest shape, but I'm better these days at calming myself down. I've never seen such a thing in my life," he repeated, shaking his head slowly.

"I understand," said Jake. He looked at Alex, saying, "You can go downstairs and help Zach keep an eye on the door. We'll call you if we need you. Eventually, you may have to drive Del here home." Alex left reluctantly as the detective turned to Del. "I'm Jake Williams, TJ's partner." He shook Del's hand, and then took out his notepad and pen. "Can you tell us what happened?" Glancing at Del, he added, "Take your time."

Del explained how he found Hardy's body, but he became visibly nervous and less coherent as he talked about the murder scene. "It's bizarre, Mr. Williams. A high school principal—who seemed such a decent man to me—sitting there with a weird grin on his face, a crazy lampshade on his head. Bizarre. Who would do such an awful thing?"

TJ watched Jake pause after writing down a few details. She always admired the way Jake could calm people down. Now he said, "Please, call me Jake. I'm sure it must have been disturbing, especially coming up on it—uh, Mr. Hardy—with no warning that something was wrong. Of course, you didn't expect to see a body. Did you notice anything else unusual when you went into his office?"

Del paused for a moment. "Let me think." He pressed his lips together. Then he said, "It was getting dark because, you know, at this time of year it gets dark early."

"Okay. Stop a minute. Does this mean the light in the office was off?"

"Yes," said Del. "I think I called out to him, but when he didn't answer I realized how dark it was, so I turned the light on because I was still by the doorway switch plate."

"Good," said Jake. "Go on."

"A lot of stuff was scattered on the floor. A coffee cup shattered into pieces and a cell phone on the floor near the doorway. The filing cabinet—something was unusual about it. Let me think a moment. You know my memory isn't as good as it used to be." He paused.

TJ leaned toward him, saying, "When you have a traumatic event, it may impact your memory. Could be when we check back with you in a couple of days you'll remember something you've temporarily forgotten. Let's try this for now: Close your eyes and focus. Envision what you saw from the time you stood at the door."

"I'll do that." He closed his eyes, waiting a full fifteen seconds. "Well, what I told you was right. His nameplate—it's wooden with a brass plate on it—was under his desk. His chair was turned like he was looking out the window. I could see his left arm hanging over the side of the chair. A few file folders were on the desk. His filing cabinet . . . Now I remember. The top drawer was slightly open, like he hadn't quite gotten it shut." He paused again, opening his eyes. "All I can remember. I think I was too shocked."

TJ added, "Great job, Del. Thanks. It always helps to hear firsthand what a witness saw. What do you think, Jake? Need to ask him anything else?"

"Yeah. How about other people in the building? Did you see anyone else or was anyone here while you cleaned?"

"Let's see, now," Del said. "The social studies teacher, Marilyn Atkins, was downstairs earlier in the afternoon, but she left before I found Mr. Hardy. Course I don't know how long he had been there. Ms. Atkins, she wouldn't hurt a fly. She's over here a lot on Sundays because she teaches history, so she grades piles of papers. We've talked occasionally when either of us took a break. Probably shouldn't repeat gossip, but I heard her husband drinks more'n he should, so maybe that's why she spends so much time here."

"Did you talk today?"

"Yes. Shortly after I got here—around one, I'd say—I stopped by her room where she was working away like mad. We gabbed a bit about the weather and the storm that was supposed to come in. It's why she left early. The storm."

"Did she seem any different than usual?"

"Can't say she did. Well, maybe a little nervous, but I figured it was because of the storm."

"Was Hardy often here on Sundays?" asked TJ.

"Occasionally. Usually when he had paperwork to catch up on or when the Packers didn't play football on Sunday," he said, chuckling. "He likes—er, liked—those Packers."

"Anyone else?"

"Not that I saw," said Del. "It's a big building with three floors, nooks and crannies, and, like I said, lots of people have keys. Too many, as far as I'm concerned."

Jake looked at TJ, she nodded, and he handed his business card to Del, saying, "If you think of anything else later, give me a call, or TJ here. Thanks, Mr. Novak. Oh—also we'd appreciate it if you would keep quiet about what you've seen or heard today. It will help our investigation. That means, Del, you cannot tell Lettie Kimball anything. Nothing. I'll have one of our officers drive you home, and you can pick up your truck later. Might be safer. You're pretty shook up." He moved over to the door, calling down to Zach Grey to send Alex Durdle back up.

"You know," said Del as he put on his coat, "I do remember something else. When I first got here, a dark sedan was parked out front. The first three letters on the plate were SAM, and then there were more letters or numbers, but I couldn't see them. Later, when I looked, the car was gone."

After they left, TJ said, "Keep quiet? Geez. If Lettie gets ahold of any of this, asking her to keep quiet would be like telling Niagara Falls to flow up instead of down."

"You know it could compromise everything if she talks."

"Oh, yes," TJ nodded, shaking her head. "Don't worry. I'll put the fear of God into her. Course it might cut down on the pie I get for a while till she forgives me."

Just then, TJ saw Ron Martinez, the coroner, trudging up the main stairway. Normally, he was a pediatrician, but he doubled as the coroner in Endurance. Seeing TJ and Jake, he said, "You must be slowing down. Usually you're about done with a crime scene when I get here. Too much pasta for lunch is undoubtedly the culprit. I keep telling you that stuff'll kill you."

"Right," said Jake, "I'll try pizza instead." He pointed to the chairs. "Have a seat while we take a first look."

"Sure," said Martinez. He sat in the outer office, pulling out his cell phone. "I'll call Woodbury. See when we can get him in for an autopsy."

"From what dispatch said, you'd better put an emphasis on toxicology," TJ said.

She turned and walked toward John Hardy's office. Putting on some gloves, she looked back at Jake. "Not much room in the principal's office."

Jake laughed. "You should know."

"Right. Ha, ha. I'll check it out first, and when I'm done, you can give it a look-see. Then we'll compare notes." Standing in the doorway, TJ surveyed the entire scene. She noted the various items on the floor, then glanced at the top file cabinet drawer partly open, as Del had described. That would mean the cabinet was not locked, so anyone had access to all the drawers. The windows were closed, the thermostat was set around seventy, and the lights were on. She checked out the files on the desk. Nothing out of the ordinary, she thought. It looked like he was writing announcements for school the next day, but he had stopped in the middle of a word. Could have been interrupted by the killer. On the corner of his desk, in a calendar book opened to today's date, was a printed note that said, "See Harrington Monday morning."

Treading softly around the desk, she studied Hardy's face. This is a strange death, she thought. It looks like he didn't stand much of a chance. Fast, fast. The items all over the floors, especially the overturned coffee cup, indicated he'd flailed around. Why didn't he call for help? Need to check the coffee cup for prints. No blood . . . no other weapons . . . his face a ghastly mask of horror. His eyes were opaque, not unusual after death. TJ could understand Del's fright. She looked over at Jake, lounging in the doorway.

"Come on in," she said, moving past the desk to change places with him. Watching her partner go through the same reactions she had, TJ thought she'd never seen a crime scene like this before. It had to be poison. What kind? Where might someone get it? What clues would it give them to the actual killer? This was not suicide. It looked as if he was disturbed in the middle of his work and, for whatever reason, took this poison—or whatever it was—willingly. It would mean the poisoner was a person he knew. She looked up and Jake nodded. Then both went back to the outer office to send in Martinez.

They compared notes while the coroner was checking out the body. Either Martinez or an officer downstairs would accompany the body so the chain of evidence would remain in place until he was safely in the hands of the Woodbury coroner who would do the autopsy.

Martinez came out, taking off his gloves and shaking his head.

"What would you surmise with your usual early crime scene lucky guess, oh doctor of little people?" asked TJ.

"Likely it's some kind of poison. My instinct tells me it may be strychnine from the looks of his muscles and face. Doesn't take long for that stuff. The victim is in agony, unable to speak. His muscles contort until he dies."

"How long?"

"Could be as little as fifteen minutes for symptoms. Maybe an hour for death."

"What about calling for help? Could he have called?" TJ asked.

"No way. He would suffer uncontrollable muscle spasms, eventually dying from asphyxiation or exhaustion from the continuous convulsions."

"Where did a pediatrician learn about poisons like strychnine?" asked TJ.

"Oh, come on, Detective. Didn't you ever read *The Mysterious Affair at Styles* or *The Sign of Four?*" he said, laughing.

"What?" asked Jake, a quizzical look on his face.

"Don't mind my friend here. He doesn't read books. Agatha Christie and Arthur Conan Doyle. Read them cover to cover. I thought this whole scene looked vaguely familiar," said TJ.

Martinez leaned back in his seat. "I can't swear to you strychnine killed him," he said, "but we'll know more after the toxicology report. Autopsy will be tomorrow afternoon in Woodbury. I assume someone will be there from the department."

"We'll flip a coin," said Jake.

"If it is strychnine," the coroner said, "it can be obtained as poison for rats, but it's highly controlled these days. Back in earlier centuries it was used to kill birds in the countryside or rats in the city. In Victorian days, they used a tiny bit as a stimulant. I guess you could say it was one of the first performance-enhancing drugs in sports . . . if you didn't take very much."

Jake said, "This history is all well and good, Doc, but how does it work?"

"It blocks a glycine receptor which stops motor nerves in the spinal cord from doing their job the way they should. It results in severe, continuous convulsions."

"That would explain the items all over the floor, as well as the broken cup," said Jake. "Suppose it was in what he drank from the cup?"

"Possibility. Of course, depending on who could get in or out of the building, the killer might have carried away the poison container after Hardy died. If it's strychnine, it doesn't take much at all," said Martinez, packing up his briefcase. "Now, I have a question for you. Why is a silly, polka-dotted lampshade with little orange balls sitting on the floor?"

TJ said, "It was on his head." Looking at the coroner's expression, she said, "Yeah. I know. Maybe a mentally ill person. Could be a way to present the body so the victim will be humiliated. My guess is the murderer thought this would be appropriate for the principal of a school, a job that usually lends itself to a conservative lifestyle and public image. Motive, so far, is a big question mark."

"This is a detail we won't put out to the public," Jake said. "Don't you agree, TJ? I don't think we want to give this murderer what he or she wants."

"Right."

"Well, one thing's for sure," the coroner said. "Whoever did this was cold-blooded, planned it in advance, and knew where he or she could get the poison."

"Do you think Hardy understood what was happening?" asked TJ.

"Oh, yes. This poison doesn't cross the blood-brain barrier, so the victim is conscious, but can do nothing about it. He can't control the muscle contractions, which eventually stop his breathing. Frankly, this isn't a way to kill someone you like. It's cruel because it causes terror and painful suffering, so if you're the victim, you're aware of it. You can't do a thing about it. It's possible the murderer watched him die." Putting on his coat and scarf, he added, "Good luck, people. You're looking for a genuinely evil person here."

TJ said, "Great! Crazy people in schools. Oh, Doc, before you go—what about a timeline? When did it happen?"

"I can tell you more after the autopsy and toxicology report are done. Tox will take a while."

Then the crime scene investigators arrived, and TJ waved them in, pointing toward the principal's office. She followed them, giving directions to be sure they bagged the pieces of the coffee cup and checked them for prints and substances. Ditto with the nameplate under the desk. Also, she had them look for a file cabinet key for prints. It was a small crime scene and, with no blood spatter to contemplate, they finished in an hour. Martinez had the funeral home attendants take the body out, and then TJ and Jake began an investigation of items in Hardy's office, skirting around the surfaces covered with black fingerprint powder. A cylinder of crime scene tape, along with an official sign, which would keep the door locked, lay out on the office counter.

TJ began methodically with the filing cabinet, whose top drawer was noticeably open. Thumbing through the files, she suddenly had a thought. "Jake, you know teachers have to get fingerprinted these days. All people who work in the building, like janitors or cooks, must be printed. We'd have everyone from here in the police database." Jake nodded as he opened folders from the bookshelves, checking out their contents.

A few minutes later, TJ announced, "Think I may have something interesting here."

"Oh?"

"This top file drawer, the one that was slightly open, has personnel files in it. Several are flagged with red file tabs. Looks like they are questionable evaluations."

"Are there many?"

"Nah. Only three, four."

"What's so interesting?"

"Look at what this one teaches."

Chapter Three

THE FOLLOWING DAY, just after noon, city workers were still plowing snow, but it turned out the weatherman was not quite accurate in predicting several inches of snow. Although the brunt of the storm went north of Endurance, even an inch of snow added a slippery layer of trouble to travel woes. Grace crept along, eyeballs glued to her car's windshield as she inched her way home from the newspaper office. Despite her concentration, she almost slid through a stop sign.

Her mind was not on the deadline for her latest historical column about the old feed store on South Main Street. Instead, she thought about the phone call a few days ago from her boss and boyfriend, Jeff Maitlin. She was not being irrational, she told herself. Whatever this mysterious trip, he seemed to indicate it had something to do with his past. "Seemed" is the right word, she muttered, as she gingerly stepped on the brakes, praying not to slide. As if I need to know why he kissed me on the one hand, and then left with little explanation, on the other.

Nervously, she forced herself to focus, checking left and right. Grace noted the street department had plowed all the recent snow into a mountain in the median, which was their common practice, but it also caused her uneasiness because she was driving next to a wall of white. This jangled Grace's nerves, and she clutched the steering wheel tightly. These white snow mounds would eventually be dumped into trucks, hauled out of town, and deposited in the countryside, but for now they made her nervous. Glancing up at the First Bank of Endurance, she noticed the American flag drooping limply from the flagpole. At least we don't have to worry about blowing snow, she thought, letting out a sigh of relief. The winter had been especially brutal in the small Illinois town, so drifting snow was the last thing they needed.

A maroon-colored car ahead of Grace stopped at the light on the corner of Main and Mulberry Street. She recognized Loretta Hildagoss, an adult now, but a girl Grace remembered as an adolescent in her high school class. *Grace always connected Loretta with the year the home economics teacher did a project involving fake arranged marriages. The "parents" had to carry around a stuffed, seven-pound flour sack that was their pretend baby. The idea was to teach teenagers that parenting was a 24/7 job, laden with lots of emotion. That "job" required more than teenage maturity. Loretta began with all smiles, but after the first day, an increasingly irritated Loretta, screaming, threw her baby out the third-floor window of the science lab. Fortunately, maturity triumphed: she got married well into her twenties and had two children—both still above ground at last count.*

Grace laughed softly, asking herself, why do I remember all these silly episodes? So many years ago, and so many teenagers . . . I suppose it's the discrepancy between their crazy teenage antics and their current adult behavior. Good thing they can't read my mind because I see them everywhere and remember when they were young and foolish.

She was still smiling when she pulled into her driveway at 1036 Sweetbriar Court, the home she and Roger had bought when they were first married. It was a Victorian house with white wooden siding above dark red brick masonry on a corner lot. Roger had put up a white wooden fence piece at the corner of the yard so Grace could plant flowers around it. Since his untimely death when the children were little, she had made various changes to the house, but its skeleton still resembled the home where they began their married lives. She perused the wraparound front porch, one of the best features of the house. Now in the winter it looked lonely and unused, but come summer, she, Deb, TJ, and Jill Cunningham would lounge on the porch in the floral-cushioned chairs or on the wooden swing, drinking margaritas or sangria. Deb got us started on the margaritas, Grace thought, smiling. She pulled into the garage and a few minutes later she was inside.

"I'm home, Lettie," she called out, smelling the savory goodness of whatever her sister-in-law was cooking today. After Roger died, his sister Lettie moved in to help with the children, and she was a fabulous cook. Her cooking was a way of loving the little family, and after she moved to her own house and the children grew up and left home, she still came to Grace's every day to do what she did best: bake and cook.

"A good thing, too," called out Lettie from the kitchen.

"Why? Something the matter?" Grace asked, standing in the doorway. Lettie had her arms crossed. Not a good sign.

"Only TJ. She came by to see if you were here. Of course, you weren't, so she stayed and had a piece of blueberry pie," Lettie said. "I don't know why that woman is skinny. How does she eat like she does but never gains an ounce?"

"She's young, Lettie. Unlike us, she's only thirty-nine, so she works off all that food on her job. We were interrupted when she tried to call me earlier, but she said she'd call back."

"Hmm. I'll bet she works it off a few other ways from the looks of the spiffy truck that's often in her driveway these days . . . at night. So, what's the latest?" Lettie said, sitting down at the kitchen table, inviting Grace, with a sweeping gesture, to sit across from her. "Here, I already made you some hot chocolate when I figured you'd be coming home."

"Lettie, you are amazing. How did you know when I was on the way home? My hours are always screwy now that I'm retired."

Lettie smiled mysteriously. "I have my ways."

"Did you put a GPS tracking chip under my car?"

"A UPS what?"

"Oh, never mind." Preoccupied with the reason for TJ's call, Grace wondered if the detective planned to check out some of the teachers. She knew many of the high school faculty, but in the past year several new teachers had been hired whom she didn't know.

"I told Gladys at the coffee shop it was an inside deal. Suppose it was a teacher? Someone you know?"

Grace laughed. "Seriously? We're talking about a high school. Teachers are supposed to mold children's minds."

"Yeah, well, in their off time I'm sure they mold other things," Lettie said. She stood up and went to the counter for a napkin, but came back with a smirk on her face. "Look at all those teachers who are doing jail time in minimum-security prisons for molding other things. I rest my case."

"You know, Lettie, teachers aren't always saints. They're supposed to be good role models, but they're human just like everyone else."

Lettie shook her head. "I don't think saints or good role models murdered the principal. I've known a lot of people in my time who were angry with the principal of a school, but I think poisoning him is beyond the bounds of sainthood."

Grace's eyes narrowed. "We have no idea who did this, and it might not have been anyone involved in the school. Lettie, you haven't talked to people about this murder, have you? You know TJ would boil you in oil if she caught you doing that."

Lettie looked away from Grace and shrugged her shoulders. "Only Gladys at the coffee shop and Mildred at the bakery. I didn't tell them anything I shouldn't say, just that I figured it was an inside job; maybe it was the cuckoo play director, or that randy driver's training instructor, or the strange French teacher. Well, actually, Mildred added the French teacher since he always comes into The Bread Box Bakery and orders croissants. Aren't they some kind of French thing?"

"Lettie. Lips zipped."

Then it was quiet, Grace drinking her hot chocolate and Lettie biting her lip.

"I was over at Del's this morning making sure he took his heart pill. Of course, he didn't listen to me when I warned him not to take that job at the high school. The building is creepy on the weekend. A homicidal maniac is on the loose, but Del won't tell me a thing. Says it's a rule from TJ." She paused, thoughtfully, tapping her fingers on the table. "I should cut off her pie supply."

"That's TJ's job, to figure it out. I mean it, Lettie. You can't talk to anyone about this. It would jeopardize TJ's case." Suddenly, Grace's phone played "Wanted Dead or Alive." She walked quickly back to the living room, where she'd left her purse, locating it before the song stopped. "Yes, TJ." Listening for several minutes, she finally said, "Sure. What time?" Then, "Yes, I can. No problem. I know those people. I'll see you at the meeting. Let me check." Then she walked to the kitchen and opened the refrigerator. "Yes, Lettie still has some blueberry pie left." She glanced at Lettie, who stuck her tongue out. "Sure thing." She hung up the phone, turning to Lettie.

"Well," Lettie said, "now what?"

Grace checked the clock. "I have to run over to the high school. Faculty meeting in a half hour, and TJ wants me to keep an eye on people's reactions."

"So, who's in charge over there today?"

"My guess is Alex Reid. Not a good situation since he is the world's most disorganized person. But in a pinch, he'll have to do." She raced around gathering her purse, electronic notepad, and car keys.

"Have you had any lunch?"

"No, but I don't have time for that. I have to run up and change clothes."

Ten minutes later, Grace was on her way across town to the high school while she munched on a sandwich Lettie had thrown together. She thought about TJ's reasoning. Grace knew the other teachers at the high school, but even though TJ was going to be at this meeting, she figured Grace might notice any unusual reactions or nervous mannerisms of people she knew better than the detective.

She reached the high school in snowy, creeping-along-the-road time, stopping in the office to check in with Ann Cummings. The crime scene tape, plus "Do Not Enter by Order of the EPD" sign on Hardy's door, gave her chills. Ann had said the meeting was in the library/learning center, so Grace sat at the side of the gathering where she could see a cross section and observe people's behavior. This had taken quite a few minutes since teachers stopped to talk to her, asking why she was there. She told them she had to cover the meeting for the *Register* and, trying to look genuine, got out her electronic notepad. TJ slipped in at the last moment, immediately moving to the back, over toward the other side of the room from Grace. Everyone talked in hushed tones and a few people had red, swollen eyes. Grace figured school had limped on today with counselors available for students.

She watched Alex Reid come in with a notebook and a water bottle. He sauntered to the front, where a small table had been placed. Setting down his items, he cleared his voice several times, said one last thing to one of the teachers in the first row, and then waited for the chatter to die down before he began.

"Ah, I think we should get started." He paused and rubbed his jaw. Then he looked up. "I'll bet you're wondering why I called this meeting," he began. No one laughed. In fact, the silence was deafening. Alex cleared his throat—twice. "Sorry, bad joke. I know we are all devastated by the death of John Hardy . . ."

Grace looked around as Reid hemmed and hawed his way through his announcements. Studying the faces of her colleagues, she noticed Evan Harrington, the chemistry teacher, regarding her. He quickly looked away. She watched as he held his head straight forward, avoided her stare, and pretended to listen to Reid. He had been a new teacher right before she'd retired, and Grace had served on several committees with him. The students loved Evan because he was young, designed unique ways to teach them chemistry, and taught his classes with a "hands on" approach. Right now, however, he sat in a rigid posture, fidgeting every so often, and avoiding Grace's stare. He occasionally stole a look at someone behind him, but she couldn't figure out whom since his eyes shifted several times.

Grace's eyes moved on to the superintendent, Dawn Johnson, who stood in the back near TJ. Johnson had been with the district three years, and Grace admired the way she handled decisions. Right now, she was leaning against the back wall, staring intently at Reid, a sour look on her face.

Grace contemplated the two administrators. Johnson was in quite a bind if she moved Reid up to the high school principal's position for the rest of the year. It was one thing to deal with the discipline problems—which Reid did now—but a totally different task to make the policies and lead the school. Grace figured Johnson would resolve this situation in the next month, bringing someone else in to be principal. Then Alex would be back at the assistant principal job, where his staff could take care of his lack of organizational skills. Ah, Grace, be charitable, she chastised herself silently.

Suddenly, her eyes were caught by a movement in the back of the room. She noticed Marilyn Atkins, a social studies teacher, who was visibly upset over Hardy's death, her eyes swollen and red. Grace could see she appeared to be having a difficult time keeping her composure even now. She didn't look up at Reid or Grace, but instead appeared to fiddle with something in her purse. Grace felt sorry for her even though they'd not been friends. She found Marilyn cold, and often students would show Grace sarcastic remarks Marilyn had written on their papers. Two seats down from Marilyn was Grace's replacement, June Jaski. Grace looked at the young, slender girl, thinking of herself when she had first started teaching. Well, not really, she thought. I already had three children and had just become a widow. In some ways, Grace envied the woman because she had her whole career ahead of her.

Then she remembered her instructions from TJ. Instead of looking to the front at Reid again, her eyes were drawn to Ellen Terry, the drama teacher. Grace had only heard about her, but it appeared she was a splash of color in an otherwise conservative crowd. Small wonder the students were drawn to her, although Grace thought her rather strange-looking. Right now, she sat in her chair, appeared sleepy, and filed her nails with an emery board. Every so often she switched the position of her feet. Then she picked at her cuticles. Grace turned her attention back to the front and Alex Reid. Better remember to write down a few notes so I'll look official, she thought.

"At this point we believe the—uh—funeral for John Hardy will be later in the week, once the coroner has released his—him to the funeral home. The police, of course, are still investigating, but as soon as we hear about the arrangements, we'll let you all know."

"Will school be dismissed so we can go to the services?" asked one of the teachers.

"I kind of doubt—" Reid looked back at Johnson, who nodded her head. "Uh, uh, that I am, well, wrong, and . . ." He flailed away at his insecurities. "Yes. Yes. We will dismiss school, but I don't yet know when." He looked back at the superintendent.

Grace watched the back of the room, eyeing Johnson as she executed a slicing motion across her neck, then pointed at TJ Sweeney. Reid introduced her, and TJ explained the police would be in the building talking to people over several days. If anyone had any information to give regarding the death of John Hardy, they could call down to the department or speak to her or Jake Williams directly during the investigation. Then she expressed her condolences since they were all sad to lose their principal and friend.

TJ's demeanor contrasted with the bumbling Alex Reid. She was all business, her crisply ironed uniform indicating her respect for her job. Her olive skin, the product of a black mother and white father, turned more than a few male heads in the town of Endurance. Speaking clearly and directly, she reminded Grace of the teenager she'd taught years earlier in this very building.

TJ—Theresa Johanna Sweeney.

Pulling herself back to the present, Grace examined her notes. She had circled five names of people she thought were ill at ease or nervous beyond the ordinary. Of course, this didn't include Alex Reid, who was always flustered and probably didn't want to have this responsibility anyway.

Everyone began to clear out of the library, but a few teachers stopped to talk to Grace. Listening to their comments, Grace thought it felt so natural, so normal to be back here in the library again. Then Evan Harrington brushed past her quickly, without saying a word. Many of her former colleagues made polite jokes about how retirement was treating her since they knew she was now working at the *Register* part-time instead of sitting on a sandy beach soaking up sun on a Caribbean island. Several mentioned how sad it was for her to be back in the building for such a terrible reason.

Grace looked around at the friends and colleagues she had worked with, some for many years. As more details eventually came out, Grace fervently hoped her trust in them was warranted. She couldn't imagine a teacher in that room murdering John Hardy.

Chapter Four

LATER THAT EVENING, Grace was driving home from the high school basketball game with her friend, Deb O'Hara. Alex Reid had gotten permission to have the game despite school being shortened by an hour. In fact, the crowd had observed a moment of silence for their principal at the start of the game. Briefly, she mulled over Hardy's murder on the way home over streets that were much improved from their condition in the morning.

"You're in a pensive mood. Still thinking about Jeff?" Deb asked.

"Oh, I don't know. Between his absence and my time back in the high school, I guess I'm a little lonely. I'd forgotten how much I missed the people I worked with all those years." She swallowed and glanced over at Deb. "Jeff's absence has . . . weighed on my mind too." Turning the corner onto Deb's street, she pulled up in front of the house, where the lights were on inside. The front porch light greeted them like an old friend. "Looks like John left the light on for you."

"Oh, he worries too much. Whenever I'm out with you or the girls, he waits up for me as if I'm an errant teenager."

"You're fortunate to have him. He's a good man. Now get in there, lock the door, and let him know all is safe and secure."

Deb shook her head quickly. "Right. Even though some crazy person is killing people in town."

"I think you're safe, Deb. I'm sure that murder was not random."

"Just the same, people are nervous." She lifted her wool scarf to cover her blond hair. "See ya," she said, climbing out and closing the car door. Grace watched her carefully plod up the sidewalk until she was up the stairs and inside. It must be comforting to have a man she loved waiting for her. Lucky Deb, she thought. Too many years now Grace had gone home alone to her empty bed.

She pulled out, driving carefully on the way home. Her mind went back to the restroom stop she'd made during the first half of the basketball game. Maybe that was why she was brooding. After washing her hands, she was about to return to the ballgame when she looked down the adjoining hallway. The English Department.

Before she even realized it, her feet had carried her down the familiar tiles, past the counselor's office, by the teacher's lounge, and to a classroom she remembered so well. She could tell from a distance the door was ajar and the lights were on. Hmmm . . . lights. Wonder why. Quickening her pace, she stopped in front of her old room, eyeing the new name taped over the door. Hesitantly, she tiptoed through the doorway. Clearly, the room was being used for a coaches' lounge, empty now during the game.

Little had changed: She saw the same student chairs, shelved books, and computer on the teacher's desk. Maroon-and-gold curtains Grace had sewn herself covered the eight windows, so she could lower the light for films during the day. She walked over to her old desk, letting her hand brush the top of it where someone had carved 2002 into the wood. She had never found out who the artist was, but she felt a pull of tenderness at its familiarity. Her lip trembled, but she drew herself back together.

Noticing the corner cabinet, Grace saw new signs and posters which had not been there before. This momentarily startled her: someone else's things. She sat down in the teacher's desk chair, smiling at the classroom. Many of the best years of her life had been spent in this room, years filled with wonder, teenagers, lively discussions, and delirious laughter. She had put the jagged pieces of her life back together here. In the far-left corner desk was where Jim Haskell had sat; now he was an English professor at Rutgers University. Imagine that!

But not all her memories were so pleasant. The seat near the door had belonged to Farley Young—a teenager she had sent out of class on many occasions. He had ended up in prison and, eventually, after his release, he'd blown himself up in a meth lab at his house. Grace shook her head. With his childhood home life, he'd never had a chance. What a terrible waste. On the back wall was the chart Ella Andrews had made about verbs. Grace knew she was married to one of the firemen in the town now. At last count, they had two kids.

So many memories, so much to be happy about. Grace couldn't venture to the post office without waving or talking to former students, now adults. But her life in this familiar room was over. That thought was finally real since someone else's possessions were in her room. Twenty-five years, and they had flown by so fast. It seemed like yesterday Roger had died, her children were small, and her students had healed her, here in this room. Now she had been retired for almost a year. This was the first time since then that she had entered this classroom. She sniffled a moment, gazing out at the silence. Then she grabbed a tissue from Ms. Jaski's desk, wiping her eyes.

She should get back to the ballgame. Deb would wonder where she was. Grace stood up, walked a few steps, took several deep breaths, and stopped in the doorway. Her shoulders slumped and she felt a thickness in her throat. Looking back into the room, she pulled back her shoulders, and then she thought to herself, it will be fine. She had a job she loved at the newspaper, and soon Jeff Maitlin would be back. She turned and sauntered down the hallway slowly.

Oh, but I so loved this life too.

You are feeling sorry for yourself, girl, she thought, as she came back to the present and turned onto Sweetbriar Court. So, stop it! You are fine. Seeing lights ablaze in TJ's house, she figured at least her friend had a little time off from the murder case. Whenever she had a big case, TJ was on it 24/7, and Grace worried about her total focus. It didn't have a great effect on her psyche—dealing with murderers, corpses, and coroners.

Once she was in her house she saw a light blinking on her answering machine on the kitchen counter. Her heart started pounding. Maybe it was Jeff, but why wouldn't he have called her cell phone? Staring at it, she hoped it was Jeff. She held her breath and pushed the button. A message from the library played: they were holding a book she had ordered. Reaching for the counter to steady herself, Grace slumped, and the tightness in her chest felt like her heart was shrinking. As she deleted the message, she smiled bitterly and her eyes filled with tears. Then her doorbell rang and she literally jumped. She wiped her eyes, checked her face in the mirror by the door, and peered out the peephole. It was TJ, whose stomach was calling for Lettie's last piece of blueberry pie. When they opened the refrigerator, they discovered Lettie had left a freshly baked apple pie.

"Which do you want? Blueberry or apple?"

TJ looked at her choices carefully. "Definitely blueberry. Last piece. Okay with you? Or did you want it too?" She sat down at the kitchen table, studied Grace's face carefully, and added, "So, what's wrong? Why the poopy face? The droopy eyes?"

"I'm fine, TJ," she muttered softly.

"That's what you usually say when you're not."

Grace warmed up coffee and set out some plates. "Oh, I'm feeling a little lonely. I stopped in my old room tonight. Of course, it brought back such memories. Made me wonder why I decided to retire. It's a momentary low point."

"Well, in that case, I think we should take a field trip tomorrow."

Grace looked up, a question on her face. "A field trip? What do you mean?"

"I've decided we need a field trip. I haven't seen Maitlin's great monstrosity of a house, so I think it's time I do. Who knows? Maybe a field trip will banish the ghosts away. You keep talking about this place, but I've never been inside."

Grace brightened. "It's been a week or two since I've been there. Sure. I'd like to see what progress Todd Janicke has made. Every time I go to Lockwood House it seems like he's created wonders. Good idea, TJ. Now I feel much better."

TJ grinned. "I wonder why people in small towns call the houses by one of the past owners' names."

"Don't have a clue. When Roger and I married, they called our house the Hamilton House, named for a family who lived there in the forties and fifties. How long does a person have to live in a house before people change the agreed-upon name?"

"Beats me. Good question. Besides seeing the work in progress tomorrow, I must see Hardy's widow, Liz."

"How is she doing?"

"Don't know. But I have questions to ask her, and she is on my list of possible suspects."

"Really? I thought you said whoever killed him must have hated him."

"What is the Shakespearean line about a woman scorned?" She raised one eyebrow. "Evidently, he'd been having an affair with someone, and perhaps she went to see him about the affair that afternoon. Her car was spotted in the high school lot by Evan Harrington."

"I can't believe that. John Hardy? He always struck me as such a straight arrow."

"Oh, I forgot. Roger was a saint who would never have strayed from the path. Unfortunately, Grace, not everyone else is in his league."

"Oh, stop it, TJ. Do you know who this mystery woman is?"

"I have a hunch, but I'd rather not say till I'm sure," TJ said, digging into her pie, avoiding Grace's eyes. "By the way, Evan Harrington is lying to me. He claimed not to know about the meeting."

"Evan?" Her eyes stared at TJ in disbelief.

"Hardy left a note on his desk to see Harrington Monday morning. When I asked Evan about the topic of their meeting, I could tell he was lying."

"Seems odd."

"Lying makes me suspicious. Must be covering up something."

"Did you get the autopsy results? Weren't they supposed to do that this afternoon?"

TJ finished the last bite of her pie, pushing the plate away. "Yeah. This afternoon. The coroner also figures it was poison, but we must wait for the tox report. He echoed Martinez. Thinks it looks like strychnine. Otherwise, the guy was in perfect health."

"What a shame. I liked John. How sad. I can't imagine dying like that, especially not John." She paused momentarily in thought. "Who could get ahold of such a poison?"

"I have my suspicions. Hardy's file cabinet had personnel files for everyone. According to Ann Cummings, the secretary, the board would be apprised of poor teacher performance at their March board meeting. We're close to the deadline."

"Really? Someone who had a bad evaluation might do such a horrible thing? Seems a bit drastic for a bad teaching evaluation, doesn't it?" Grace popped the last bite of apple pie into her mouth. She waited for TJ to take another sip of coffee, and then added, "TJ?"

"No telling what a person might do if he thought he would lose his livelihood. The file cabinet drawer was slightly open, and I found plenty in those personnel folders. One of the negative evaluations was for Evan Harrington, the chemistry teacher." She looked up at Grace, waiting.

"Evan? No. Can't be. The students love him. I can't remember him ever getting a negative evaluation."

"I knew the Grace Kimball defensive proclamation would be the next thing out of your mouth. What else do you know about him?" asked TJ.

"I know when my neighbor Janet Grant's boy, James, took his class last year, Evan tutored James for hours after school because he had a math disability. Of course, math is indispensable for understanding chemistry problems. Evan was tireless in helping him. I always thought of him as one of those teachers who went above and beyond to help kids and make them feel special. Hard to believe he'd do such a terrible thing. Evan doesn't have a mean bone in his body."

"Did you know he does a quasi-CSI unit in his chemistry class these days?"

Grace stared at TJ. "No. I had no idea."

The detective chuckled. "Since all the television shows about crime scenes began, everybody's kids want to be forensic scientists so they can go testify in court. Harrington does a mini-CSI unit, creating a murder so they can try to solve it."

"Doesn't sound like a reason to be suspicious. It actually seems like a great way to get kids interested in science."

"Oh, I agree, Grace. I went in to see him today. He has a cabinet filled with chemicals, but he keeps them locked up. For this CSI unit, some of the bottles are filled with poisons. He says he needs them to show kids what they look like. He gives the future forensic experts a set of facts about the victim's remains, and they must figure out what killed the dead guy. Guess which bottle was missing?"

Grace pulled in her breath and gasped. "Oh, no, TJ. That can't be. Who else has a key to the cabinet?"

"Good question, Grace. All the teachers in the science department have keys to open all the locks on the third floor."

Grace rubbed her jaw, a nervous habit. "What about anyone else in the building?"

"The janitors and the administrators have master keys which will open anything. But I hardly see Alex Reid with enough intelligence to even figure out how to find the poison cabinet, let alone know it exists."

"Where does Evan keep his key? With his other keys?"

"He says he has two chemical cabinet keys. One is with his building keys on one of those things that hangs around your neck," TJ said.

"A lanyard." Grace sighed. "I have so failed you on vocabulary."

"Don't worry, Grace. I don't have to use fancy words to write my detective reports. I'm the Ernest Hemingway of detective report writers. All verbs and nouns."

"So where is the other?"

"Key? Conveniently missing from his desk drawer until recently."

"Since when?"

"Last week," said TJ. "He began to sweat, staring at me with one of those deer-in-the-headlights looks. I waited for him to ask if he needed a lawyer yet."

"Does he?"

TJ shook her head slowly. "Not yet. But the noose is definitely tighter."

"Did you ask him about the bad evaluation?"

"I did. In fact, it was, I'd say, the climax of the interview. He claimed he'd had nothing but positive evaluations, and this is the year he'd get tenure. Says Hardy told him he was good."

"So how does that make any sense?"

"I showed him the red-flagged evaluation from Hardy's filing cabinet. I pointed out a few statements Hardy had written which made it sound like they might hold off on giving him tenure. Along with the evaluation, the file contained a list Hardy had organized—a bulleted list—which prioritized his upcoming actions to remedy Harrington's shortcomings. But first, of course, Hardy wrote a note to himself to talk with the superintendent. I don't think he'd done it yet because a quick call to Dawn Johnson revealed they made a plan to meet next week to discuss evaluations."

"You know, TJ, schools are filled with lots of forms and paperwork. Evan would have had a copy of this bad evaluation. But he denies he knew about it?"

TJ poured a little more coffee into each of their cups while checking a text that just dinged on her cell phone. She closed the screen and looked up at Grace. "You are so right about copies. He said to me, 'I'll prove it to you. I'll show you I have had nothing but good evaluations. Here, I'll get my most recent one.' He pulled some folders out of his desk. Thumbed through them. One of the labels said 'evaluation,' so he took it out and set it on a lab table. I opened the folder. It was an exact duplicate of the red-flagged one I had in my hand."

"What was his reaction?"

"If I didn't know better, I'd say shock. His eyes widened and he was momentarily at a loss for words. Said he'd been down to see Hardy a week earlier about his evaluation. Claims it was all positive. Hardy assured him he wouldn't have any trouble with the tenure designation. Harrington slipped the eval copy in his desk folder and forgot about it. He claims this file, the one on the table, was not what Hardy had given him. Of course, now that Hardy is dead, I'll have a tough time confirming any conversation, especially when the bad evaluations match."

"Do you have enough to arrest him? Could someone be setting him up?"

"Good question. It's an awfully elaborate plan if he's being set up. I don't know what Hardy wanted to see him about on Monday morning. The timing is suspicious. Problem is, I can't put him at the scene. He said he drove by the school and saw Liz Hardy's car. Why would he be driving down the alley behind the school? It's the only way he could have seen her car."

"I'm sorry, TJ," said Grace, shaking her head. "I just have a hard time picturing Evan Harrington as a cold-blooded, premeditated killer."

"I've heard those words pass your lips on several different occasions when someone you thought you knew was in trouble."

Grace rolled her eyes, reminiscent of her high school students. "Haven't I always been right?"

TJ didn't say a word, but a pained expression on her face was enough.

"There. Besides my expertise in gin rummy, I'm also right about your suspects."

"Not sure you are this time, Grace. The fingerprint IDs came back today. Since we have every teacher in the police files, it isn't difficult to figure out who's who."

"Well, who's who? What did you find?"

"Two sets which are definitely suspicious. Another teacher's prints were on a flower vase on the bookshelf. Then, on the coffee cup on the floor in pieces, we found fingerprints that matched Evan Harrington's."

Chapter Five

EARLY ON TUESDAY, Grace sat in her car, the heater running, and stared at Lockwood House. Jeff Maitlin had purchased all four thousand-plus-square-feet of this huge old Victorian built in the late 1800s by Judge Charles Lockwood. Now, he was having the Victorian renovated to its 1800s appearance because it had, unfortunately, been divided into apartments back in the 1950s. Frankly, it hadn't been maintained well since the late 1930s. A local renovator, Todd Janicke, was restoring the inside, but the outside would still need attention once the Midwest weather warmed up in the spring. Grace took a last sip of her coffee, examining the house from her car window as she waited for TJ Sweeney.

Lockwood House was three stories high, boasting several gables and a pointed tower over a third-floor window. The porch roof was supported by three pillars, while the spindles which enclosed the porch sat at odd angles, a few of them missing. The wooden siding would need to be patched and painted, but the roof would have to be completely replaced. Jeff had plans to eventually move in, operating it as a bed and breakfast, so people who returned to Endurance College for special events would have a historic place to stay. Glancing at the porch, however, Grace realized his goal was a long way off.

TJ's truck came around the corner as Grace set her coffee cup down and opened the car door. She watched as the detective parked her truck, turned off the lights and music, and trudged over through the snow. "Time I saw the inside of this monstrosity."

"Oh, come on, TJ. Use a little imagination. It will be beautiful."

Sweeney glanced up at the porch, roof, and siding, shaking her head. "He must be either a millionaire, or else he launders drug money."

"I can't imagine either of those is true. But you're right—it's going to take an awful lot of money to put Humpty Dumpty back together again. Even though Jeff's gone, we can see how Janicke is doing with the work."

"You still have no idea where he gets his money, or why he came to this tiny town from New York City. You have too much faith, my friend."

"But I fell immediately for his blue eyes."

"Right. I've only heard about those fifteen or twenty times. Let's see. Bluebonnet? No, cornflower blue. I don't even know what blue cornflowers look like."

Grace laughed while they picked their way across the slippery street, up the stairs, and into the house.

She called out, "Hey, Todd. It's me. Grace." They heard footsteps; then the pocket doors into the front hallway opened, and a blond head stuck through the opening.

"Hi, Ms. Kimball! You brought Sweeney with you. TJ Sweeney, the most feared fighter on the playground at Gardner Elementary."

TJ smiled, shaking his hand. "No different now, except I get to carry guns with live ammunition."

Todd Janicke's jeans and insulated vest were covered in plaster dust, and some sawdust sat precariously on the curly ends of his hair. His left hand held an electric screwdriver, while his other hand pushed the pocket doors open. "Come on in." He turned, walking back into what had once been a front parlor.

TJ tapped Grace on the shoulder, whispering, "Mmmmm . . ." She nodded toward Janicke's well-defined biceps stretching the soft material of his waffle shirt. Softly, she murmured to Grace, noting, "Nice shoulders, manly power tools, but married . . . Crumb." Grace shook her head, a wry smile on her face.

They walked into a main room that would have been a front parlor. A wall had been taken out on the north end to make the two parlors into one huge room, perhaps in the 1950s. Now the front and family parlors would be their own spaces once again.

"This is amazing," Grace said, her eyes studying the demolished room.

Janicke wiped his arm across his forehead, leaving a trail of plaster dust on his face. "Yeah, well, I came across some problems I hadn't counted on, so I'm a little behind where I'd like to be."

TJ scanned the room, shaking her head. "This might be a lifetime project. Are all the other rooms like this?"

"Some are not so bad, but Mr. Maitlin is always particular about how he'd like this done, and that's the only way I roll."

"When do you think that will be? Done, I mean?" asked Grace.

"My guess is by the end of the year. Course I'm not doin' it all myself. Several of my buddies come over when I need more than two hands. I have a couple of guys on another job; I'll move them here when they're finished."

TJ glanced questioningly at Grace, then turned to Janicke. "So, Jeff won't live here for a whole year?"

"Oh, no. The rooms I'm working on now will be in decent shape by late spring, and he can move in while I'm working. I'll finish an upstairs bedroom. He'll be gone during the day, but he's already had some appliances brought in for the kitchen."

Grace said, "I had a call from Jeff, and he should be back in a few days."

"Oh, good," said Janicke, his voice registering relief. "I want to show him several problems where I need to get some decisions." He checked his watch, saying, "Well, gonna head out and have some coffee with the guys down at The Depot. You two feel free to stroll around all you want. I've taken out paneling and carpet, and most of the windows are stripped down to the essentials. I'll put in plaster, lath, insulation, sheetrock. It's a bit of a mess right now. The chimney and fireplace had to have more work than I anticipated. You'll need to watch where you walk. But, she's coming along fine." He smiled, looking around. "Going to be a proud lady once again, eventually."

After Janicke left, TJ said, "Well, hundreds of thousands of dollars eventually, plus Janicke will be able to retire." She examined all the windows. "Are you sure Jeff didn't rob a bank in his past life?"

Grace laughed, twirling around to get a panoramic view of the parlor. "This is really something. I can't wait to see the finished product. Come with me while I show you the kitchen and the upstairs. You can see where I found Olivia's diary."

As she gave TJ a tour of the broad staircase that led up to the second floor, Grace pointed out the old black metal gaslight fixtures, along with various changes Jeff planned to make. They spent a few minutes in the front bedroom, where Grace had found the diary of Olivia Lockwood, the young wife of the judge who built the house back in the 1890s. The diary was hidden beneath a squeaky floorboard in the front bedroom, the noise causing Grace to unearth it a month earlier. She had read the girl's account, and now Sam Oliver, the history department head at Endurance College, was studying it.

After pointing out what Jeff planned to do on the second floor, Grace took TJ still higher to the ballroom on the third floor. Like the other rooms, it appeared tattered and neglected, but the ceiling held a chandelier surrounded by paintings of cupids or angels which were barely visible beneath the grime. Grace thought it would have been so grand in its day. Then they took the servants' back staircase down to the kitchen and dining room on the north end of the house.

On her way down the stairs, Grace suddenly realized Jeff was everywhere in this house. After he signed the papers, he couldn't wait to take her around each room, seeing the old decaying mansion through the eyes of a dreamer. She remembered their kiss on the huge stair-case leading up to the ballroom, and how he had held her hand, pull-ing her through each room as he had talked excitedly about the changes. Then there was his boyish enthusiasm as he lovingly caressed the mahogany woodwork of the front staircase, his smile and laughter as he pointed out the old gaslight fixtures, his plans for the hallways, and his descriptions as he focused on fireplaces, chandeliers, and wallpaper ideas. The tiny lines around his cornflower-blue eyes wrin-kled from the grin that spread over his face as he had explained each of his ideas. She was sure he would be back. He'd already invested thousands in this mansion.

She had been alone for so many years. Oh, she had gone on dates with other men over those years, but nothing had come of those rela-tionships. They simply weren't Roger. The men she'd seen were somewhat interesting, often kind, but she felt no spark, no impulse that told her she'd like to spend the rest of her life with any of them. Not, that is, until Jeff Maitlin came along.

"So," said Grace, putting her last thoughts about Jeff into words. "I think it's exciting he's decided to stay here in Endurance."

TJ nodded her head. "I hope you're right, Grace. I know how much you want that." Then moving across the dining room, she pointed at some papers, asking, "Is this mail?" She walked over to the pile of envelopes and circulars on the floor.

"Yes. It comes in through a slot, but Todd or I have piled it on the table over here."

TJ gathered up the envelopes, credit card opportunities, and store ads, straightening them out. "Hmm . . . What might this be?"

"You're being snoopy."

"Of course I am." She pointed to her badge. "Police detective."

"Let me see." The heavy manila envelope was packed full, with $8 worth of postage on its corner. The return address said, "Atkins, Pheiffer, & Genler, Law Offices," and was postmarked Chicago, Illinois.

"If he's in Chicago, he's only about three hours away."

"I'm sure that's not true," said Grace, slowly. "He's been gone too long to be so close." But she stared at the address.

"We'll see. I have my concerns about this mystery man in your life. You've hardly known him longer than a few months, and then he disappears."

Grace sat down on a packing box in the middle of the front parlor while TJ stared out the window into the cold, Illinois snowdrifts. Grace had known TJ for a long time, so she could tell her friend was holding something back. "It's your job, TJ. It makes you suspicious of everyone. So, what is it?"

"I had hoped he'd be back by now so he could tell you himself."

"What? Tell me what? Have you been snooping? You know I told you not to bother. He'll tell me at some point."

"Right, like he's done so far." She turned away from the window, walking over to Grace. "Yeah, I did do a little snooping into his background. Someone has to watch your back."

Grace considered for a few moments whether she wanted to know what TJ had found out. She and Jeff had just begun to date when he disappeared. Unlike her sister-in-law, Lettie, Grace was more reticent when it came to asking people about their personal lives. If Lettie had been dating Jeff, by now she'd have known the location of his measles vaccination and what year he got it, as well as its cost.

"Oh, all right. What do you know that I don't?"

"Good thing you're sitting down. I did a tiny background check on him."

"And?"

"And . . . his parents . . . were murdered."

Grace gave TJ an incredulous stare. "What? Murdered? You mean killed intentionally? Oh, TJ? Why? How could that happen to them?"

TJ looked at Grace. "Intentional—yes. I discovered that quite quickly when I investigated where he'd been. The speculation at the time was that his father defended Mafia guys. In other words, he was connected, and both parents were shot execution-style."

"What? TJ, that's horrible! Those poor people. Please tell me Jeff didn't find them. How could he survive that? How old could he have been?" She paused, thinking about the detective's revelation.

"His father was a Chicago attorney, and his mother was one of those charity mavens. They were found murdered in their home in July 1961. Many of his father's clients worked for the mob. At the time their influence in Chicago was high—money-laundering, bookmaking—and it appears Jeff's dad was in the thick of it."

Grace raised her hand to her mouth and asked in a shaky voice, "What about Jeff? Why wasn't he killed too?"

"He was away at the time. Summer camp."

"Did he have any brothers or sisters?"

"No, only child. His grandparents raised him somewhere else."

"Well, it explains why he said he grew up in a small town. He told me Endurance reminded him of those years." She put her hands in her lap and looked down at them, softly shaking her head. "Poor Jeff. No wonder he's been so alone. I can't imagine how anyone could deal with such a horror."

TJ's cell phone began to play the doleful hymn, "Precious Lord, Take My Hand."

Grace looked up at her friend and raised an eyebrow. "Hymns?"

"It's my mom," said TJ. "I'll call her back in a few minutes."

Grace's voice indicated a new resolve. "Jeff will be home soon. I think I need to come up with a way to get him to open up to me. That poor man. I know him and he won't want my pity. TJ, don't say anything to him."

"Don't worry. Mum's the word, but you'd better get some answers soon before I get annoyed and take matters into my own hands." She scowled and uncrossed her arms, pretending to examine a piece of woodwork.

Grace pulled her phone out of her pocket, checking the time. "Oh, I need to get home. Lettie's expecting me to show up because we've hardly seen each other in the last day or so."

"I think you should consider putting her on Maitlin when he returns. She'll get every detail out of him about his history." TJ zipped her jacket, then searched for her gloves.

"Before you go, where are you on the suspect list for John Hardy's death?"

TJ started for the doors to the front hall entrance. "The grieving widow, Liz, is high on my list. Lots of life insurance money there just waiting to be transferred into her bank account. Then we have that other thing."

"What other thing?"

"A covert affair between Hardy and a woman not named 'Liz.'"

"Oh, that."

"Ah, yes, Grace. Hard for you to believe but true. Many a woman scorned has taken matters into her own hands, or hired someone to take care of the 'till death do us part' item in the nuptial contract."

Grace smiled. "TJ, you'll rue the day you kept all those guys at arm's length. When it comes to marriage, you are one cynical woman."

"Oh, please. Can you blame me? It takes someone who isn't trusting to be a detective, which means suspicion seems to spill over into other parts of my life." She looked around. "Well, Grace, my professional opinion is this house needs a little work. Thanks for the tour. I think I'll head back to the station."

When Grace pulled into her garage on Sweetbriar Court, she was still shocked at what TJ had told her about Jeff's history. She considered it on the short drive home. What a horrible thing for a boy to understand or live with. How old could he have been at the time? 1961. Maybe eleven or twelve. No wonder he didn't want to talk about his past. Did they ever catch the people who had done this horrendous murder? What about his grandparents? Could they still be alive?

Grace added up the years in her head. Probably not.

Turning off the car, she sat for a few moments in the garage, feeling the air become colder. She wondered how his parents' murders might have affected Jeff. Maybe that explained why he had never settled down or married or had children. He was so kind, so affectionate, and when it came to the newspaper, he was decisive about how to increase the readership. Maybe he was driven by this . . . this incident—what would you call it?—this horrible memory from his past. But that was so long ago. She put her keys in her purse and collected her belongings to take into the house.

Lettie puttered around Grace's kitchen as if it were her own because Grace was a terrible cook; she was still hoping to keep Jeff Maitlin ignorant of her secret. Grace loved her sister-in-law, but Lettie could be aggravating. Yes, just a bit.

The delectable aroma of Lettie's latest confection hit her nostrils as soon as Grace opened the back door. "Oooooh. What is this lovely smell?"

"A chicken and rice casserole. I made more than enough, so if TJ comes over again tonight, you'll have plenty for dinner."

Grace pinched a little flake of pastry from the casserole dish cooling on the stove, popped it in her mouth, and said, "How did you know she came over last night?"

"Oh, please. That is too easy."

"Really?"

"You go to basketball games when Deb or TJ can go too, and you left a basketball program on the hallway table with yesterday's date. Since you've become involved in this murder investigation, you've gotten back in touch with the high school folks. After all, Grace, you'd never do a job—not even your newspaper stories—where you couldn't investigate and do it thoroughly. And, finally, you love a good basketball game. The Endurance Eagles have won everything in sight lately. Plus, check out your horoscope in yesterday's paper." She walked over to the table, picked up the *Endurance Register*, opened several pages, folded them back, and pointed at the horoscope section. This was Lettie's favorite part of the paper, a section she believed in religiously. "See, look at Libra."

Grace picked it up and read aloud, "You need to get out of the house more and talk to people. Try a sporting event to lift your spirits. Keep your wits about you because some people are not what they seem." She paused a moment, rereading the last sentence.

"See? Horoscopes know everything," said Lettie. Suddenly, she jerked her leg sharply in surprise, saying, "There, there. Eliot. I'll get your lunch too." TJ's cat, Eliot Ness, had been commandeered by Lettie, who taught him to do silly cat tricks. This had proven quite helpful on one deadly occasion.

"Well, I think I'll go upstairs, freshen up, and change clothes. Meeting Deb and Jill. You and Del going out tonight?"

She remembered when Lettie first met Del Novak at the kitchen door with an iron skillet in her hands. It was World War III. But eventually he won her over with his soft, quiet ways. "Nah, we're playing poker with his buddies tonight."

"You too? Playing, I mean."

"Sure. Who do you think always wins? And besides," she added, "I bring the scotch and cigars."

Chapter Six

AFTER LEAVING LOCKWOOD House, TJ Sweeney parked her patrol car in front of Liz Hardy's. Grace was meeting Jill Cunningham and Deb O'Hara at The Depot for lunch. Gnawing away at TJ's thoughts was her concern for her old teacher, mentor, and now friend. With this murder investigation on, TJ was torn in two directions: finding the killer or killers, and keeping an eye on Grace, who always managed to get into the thick of things without regard for her own safety. It wasn't that Grace was a child who needed looking after; she just believed too much in the goodness of people. TJ admired her empathy, but she also knew it had often resulted in Grace's good intentions leading her straight to disaster.

"See, here I am again," she said out loud to her windshield. "I need to think about Liz Hardy, and instead I'm worried about Grace." She pulled her keys out of the ignition, checked for her badge, touched her pocket where she kept a notepad and pen, and looked at the Hardy's house. It was a brick, two-story home in the newer section of town. Now in the winter, the flower gardens on either side of the porch were covered with snow and a shovel had been leaned against the side of the front steps. In the yard was an abandoned sled, deserted for some time by the looks of the snow crusted on it. The sidewalk needed some attention, but TJ figured the Hardy household was a bit disorganized since they were dealing with grief at this address. She wanted to come during the week to question Ms. Hardy because the children would be in school.

TJ lifted her hand to knock on the front door of the closed-in porch, but then she saw a doorbell. It rang with a *Jingle Bells* melody—evidently unchanged since Christmas—the last notes echoing in the cold. As those musical notes died away, Liz Hardy's face, wearing a pinched expression, peeked out the window of the door inside the porch. Well, thought TJ, at least she recognizes me. She ushered the detective in, indicating an area in the vestibule where she could leave her boots and hang up her coat.

"Detective Sweeney. How nice to see you. I figured I would be at the top of your list. Isn't it always the discontented spouse?" She gave TJ a studied, practiced smile, indicating a chair in the living room, and TJ sat in the wing chair, close to a fireplace with no fire and an almost empty firewood rack nearby. The house was totally quiet: no music, no television, and no sounds whatsoever. TJ looked around. The room held matching chairs, a sofa, an ornate mirror on one wall, and pictures of the children on various tables. On the coffee table were magazines, three or four coffee table books, and a small pile of unopened mail.

"Yes, ma'am. I stopped by because I have a few concerns to address. How are you getting along?"

Liz Hardy sat down across from TJ, pulling together the sides of an expensive cardigan sweater for warmth. "As you might expect. Lots of legal estate questions after my husband's death for me to deal with." She paused, crossing her arms in front of her. "May I assume you are closer to finding his killer?" She stared at TJ as if she wished her to come up with the killer's name on the spot.

"Making progress, Ma'am."

"Oh, call me 'Liz.' 'Ma'am' sounds like an old lady."

TJ looked up from her notepad. "All right. Liz it is. Let's start with your husband's behavior just prior to his—his death."

Liz Hardy proffered an ingratiating smile that told TJ the woman had already considered how she was going to handle this expected interrogation. "Oh, Detective. You don't have to put on kid gloves for me. John and I hadn't been sleeping together for months before his death. Furthermore, I could care less about what you think of my lack of grief." She frowned and looked up a moment as if considering what she would say next. "Before his death—murder—he was just like he usually was. The good, highly principled, respected leader of Endurance High School." Her last few words were heavily laced in sarcasm.

"Ma'am? Er—Liz. What exactly do you mean by that?"

"My husband, Detective, was having an affair with one of his employees, for lack of a more descriptive word."

The woman's voice was tightly controlled, TJ thought. "You know this because—?"

"I confronted him, of course. He'd been spending less and less time at home. The children began to think of him as a stranger. Oh, he always had an excuse . . . his job called him away . . . he had to be at an out-of-town basketball game . . . he had a meeting with other principals in the conference . . . blah, blah, blah." She waved a hand dismissively.

"Did you fight about his absences?"

"Fight? I wouldn't exactly call it fighting. I yelled while he simply put on his coat and left. After all, that's the way men handle things, isn't it?"

"But you said you confronted him."

"I certainly did." TJ watched Liz Hardy's eyes narrow and her voice grow more intense. "I spent years working my fingers to the bone to put that man through graduate school so he could have an administrative job which would pay more than peanuts. It would mean more money for us, and he could move up to a superintendent job eventually. So how did he repay me? He had a fling, sleeping with this sleazy teacher who was on his own staff. She's married. Why did she think it would be fine to break up my home?"

"What proof did you have that he was having this affair?"

She walked over to the fireplace mantel and picked up a cigarette from an old-fashioned box, lighting it with a match that she threw in the fireplace. "I don't often smoke. Never in front of the children. But sometimes I just need something to lower my anger level. To answer your question, I knew about the affair because earlier that week—was it only four days ago?—I got a letter in the mail. Oh, it wasn't exactly handwritten. It was high drama." She flicked some ashes into an ashtray she produced from the mantel.

"You know, those movies where a blackmailer sends a note to someone with letters cut out of a magazine. Well, that is exactly how this letter had been put together. It said John was having an affair right under my nose. At first I thought it was a joke, someone playing a prank on the principal's wife. Then I began to consider the possibilities—all those nights out when he came home ridiculously late. Can you imagine for one minute how I felt? Do you realize how small this town is? I'm sure the gentle, understanding townsfolk would think it was my fault. I wasn't making him happy enough, or I wasn't giving him what he wanted. I can hear the gossip now."

"Do you still have this letter?" TJ asked.

A sweeping gesture with her arms accompanied her voice. "Why would I keep it? For old time's sake? Because I'm sentimental? I didn't keep it. I confronted him with it, and then threw it in the fire."

"What was his reaction?"

She smiled like the Cheshire cat in *Alice in Wonderland*. Then she looked directly at TJ again, her eyes cold and determined. "Of course he denied it . . . at first. But John was never good at lying or poker. I knew it was true the minute I saw it in his eyes, and he knew I saw it. So, he confessed. Yes, he'd had an affair, but he'd end it. Break it off. After all, as I said, it's a small town—he'd probably lose his job. A teacher like Marilyn Atkins might get away with it in this day and age, but not a philandering principal. 'Fine,' I said. 'You do that. But don't expect to come near me again. After all, I don't know where you've been, so I don't need to get any of those STDs from some whore.' " To emphasize her point, she ground out the stub of the cigarette in the ashtray and turned toward the fireplace, her head down.

TJ simply looked at her rigid back, waiting for her to continue, the silence lengthening between them.

Then Liz Hardy turned around and said, "I know, looking back now it was a brutal thing to say. But I meant it. He was willing to throw away twenty-two years of marriage on a little trollop like her."

"Was that why you came to the school Sunday, the day he was killed?"

"Exactly. I knew they were together. I was sure of it, and I didn't want to confront him in front of the children, so I figured I'd catch them together and tell him our marriage was over, done."

"And—?"

"Her car was there in the parking lot. I had a key to the doors in the building—he had an extra key at home. When I got to his office he was alone, writing something. I asked him if he'd ended it. He said 'yes.' 'Good,' I said. Then I added a lot of words I didn't mean. But I was so angry, so mad at his betrayal. When he stood up and came across the room, I picked up the closest thing—I think it was some kind of wooden thing, a nameplate—and I threw it toward him. It hit a file cabinet, landing on the floor, not even grazing him. I told him to stay away from me. Then. Forever. I was so humiliated, so angry."

"How did you leave him?"

She stared at TJ, confusion on her face. "You mean, was he dead?"

"Yes."

"No, unfortunately. I stormed out of his office and left the way I'd come in.

"So, alive?"

Once again, her eyes narrowed and she forced her voice to be calm. "Of course. Really, Detective Sweeney, I'm not a murderer, despite what you might think."

"Do you remember what time this encounter was at the school?"

She took a deep breath. "Sometime in the noonish area. My daughter was at a friend's, and my son was watching a basketball game on television. I believe I slipped out around noon."

"How long were you there?"

"Truly, Detective? You expect me to remember? I have no idea."

"Did you take anything with you to this meeting?"

"What do you mean?"

"A box or a bag or your purse?"

"Why would it matter?"

"Answer the question, Ms. Hardy."

"Liz." Again, the smile.

"Liz."

She had long ago dumped the remains of the first cigarette into the fireplace; now she lit a second cigarette from the box on the mantel and smoothly blew out the smoke, saying, "No."

"Nothing?"

"Nothing. Why? Does someone say I did?"

"Just trying to get the whole picture."

"Oh, you mean did I happen to come upon some poison and carry it along with me, asking him to take it?"

TJ smiled now. "I believe you're a little smarter than that, Ms. Hardy."

This time she didn't correct TJ's use of her last name. She drew deeply on her cigarette, blowing out a smooth cloud of smoke.

TJ said, "Tell me, Ms. Hardy, about your husband's will."

"The usual. I get his estate to help raise our kids. Alone."

TJ jotted down her answer, mostly delaying her next question. "Life insurance? Did he have any?"

Now Liz Hardy threw the second cigarette in the fireplace and sat down across from TJ. "You obviously already know or you wouldn't be asking me, would you?" Her smile again.

"I do happen to know your husband took a life insurance policy out about six months before his death. Two million dollars, with you as the beneficiary."

"Correct. With all the school shootings in this country, I believed he owed it to his family to make sure we weren't destitute. You know, they often go after the principal, these shooters."

"I assume the policy payment is being held up pending the investigation?"

"You assume correctly. Two for two. So, if you'd hurry up, get on with this investigation, and find out who really killed my husband, you would assure my children don't starve."

"Oh, please, Ms. Hardy. You worked before you met your husband. How did you put him through graduate school? You must have had a job."

"I did."

"And—?"

"My job?"

"Yes, what did you do?"

Again, a silence fell between them. TJ waited, watching the question play out on Liz Hardy's face. She seemed reluctant to answer it. But then she looked TJ in the eyes, daring her to accuse the scorned woman of murder. "I was a pharmacist. I met him when I was in pharmacy school."

Chapter Seven

GRACE STOPPED IN front of The Depot, a restaurant opened earlier in the winter by two of her former students, Camilla Sites and Abbey Parker. Amid much applause from the town, the women had started the restaurant, creating a pleasant aura for dining and inventing a railroad theme for their décor. Endurance had a long history with the railroad, and the brick building on South Main Street was the perfect place for them to exploit the town's history while also preparing mouth-watering food. Grace stared at the oval-shaped, wooden sign with its old-fashioned gold letters on the wall beside the doorway. Then she broke into a huge smile as she thought of Camilla and Abbey. They were not the top students she'd ever had, but they both had large doses of determination.

They had added recessed lighting fixtures with huge pots of plants hanging from the ceiling, lighted by the new skylights. The interior was decorated in dark green with white contrasts highlighting unevenly faded red brick, some of it from the original depot, which had been built a hundred and fifty years ago. Grace and her friends agreed The Depot would be their spot for occasional lunches and coffee after basketball games.

She pushed open the door, hung up her coat, and walked over to a table where Deb O'Hara and Jill Cunningham were sitting.

Jill said, "It's about time we managed to get together. February is early tax season at the accounting firm, so this may be the last time I see you for a while." She sighed. "You know, I'll be under huge stacks of papers for the next two and a half months."

"I saw you run past the house this morning, all dressed up in your winter running gear. How do you manage to do it every single day?" Grace asked.

Jill shook her head slowly. "Self-preservation. Between taxes and food that goes right to my hips, I fight off the stress, as well as the calories, with my runs. You should try it, Grace."

"Don't think so. An occasional jog with TJ last summer convinced me I'd never be able to keep up a schedule. Breathing is important too."

"By the way, Grace, we already ordered for you. Your favorite: A Train Wreck Burger and The Ties that Bind. I'll help you with the ties—er, fries," said Deb.

Grace rubbed her hands in anticipation. "It's been ages since I've been out to eat with you guys. Sorry about TJ. She's working day and night. Otherwise, I know she'd like to be here."

"Yeah, I believe it," said Deb. "The whole town is on edge about John Hardy's murder." She lowered her voice and added, "I've heard hints, here and there, that we're going to see a public meeting pretty soon. Parents are worried about their kids. At least murder is a good reason to be a helicopter parent—"

"As opposed to—" said Jill.

"Oh, bringing milk and a birthday cake to school for their high school son's birthday," finished Grace, "or protesting some PE dress requirement because their kid is too lazy to change clothes. Frankly, my children would be totally embarrassed if I'd done any of the above back in the day."

Jill looked around at the nearby tables, making sure no one was listening. "I heard John Hardy was found with a lampshade on his head."

"Really?" Deb turned to Grace, her eyes opened wide. "Is that true?"

"How would I know?" Grace's brain began to calculate how that piece of information got out. The killer? Del? One of the younger cops?

"And—" said Jill, "one of the college interns at the accounting firm said she heard that Hardy had on a radio playing 'Creeping Death' by Metallica."

"Geez, this is just the kind of dumb thing which escalates all over town. I doubt any of it is true," Grace said.

"Has TJ confirmed those details?" They both looked expectantly at Grace.

"No," she said, hoping to protect her position as TJ's sounding board. "She never tells me anything about cases." She crossed her fingers on her lap, hoping to be forgiven for little lies. "Alex Reid is now in charge, well, nominally in charge at the school. In another week, the school will be run by the inmates with him *nominally* in charge."

"I thought he was good with discipline," Deb said.

"I think maybe he is," Jill answered. "But how can he manage everything? After Deb was the secretary at the junior high with him, we know he can't manage to keep anything in order."

A waitress came up to them, unfolding a temporary food stand. Abbey Parker followed with a tray of dishes, wonderful food fumes trailing along beside her. "Hi, ladies. Good to see you back."

"Looks like you have a full house, Abbey." The blonde fireplug of an owner blew her hair out of her eyes, setting the tray on the food station.

"Yes, we're doing quite well. Camilla hasn't even had a reason to throw a fit lately. You know what happens when she gets frustrated, Ms. Kimball."

Grace rolled her eyes and nodded. "Yes, I remember that. I get a phone call to come over and calm her down before she puts her fist through a wall." She glanced around. "I must say bricks would be more challenging than drywall."

Abbey laughed, setting plates of food on the table. "So, what's the latest on the murder investigation? TJ got any leads?" asked Abbey. She leaned back on her heels, hands on her hips.

"Not that we know of," Deb said. "She keeps information close. We haven't seen her much, but I'm sure she's working ridiculous hours."

"Sounds like her," Abbey said. "Well, anything else I can get for you?"

The three friends examined their plates. "No, I think we're good," Jill said. "Thanks, Abbey. I'm so happy to see all the business."

"Boy, we are too. Well, enjoy!" She picked up the heavy tray, folded the serving station, and was about to go back to the kitchen door. Instead, she turned back and whispered to them, "Notice the merry widow over there?" She moved her head to her right and they followed her movement. Liz Hardy, dressed quite expensively, was sitting at a table with her lawyer, Simon Barclay.

"Hmm . . . ," said Deb. "She's cut her mourning period rather short, as in two days."

"He is a good catch," said Jill. "Solid balance sheet. Probably owns half the town and single—"

"Sure, if you don't mind two former wives and a solid prenup," said Deb.

Grace watched Liz laugh at something the handsome Barclay had said and then speak earnestly to him, putting her hand over his on the table. "The times they are a-changing," said Grace. "His great-grandfather oversaw Olivia Lockwood's estate back in the late 1800s and into the next century. He, however, was known far and wide for his ethics."

Abbey left and they turned back to the table. All three of them put their napkins on their laps and began to dig into the plates of food, oohing and aaahing. Loud laughter erupted from a table across the room. Grace looked up and recognized four teenagers who had graduated last year when Grace retired. *Inseparable in high school, they all got a three-day suspension for turning John Hardy's car upside down in the parking lot. They said it was just for a prank their senior year. TJ reported they'd camped out at Lake Simpson, gone fishing, and declared it was worth the three-day vacation "just to see Mr. Hardy's face."* Now it appeared the four were still together.

When Jill and Deb came up for air, Grace asked, "What kind of community parent meeting did you hear about, Deb?"

Deb wiped her mouth with her napkin and set it back on her lap. "I'm surprised Lettie hasn't mentioned it since she usually knows everything. It's going the rounds that the high school parents are seriously worried about the safety of their kids in the building if we have a crazy killer running around. I can understand, and I'm thankful my kids are out and gone. As it is, our own children have called home several times to check on us, suggesting neither of us goes in the building. Word gets around fast, evidently all over the county."

"Well, that's a new one. Kids worrying about their parents being knocked off," said Jill. "But we know you'll still go to basketball games."

"Sure. What do my kids know? Didn't I raise them without one broken bone or serious accident?" She paused, setting her fork down. "Actually, I almost called TJ. Janice Tupper came into the Historical Society on Monday morning. Said she saw Evan Harrington's car at the back of the high school Sunday afternoon . . . you know, she lives in one of those houses on the other side of the alley shared with the back of the school. Her location means she sees some really interesting events from her vantage point."

"Such as?" asked Jill.

"Oh, kids making out behind the school, smoking pot. One time the Adderson boy practically undressed his girlfriend against the back wall before Janice marched over and told him he should be ashamed of himself."

"Sounds like Janice," Grace said, laughing. "I'm surprised she didn't call their parents."

"She did."

"At least someone is keeping an eye on the community's values," Jill said primly.

"Ah, Jill," said Deb, her voice lowered. "Didn't you have a tussle or two out behind the building in your younger years?"

"I can assure you I did nothing of the kind," Jill said, her face twisted into a slightly indignant rage.

"Oh, come on, you two," Grace said. She wondered how she ever became friends with two people who were like apples and oranges. Deb could down six margaritas while dancing on the countertop at Patsy's Pub. Grace had actually watched her. Then we have Jill: prim and proper accountant, daily runner, and woman of tremendous willpower. No smooching behind the school for her.

"So why is it such a big deal that Janice saw Evan's car?" asked Jill. "He's one of the favorite teachers, if what I hear is accurate."

"It's what he teaches," Deb said, picking up another fry from Grace's plate and popping it in her mouth.

"Chemistry? Why would that be a problem?"

"Word has it John Hardy was poisoned," Deb said, lowering her voice again. "A chemist would know how to poison people; besides, if his car was there, he was on the spot when the murder took place."

No one said a word after this proclamation.

Grace added, "I heard, via the grapevine, the kids are working on a play they'll perform in a couple of weeks. That eccentric drama teacher, Ellen Terry, is directing it. You know, she's the one I told you about who started teaching last fall. Very unusual woman."

"You can say that again," said Deb. "She put on a whacko play in the fall. John refuses to go with me anymore. She has a strange sense of humor."

"I've heard the kids like her," Grace said.

"According to you, Grace, they like the chemist who knows about poisons too," remarked Jill. "What does it say for their ability to make good choices?"

"Oh, Jill, let loose a little," said Deb. "The drama group is a great place for kids to go find themselves."

"Are they lost?" Jill asked.

"All right, you two," said Grace.

Jill shook her head. "Sorry, ladies. I've had too much work lately, too many things on my plate." She turned to Deb, repeating, "I'm sorry."

Deb said, "That's fine. We understand. Would it help if I ordered a brownie and ice cream, forcing you to split it with me?"

"I'd have to slog an extra mile tomorrow, but it might be worth it."

"So," said Deb, "what play is the drama teacher doing?"

Grace looked at both and said, "Only a play Ellen Terry could pick, given the timing."

"Well, give," said Jill. "*Our Town? Auntie Mame? The Man Who Came to Dinner?*"

"None of the above," Grace said. "Think about it. What would the most totally inappropriate standard high school play be, given the circumstances of last weekend?"

Silence around the table.

Then Jill said, "*Arsenic and Old Lace.* Please tell me it's not."

"Bingo!" said Grace.

Chapter Eight

AFTER JILL AND Deb left, Grace sat for a few moments, lost in thought, drinking her after-lunch coffee. Ellen Terry was hired at the last minute in the fall as a speech and drama teacher. Grace was aware she was a late, desperate hire. However, Grace knew John Hardy. He was a straight-arrow, follow-the-rules kind of person at work. Well, yes, Grace thought, he did have a sense of humor, but when it came to his job he was quite a serious man. He was a polar opposite to Ellen Terry, from what she'd heard of the drama teacher.

She drained the last of her coffee, reached down to grab her purse on the floor, and started toward the cash register. That was when she saw Bob Godina sitting at a table by himself, stirring a cup of coffee. Walking over to him, Grace pulled out a chair.

"May I join you?"

Bob looked up, smiled, and said, "Oh, Grace. Sure." He wiped his mouth with a napkin, adding, "I'm not playing hooky. Honest. I had an appointment, but I don't have to be back at school until two. It's nice to see you. I miss you up at The Big House."

"Me too," said Grace. "Miss you all, that is. I was at the library meeting and saw how upset everyone was. I'm so sorry about John's death. It hit a lot of people very hard, I'm sure."

"True." They were both silent a moment.

"How are things going on the second floor in the earth science classes? Good year? Great classes?" asked Grace.

"I'm doing fine, Grace. You know I only have this year and next until I retire like you. Got any advice?" He ran his fingers through his abundant silver hair, taking a deep breath.

"I think you have to keep busy and do something you love."

"Like your newspaper job?"

"Oh, yes. It's been a godsend. Otherwise, I'd be at home snapping at my sister-in-law."

Bob laughed, and little crinkles appeared around his eyes.

"As it is, I'm watching the murder of John Hardy from afar and wondering what's going on at that school I loved."

He sighed deeply. "I wish I had been there Sunday. Maybe I could have stopped it."

Grace lightly put her hand over Bob's hand, resting on the table. "I'm sure it would have been impossible for you to do anything, no matter your good intentions. Besides, you might have ended up on the floor of the office, dead. Whoever did this was a malicious, inhumane killer."

"I suppose you're right," he said, with deliberate slowness. "That was the day of the storm. Whoever killed John must have been someone from the outside. I can't believe anyone I work with would have done such a terrible thing." He thought for a moment. "He didn't have enemies."

"Let's get off this morbid topic. How is your year going?"

"The students are wonderful." His voice seemed lighter, and he sat up and looked at Grace, sharing a topic they both loved. "I have two sections of earth science that are the best I've had in years. The juniors are a strong class, highly competitive, so that makes it fun and much more interesting—as you know. The other classes are, well, not bad."

"Great. I remember years like that."

"Kind of makes up for some of the . . . other things."

Grace put her purse down on the floor, motioning to Abbey to bring her another cup of coffee. "What do you mean?"

"Oh, I don't want to sound like a Danny Downer," said Bob. "The high school isn't the same as it used to be, you know, when veteran teachers like us were there, and we didn't have so many new people."

"What's the matter with the new people?"

Bob had Abbey refill his cup when she brought Grace's coffee.

"Oh, just leave the pot, please, Abbey. I'll probably be jittery and jumpy all afternoon after so much coffee." Grace smiled and dumped in a little sugar, waiting for her colleague to continue.

Bob's shoulders slumped. "I don't know, Grace. It's just lots of things. I don't want to say these young, new teachers are alike—they're not—but sometimes I wonder about their lack of professionalism."

"Really? Like what?"

"Well, here's an example. I was sitting in the lounge at lunch and one of the new teachers was talking about her summer school class. She said she'd had to take a class to add some certification hours, so she picked a drama course thinking it would be easy. 'You know, plays are much faster to read than novels.' Honest, Grace. That's exactly what she said."

"Right."

"Then she said she realized she'd made a horrible mistake when the professor came in the first day and said they were going to read fifteen plays. Her reaction was, 'You have to be kidding. Fifteen? I've never read more than two plays in my entire life, if that.' She went on to explain that she found study guides for several of the plays, and a book of play summaries and read those. She passed the class with a 'C,' and it was good enough for her. Grace, I was appalled. Here is a woman who is teaching students, but she herself is totally dishonest, not to mention lacking any intellectual curiosity. Her attitude shocked me. Where do these so-called 'teachers' come from, and how did they get through college classes, well, except by cheating?"

"Surely she's an exception."

"I'm not so sure, Grace. You and I are 'old school.' We believe in promoting intellectual curiosity, pushing students hard to do their best, and not simply giving them easy grades. That's changing now. Sometimes I think these new teachers see teaching as a business, one where you don't take any papers home at night, and you leave practically before the students. With that kind of attitude, so many kids fall through the cracks."

They both drank their coffee, sitting for a moment in silence.

"I have a prep period with several people, one of them being Ellen Terry, the new drama teacher," Bob said. "Thank goodness she doesn't show up in the teacher's lounge often because I can't get anything done once she arrives. No one can. We just leave with various excuses at differing intervals. She's loud and obnoxious. I can't figure out how she ever became a teacher.

"Of course, the teenagers are always entertained by someone new, young, and interested in pleasing them and being liked. Ellen Terry asks too many obvious questions for a person who's been teaching for a while. She's seriously mixed up by the new evaluation process, but then, to be fair, a lot of us are."

"New?" Grace said.

"Yes. It goes hand-in-hand with the loss of tenure in a couple of years. We must have a better way to evaluate teachers. The state is pushing it."

Grace nodded her head. "If tenure goes, what happens? They can get rid of bad teachers more easily, but where is the protection for good teachers?" Grace's voice became stronger, picking up on Godina's unhappiness. "The best are often the veterans who make the bigger salaries."

"Exactly right. It's a matter of trust. Nowadays, trust is a rare commodity." He stirred his coffee and thought for a moment. "It's about recall rights too, Grace. Often the cash-strapped state doesn't make payments, and teachers must be let go until the board sees if the program money will be available. So, who will the board call back first—a teacher paid $28,000 or a veteran paid $45,000? With tenure, seniority mattered. Enter the new evaluation system. Now it won't."

"Is this evaluation policy a subject people have been arguing about?"

"You better believe it. It was under debate last summer when we had some meetings, plus throughout the first semester. We finally hammered out a system, but, of course, it has possibilities for unfairness."

"Any evaluation system would when you're dealing with humans."

"Sure," said Bob. "I don't know where this new policy is going to go now with John Hardy gone. At least he was reasonable and had been a teacher in the past. Unlike some administrators, he remembered the classrooms he came from." He poured the few last drops of coffee into his cup. "I think John was under a great deal of pressure."

"Why would you say that?"

Godina seemed to take a rather long pause before he continued with an answer. He scanned the room and, seeing no familiar faces, said, "I heard he was concerned about a person on the faculty cheating on their test scores."

"Cheating?"

"The new evaluation also includes student test scores."

Grace's voice rose. "What?" Then she looked around and lowered her voice. "Why?"

"State law. We have to show students are making progress somehow."

"But you and I both know we've watched students make beautiful patterns on their answer sheets. It's easy to do with those bubble sheets."

"Now they're doing it on their electronic notepads. The tests mean nothing to them. If they fail the standardized test, they still graduate because it doesn't affect their grades. Why do well?"

"You're saying this determines whether you're a competent teacher?" said Grace, shaking her head.

"Yes, but it's only one part of the evaluation, Grace. It doesn't count as much as actual observation in the classroom. That's another story. All kinds of domains and questions for administrators to answer as they watch teachers teach."

"Thank goodness it counts more than the student test scores. So where do the tests come from? Is it possible to cheat on them?"

"Part of the test is the standardized one; it would be difficult to change those answers. Now that we're doing computerized tests, it's not easy to change test answers. But we also use local tests made by teachers, and those tests should show improvement from early in the year until later in the year. The teachers grade them, turning in the scores."

Grace shook her head. "Of course, they show improvement. The students haven't had the material yet at the beginning of the year. Any fool could make that happen. Just more jumping through hoops."

"Rumor has it that Hardy suspected someone of changing his or her local test scores."

"Wow," said Grace. Then, almost as an afterthought, she added, "I wonder if that's what he wanted to talk to Evan Harrington about."

"Evan?" His eyes widened and he touched Grace's arm. "Why?"

Grace had to backtrack to get out of this slip of the tongue. "Oh, I heard the police found a notation on John's desk calendar to talk to Evan on Monday. It's probably a rumor flying around town. You know how that goes."

Bob slowly shook his head. "I can't imagine Evan Harrington would cheat on test scores. He's just not that kind of person."

"How do you know? What if his job depended on it? You talk as if this new system would warrant that."

He was silent for a few seconds. "I know Evan well, Grace. We have a prep period together and teach in the same department. You get to know people when you're thrown together with them. He's very innovative. The kids like him, John Hardy likes him, and I can't imagine he would have a problem with test scores. He wouldn't cheat."

Then they were both silent, lost in thought.

"Are the mailboxes still in the teacher's lounge?" asked Grace.

"Sure. If he checked his mail for a note on Friday and found one from Hardy, he would have said something." Godina paused thoughtfully. "I don't remember anyone delivering him a note from the office during his prep period either."

"Well, I imagine I just heard a rumor. This town is rife with them."

Bob nodded his head, beginning to put his coat on. "I need to go, Grace. Remember, I'm still teaching," he said, picking up the mood.

"You're going to the funeral Friday, I'd guess?" asked Grace.

"Yes." He looked away from her. "It will be difficult."

"Maybe the teachers can lean on each other."

Bob hesitated a moment, and said, "Yes, you're so right."

After paying her bill, Grace thought about the changes Bob had brought up. Not gone a year, she thought, and already the climate at the school is changing. If Bob Godina is right, this new system is pushing the change and driving a wedge among the people she fondly remembered.

Chapter Nine

THE AIR FRIDAY morning was fresh and crisp with no hint of snow or storms. What a perfect day for a funeral, Grace thought, if you had to have one in the winter. She remembered her own father's funeral years earlier in Indianapolis. His was in February too, but overnight they had an ice storm, stranding many of their friends in airports all over the country. But not today, she thought. Sitting quietly in the church, her hands folded in her lap, Grace tried to forget that memory by watching the mourners.

Liz Hardy was immaculately dressed in a black silk suit, keeping close to her two devastated children, one in junior high and one in elementary school. Watching the grieving family, Grace found John Hardy's violent death so unfathomable. TJ would tell her about evil, even in small towns, but Grace didn't want to believe her.

She could see the district's faculty had turned out, and she also noticed TJ standing quietly in the back, observing the crowd. Out of the corner of her eye, Grace saw the entire coaching staff, plus Alex Reid. They sat in a starched, suited, and neck-tied group, uncomfortable without their shorts, T-shirts, and sneakers.

Other mourners caught Grace's eye. Marilyn Atkins sat in a back pew, red-eyed as usual, but without her husband. Del Novak came alone, quickly leaving after the service. He was probably nervous that he might have to see Hardy's horrible grinning face again, but the family had chosen to have a closed coffin. Overflowing flowers of every imaginable kind covered the casket, with plenty of colorful blooms sitting in spaces at the front of the church.

After the service, Grace elected not to go to the cemetery or stay for the bereavement lunch in the church's social hall. She needed to steal away home, have her own lunch, and pick up her notes so she could get down to the *Register*. As she was walking to her car, she felt a hand on her shoulder. Turning, Grace saw a disturbed Evan Harrington.

"Grace," he said, his eyes matching his pleading voice. "I know you and TJ Sweeney are tight. Do you think you could put in a good word for me?"

Grace smiled, played dumb, and said, "A good word? What do you mean?"

"She's questioned me twice now," he said and swallowed nervously, looking away. "Believe me, Grace, I had nothing to do with this. You know me. I couldn't kill a fly, let alone poison somebody, especially not John Hardy. He was great to me."

"I think if you didn't do it, Evan, you have absolutely nothing to worry about. TJ is really good at her job. She pokes and pries at everything, trying to find out the truth."

"She seems to do a lot of that specifically with me. I wasn't even there, Grace." He cleared his throat. "Yeah, I did stop into the building on Sunday, but it was to pick up the lab reports I'd left on Friday. I slipped in the back door and up the back stairs. Didn't go anywhere near the main office. I couldn't have been in the school more than five minutes, tops."

"Did you see anyone else?"

"No. Hardy's car was in back where he usually parks, plus another one with his wife's name on the plate. I think I saw a car in the student parking lot." He pursed his lips, picturing the scene in his head. "I guess I didn't pay much attention at the time since I was in a hurry."

"Makes sense, Evan. But it means no one saw you either. I suppose TJ asked you where you were on Sunday."

"Yeah, of course. But I didn't mention I stopped into the building because I was afraid it would put me at the scene. She's already suspicious enough. After all, I'm the man in the school with the chemicals, although the janitor's closet has chemicals too. It's not just me. And incidentally, I don't see anyone questioning him."

"I hadn't thought about you and chemicals. Does anyone else have access to wherever you keep those chemicals?"

"Of course. The other teachers on my floor do, as well as anyone with a basic AC314 key. It's a common key." He paused. "Oh, and I also keep a second key in my desk drawer."

"Could someone get into your desk drawer? Do you keep your office locked?"

He paused a moment, combing his fingers through his hair. "Oh, Grace, you know what it's like. Since I teach five classes, I go in and out of my office to grab things I need. I pop downstairs to copy papers or stop in at the main office or take a bathroom break. Geez, I forget to lock it half the time. Yeah, I know I shouldn't be so casual about locking up chemicals or poisons with teenagers around. I made a pledge to myself to work harder on that."

"You have the carelessness going for you then."

"How do you mean?"

"They can't prove you alone have access to your chemical cabinet. Of course, if they find your fingerprints on a bottle of poison that matches whatever the autopsy finds, now that might be a smoking gun. When was the last time you opened the cabinet?"

"The poisons specifically? Not since last spring. I do a special CSI unit in the spring."

"Can you think of anyone else in the building who might be so angry at Hardy that he would do this?"

Harrington shook his head, responding thoughtfully. "I can't imagine anyone I teach with could be a murderer."

Grace smiled. "I used to believe that about people I knew too, but look where it got me last month. I ended up right in the middle of a murder investigation, trying to prove a former student could never have murdered her husband." She hesitated, considering what else she could say to help Evan while not betraying TJ's conversations with her. "I struggle these days not to think the worst of people; it's sad because it's not who I always thought myself to be. Well, for what it's worth, I'll share some advice. I think you should search through your memory, especially over the last few months. Consider details. Sit back and let your mind travel through those months. Sometimes a memory will come back to you that you didn't think was important at the time."

Evan looked up at her, touching her arm. "Thanks, Grace. I feel better already. You always were a real friend to me, especially when I first came to teach here. It was tough to move into a new district where I didn't know anyone, but you went out of your way to be helpful. You didn't have to because you were heading toward retirement. I'll never forget that." His eyes dropped, embarrassed by revealing such a raw emotion. He cleared his throat, backing up a step. "I'll do what you say: try to relax a little bit. Maybe you're right. After all, the brain works in very mysterious ways! Chemicals, you know, and electricity."

"Good luck. Evan, trust TJ to figure this out. She'll get the right person."

Grace watched him walk back to his car, his shoulders slumped, his gait slow. She believed in her heart of hearts Evan Harrington could not have done this terrible thing. But then she considered that TJ always told her she was too trusting. Which is it? she thought. She realized Evan didn't mention the strychnine was gone from his cabinet. TJ told her that. Should that lapse make her trust him less?

She turned onto Sweetbriar Court and saw a police squad car parked down at the end of the street in front of Ardis Brantley's house. Oh, no, not again, she thought. After putting her car in the garage, she decided she'd walk down and see what was happening. Maybe she could help.

Trudging down the snowy block in the car tracks, she saw Ginger Grant coming out of Ardis' house, followed by a policeman. It was Ted Collier, the guy the other cops called "Mr. Chivalry" because he was always so sympathetic and kind to crime victims. Before Grace got to them, Ted started his car, driving cautiously down the street. He waved at Grace, but didn't stop. Again, Grace thought about how comfortable it was to live in a small town where people helped you.

"What's up?" she said to Ginger, who was walking Ardis's English cocker spaniel, Stella, on a red leash. Ginger had been Grace's student a year ago, before Grace retired. An intelligent girl with strawberry blond hair that waved slightly, she had dark brown eyes like Grace.

Ginger's face lit up. "Hi, Ms. Kimball. It's okay. Ms. Brantley's fine, but I think occasionally she gets nervous or needs someone to talk to. Officer Collier said he was doing a wellness check since they'd been to her house about the fire alarm. I try to stop in too. It's a little harder for me to get down there to walk Stella when I'm in school, but today, you know, school was out for the funeral, so I had some time to stop by."

Grace had forgotten Ginger's bubbly voice and endless energy. "You are kind to check in on her, Ginger. Makes me feel guilty."

"Oh, but you take care of everyone else. I miss you at the high school, and I'm reading a great book right now. You'd know it— *Crime and Punishment*. I got it from the list of college-recommended books you gave us last year."

"Wow. Dostoevsky. Pretty dark. What do you think so far?"

"I think people's minds are weird. Here this guy murders someone he doesn't even know to see what it feels like, then suffers from terrible guilt. I know it was written long ago, and this guy is Russian, but it seems to me like lots of people do that kind of thing today, but they don't feel guilty, do they? You see it all the time on the news. I mean, look at Mr. Hardy. Somebody killed him, but I don't see anyone turn up at the police department to say, 'Gee, I feel guilty and I did it.' " A pained expression on her face followed this literary assessment.

"That's a very good point, Ginger. What do your friends at school say about all of this?"

Ginger reached down a moment, petting Stella's soft caramel coat. Then she stood back up and said, "Well, depends on who you ask. Nobody's sure what to think. I mean, well, what if it's a teacher? Geez. Can't imagine a teacher who would do such a terrible thing. Why, Ms. Kimball? Why would a person kill Mr. Hardy? I always thought he was a great guy. He'd be in the hallways between classes talking to everyone because he knew all of us by name, even though there must be seven hundred kids at the high school."

"Are your friends nervous about it?"

"Well, again, depends. My mom says some of the parents are saying they may keep their kids at home until Detective Sweeney figures it out. I think that's dumb."

"I wish I had answers for you, Ginger. I don't know who did it, and I know most of the teachers in the building, except for the new ones. Seems hard for me to believe too. But I have faith in Detective Sweeney, and since she lives right here in the neighborhood, I'm sure we're safe."

Ginger's eyes sparkled and she grabbed Grace's arm. "I forgot to tell you the best news of all, Ms. Kimball. I'm going to be in the junior class play. Ms. Terry picked me for what she calls 'an old water chestnut' called *Arsenic and Old Lace*."

"I think the phrase 'an old chestnut' means a play that has been done often. Perhaps it doesn't seem like such a great choice after Mr. Hardy's death."

"But we've practiced it already for about three weeks. The blocking is done—you know, figuring out where we should stand or where we move. Memorizing is next. We didn't know something terrible was going to happen, but we already have too much time invested to stop. I'm sure glad we weren't in the school on Sunday."

Grace patted Stella's smooth, silky coat and looked up. "What part do you have?"

"I play the part of Abby Brewster. She's one of the wicked but lovable elderly aunts who poisons people. It's so hilarious because Ms. Terry knows that a killer is not who I am. A little weird, Ms. Kimball—she told me to have fun with it."

Grace smiled. "I'm sure she was joking, Ginger. It's been a long time since I've seen that play. This is one of those stranger-than-fiction things, I mean, the fact that she would do this particular play when Mr. Hardy just died." Grace stopped herself before revealing he'd been poisoned, because she wasn't sure how much to say. It was likely, however, that everyone in town was aware of how he died, except for the underbelly of gossipers who undoubtedly had him stabbed, shot, or thrown down the stairs in their discussions. Small towns were hotbeds of inaccurate information, the more salacious, the better. Endurance was about the same as any other, she supposed. She glanced at her watch.

"Oh, dear, I need to go. Well, you must keep me updated on *Crime and Punishment*. I wonder how it will end."

"Now you're kidding me, Ms. Kimball. You know how my book's going to end. You've read just about anything I could quiz you on, I think." She paused. "I'll take Stella along with you past your house. She needs some exercise, so I thought I'd at least walk her to the end of the Court. I'll keep you up to date, and you must come see our play, of course."

"Absolutely. Take care of yourself. I miss seeing you too at the high school," Grace called to her.

Ginger waved enthusiastically and went on down the street, Stella trotting happily in front of her, excited to be out of the house. After Grace closed her garage door, she ambled into the house, stopping in her kitchen. It was obvious Lettie had been here because lunch was in the refrigerator, and a casserole sat next to it, covered in plastic wrap, ready to put in the oven for dinner. She always left Grace very specific instructions for the oven temperature as well as how long to cook the food. She taped them on the plastic. This time she also left a message to "take off the plastic wrap before you cook it. You remember what happened last time you left the plastic on. Geesh! What a smell!" Grace shook her head and chuckled.

She had obviously been distracted a month earlier when she put the dinner in the oven and left the plastic on. The next thing she knew, she smelled something smoldering, and when she opened the oven, smoke billowed, the smoke alarm went off, and the Chicken Delight Casserole was definitely not delighted. Cooking was simply not a household job she would ever understand. It wasn't that she was stupid.

When she and Roger married years ago, it became painfully clear she was not going to be Mrs. Homemaker, unlike many of the wives who lived near them and could throw together a feast, watch three children, and have a spotless house. Grace thought those women were like one of the 1950s television commercials for the perfect wives using the newest appliances. As time went by, she became somewhat proficient at tuna casseroles or homemade pizza. Thank goodness Roger was the epitome of patience and understanding. But wasn't that what you were supposed to do when you loved each other? Take the bad with the good, forgive, and let each other grow?

Chapter Ten

LATER THAT EVENING, Grace perused the *Register* for errors and ty-pos, and finding few, she gloated. See, Jeff Maitlin, we can keep this newspaper afloat without you, she thought. She had remembered to take off the plastic wrap from the casserole, eating way too much of Lettie's tasty dinner. Now she was ready for a cup of warm tea and an old movie.

Sitting down in her recliner, she put the teacup on the table, grabbed the remote, and switched the television to a movie channel. She had just begun to watch *The Way We Were*—one of her favorites—with Barbra Streisand and Robert Redford. Too bad it wasn't a DVD or she could put it on pause long enough to simply stare at Robert Redford in his white uniform at a New York City bar. No man de-serves to look that handsome in a uniform. She sighed. Then the house phone rang. She glanced at her clock. It was seven p.m. Couldn't be TJ because she'd call Grace's cell. Could be a robocall or someone who wanted to sell her something. She checked the phone, and since it was a local number, she picked up the receiver.

"Hello."

"Grace, thank goodness you're home!"

It was a man's voice, vaguely familiar.

Grace's eyebrows furrowed. "Who is this?"

"Evan. Evan Harrington. I need to talk with you, Grace. I took your advice. I remembered something. I wasn't thinking about Hardy at all. That's what's so strange. It came to me out of the blue. It's really important."

"Well, what is it?"

"Grace, someone is trying to frame me for John Hardy's murder—first, a bad evaluation which I'd never seen, then my coffee cup stolen from the lounge and left in Hardy's office. It's been missing for a week. We need to talk in person, and it would be better away from the school grounds. Sometimes I think these walls have ears. Can you think of a good place to meet? I'm at school right now."

Grace checked her watch. "Well, all right. How about the little coffee shop down on the Square? It's still open."

"Perfect. I—I'm sorry to call you about this, but I didn't know who else to call."

"Why not Detective Sweeney?"

"Grace, she already has me one foot in prison for the rest of my life. No, I'll meet you at the coffee shop in, say, fifteen minutes?"

"I can be there, Evan. I'll put on my coat, and I'm out the door as soon as I hang up."

"Grace . . . I don't know what to say. Thanks. I appreciate your help so much. You're a lifesaver. Just need to pack up my stuff before I go down to the car. See you in a few minutes."

Ten minutes later she had parked and ordered coffee at The Coffee Bean, owned by one of her former students, Sissy Brock. *Sissy could have been a poster girl for STEM programs, long before the acronym became popular for girls who were good at math, technology, and science. Sissy and two of her friends figured out how to make the very volatile nitroglycerine in the high school chemistry lab. Forced a full school evacuation. Fortunately, they didn't add one ingredient, which prevented the demolition of the high school and surrounding blocks.* She assumed Sissy was more careful brewing coffee.

Only one other person was in the shop, sitting in the back. It was a cozy little business, with all kinds of coffees and teas. Grace ordered a French press, light roast coffee with a shot of caramel. She looked around at the tables and noticed an area of comfortable, stuffed armchairs, arranged in groups so customers could have conversations. A sign on the wall said Wi-Fi was available, and that brought in quite a few college students or professors who liked to drink coffee while they worked on their papers.

Grace set her coffee down on a table close to the front window where she could watch for Evan. What did he remember? She looked at the clock over the counter. 7:15.

Gazing out the window across the Square, she watched the old-fashioned historic lights, spreading a warm glow through the misty night. Three creamy round globes adorned the top of each light pole, their lights reflecting on the store windows on the quadrants of the Square. She observed the dark front of Gimble's Paint and Wallpaper Store. The last time Grace had called the paint store to ask about whether they still had cement sealer for her porch, Mandy Thompson answered with, "Gimble's Paint and Wallpaper Store. This is Mandy. How may I help you color your world?" What a clever thing to say to customers, Grace thought, smiling at the memory.

Her eyes strayed to the Second National Bank of Endurance, under new management since the difficulties from earlier in the winter. That reminds me. I need to give Emily Folger a call and see how she is. Grace had kept in touch with Emily since her life fell apart when her husband was killed.

Next to the paint store was the Endurance Public Library, a single light burning over the doorway. How many hours she'd spent there with her three children, Roger Jr., Katherine, and James. What sweet memories we have from those times. She was glad Roger brought her here to his hometown when they got married. She took a sip of coffee. It was such a lovely place to bring up our children. The bell on the coffee shop door jangled, causing Grace to look up, expecting to see Evan. But it was Jane Randolph. Grace knew her because she worked at the courthouse. *Jane Hillman, later Randolph, had graduated as the valedictorian of her class. Let's see. Probably twenty years ago.*

She stared at the clock again. 7:25. Where was Evan? She stirred her coffee for the fourth or fifth time and checked her phone, but she didn't have his cell number because he'd called on her house phone. Technology. Much good it does me in this situation! He might be between here and the school by now. She determined she'd wait until 7:45, then drive by the school to see if his car was gone. Finishing her coffee, she frowned and peered anxiously out the window into the darkness. By 7:50, she figured he wasn't coming.

Driving past the school, she saw lights in the top-floor hallway windows. That was where the science lab was, but then the night janitor might be up there working too because his battered brown Ford was parked out in front. She studied the parking lot as she drove by, but it was deserted, its tall mounds of snow standing like sentinels on the easternmost corners. Well, she thought, where did you go, Evan? Pulling into the alley behind the school, she peered between the ends of the building addition. The outside night lights glowed in a straight line all the way down the brick school wall, and Grace could see Evan's dark blue Ford in the spot where John Hardy often parked. That's strange, she thought, biting her lip.

She pulled out her cell phone, punching in TJ's number, and the detective's voice came on the phone after three rings. Grace could tell she'd been napping because she sounded groggy. After explaining the situation with Evan Harrington, Grace asked if TJ could come meet her. But how would they get in the school?

"I've got a master key, Grace," said TJ. "Johnson gave it to me because it was easier than making people let me in all the time. I'll drive over and meet you in back. It could be he's up in his lab and just forgot the time."

"I don't think so," Grace mumbled. "He seemed very interested in talking to me about something he remembered." She paused and took a breath. "I'll wait here behind the school, but hurry, TJ."

"You stay in your car and be sure to lock the doors. I'll be there in no time at all."

Ten minutes later, TJ's truck cruised around the corner of the building, and the detective pulled in next to Grace's car. Together they unlocked the back door of the high school, TJ in the lead. She'd told Grace to stay behind her, checked the magazine in her gun, and went through the door, alert for anything. The building was quiet, except for the furnaces, which thundered every time the fans came on. They walked the length of the lower-level hallway, their footsteps on the tiles sounding muffled from their snowy shoes. Up to the main office. Another set of stairs took them to the top floor, Grace huffing and puffing a little after two flights of stairs. TJ, of course, could have doubled her speed without breathing hard, Grace thought. All the lights were on in the second-floor hallway. No janitor in sight.

"He could be on a break down in the janitor's room," whispered Grace. "Maybe he was up here, left on a break, and that's why the lights are on."

They walked down the long hallway to Evan Harrington's lab, finding the door closed and the lights off. TJ used her key to open his room. Moving cautiously, she signaled Grace to stay back in the hallway. She flipped on the switch inside the door. Instantly, all four banks of lights came on in the lab area. Nothing. Grace peeked around the open door, watching TJ walk farther into the room, looking behind lab benches. Then she turned toward Evan's office, which was attached to the far end of the lab, unlocking that room too.

"Nothing. Come on in, Grace," she called.

Grace moved toward TJ and glanced around, opening the closet door near Evan's office. Her eyes squinted. "This is strange. He always hung his coat in this closet, and he'd have his briefcase with him. They're both gone. Still, his car is out in the parking area behind the building."

"Then he has to be here somewhere." TJ rubbed the back of her neck and scowled. "If he left his office, heading downstairs, which stairway would he take? I'd guess the back stairs. It's the only way he would leave unless he went out the front, which would be stupid with his car in back. The outside door we came in opens into the lower hallway, but it doesn't access the back stairs. Come on, let's try the back stairs and see where he might have gone from there."

Locking all the doors, they trudged back down the stairs, which extended from the third floor to the basement at the building's south end. Night lights shone dimly on the stairwells. On the second floor, TJ stopped, pausing to look through the glass panel in the door to the landing, a door that opened into the main-floor hallway. It was dark; nothing was moving clear to the north end of the building. TJ turned and started down the last flight, Grace following close behind. Suddenly, Grace bumped into TJ with an "umph." She heard the detective pull in her breath, saw her shoulders tighten, and felt her put her hand back to Grace's waist.

"Go back to the landing, Grace." Then she started cautiously down the stairs. Ignoring her, Grace crept behind TJ, staring ahead at the lights outside the door on the end of the building. What was TJ seeing? The stairwell below was bare, painted a neutral institutional gray. The metal railing on the stairs was cold to the touch.

Grace tried to see around TJ's back, but to no avail. Her leg muscles tightened, sensing the detective's caution. Following TJ's movement, she shifted her gaze to the stair railing on her right. That's when she saw Evan Harrington's open briefcase, its contents strewn all over the floor. Then she stuck her neck out to see around TJ and gasped. At the bottom of the stairs was Evan Harrington, his eyes staring skyward, his neck twisted at a strange angle, and his feet still lying on the lowest three steps.

Chapter Eleven

GRACE STARED AT the clock on her bedside table. 2:45 a.m. She turned over, plumped and repositioned her pillows, and pulled up the covers, but to no avail. Evan's lifeless eyes and the horrible picture of his crumpled body kept floating through her brain. She couldn't get the image out of her head. Over and over her thoughts replayed the scene at the bottom of the stairwell as if it were on a loop. How does TJ do this? She wondered.

Her thoughts went back to the school. After TJ turned, telling her to sit down on the top step or return to the hallway on the landing, the detective carefully advanced down the stairs, not touching the railing or the wall. Grace slowly lowered herself to the step and observed. TJ bent over Evan carefully, keeping her balance as she examined his body from above at different angles and then, finally, checked for a pulse. Then she watched TJ turn her head and look up at the wall above the landing and behind Grace. Following the line of TJ's sight, Grace saw above her, perched on a small shelf over the landing doorway, a camera, aimed down at the stairway.

Grace stared at the camera and then turned back around. She saw TJ pull a cell phone out of her coat pocket and call the police department, asking Myers to assemble Jake Williams, the coroner, and the CSI team. Then, as an afterthought, she told him to call Dawn

Johnson, the school superintendent, to let her know another death had occurred in her building.

Cautiously, TJ came back up the stairs, unsmiling and choosing her words with care. "Grace, I want you to do two things for me."

"Yes, TJ." Grace's voice echoed in the stairwell, a rote reply as shock had set in.

"Find the night janitor and tell him to stay out of this entire area of the building; then go home and lock your doors. I mean that, Grace. Lock your doors. I'll talk to you as soon as I can get loose." She started down the steps, but then Grace saw her stop, pause, and come back up to the landing. Her voice took on a kinder tone. "I'm sorry, Grace. I know he was your friend. You've already defended him to me with the loyalty I've grown used to hearing from you." She smiled, leaving out her usual cynical reply. Now her words were tinged with sadness. "If this turns out to be anything but an accident, I'll admit you were right to believe in him." She pulled Grace to her feet, looked in her eyes, which were blinded temporarily by tears, hugged her, and told her sternly, "Get yourself together. I must stay with the body, so I need your help. Go find that janitor, and then get home before the emergency vehicles block you in."

Grace rolled over in her bed, staring at the clock again. 2:53. Closing her eyes, she tried to get the vivid pictures out of her head. This is useless, she thought, with a heavy sigh. She moved over on her back and studied the ceiling. She had driven through the dark streets, tears streaming down her face. She kept replaying Evan's call—"You went out of your way to be helpful. I'll never forget." That thought switched to his voice asking for help when he had called her only a few hours earlier. She counted it up in her head. Almost eight hours. He was alive then and needed me. What was it he remembered? Was someone else in the building, someone who overheard him?

Thanks, Grace. You're a lifesaver. "Well, I guess I wasn't," she said out loud, tears filling her eyes again. She reached for a tissue, wiped her face, and sat up. Her bed was close enough that she could just see out the window. The streetlight shone on the glistening snow, and not a car was in sight. With no wind, the street was perfectly calm. She stared silently out the window.

3:01. She lay down once again, pulling up the covers. Her legs were restless and her mind wouldn't shut down. He trusted her. She would never believe Evan could have killed John Hardy. Again, she recalled all the evenings when she left the building as the day was starting to get dark, and Evan was still grading papers in the teacher's lounge or running off copies. Does a person like Evan murder people? Grace remembered her last year when the Coates boy was having so much trouble at home. Evan let him hang out in his room and listened to his troubles day after day. That's what Grace meant when she told TJ that often teachers help kids from falling through the cracks. Disappearing into silence. Surely a person like that doesn't murder people.

Then she remembered her conversation with TJ about being too trusting. Whom had Evan trusted too much? Had he figured out who took the poison from his cabinet? Had he remembered a significant conversation with someone? What was he going to tell her at the coffee shop? Maybe his death was an accident. He might have slipped on the stairs if his shoes were wet from coming into the school. How long had he been at school before calling me?

3:10. Grace finally decided she didn't have any answers, and she wasn't going to get any sleep. Putting on her bathrobe and slippers, she trod softly down the stairs. A cup of warm tea would do the trick, she thought. Twenty minutes later she was asleep in her recliner, a blanket up to her neck, the tea cooling on the end table, and the television running quietly in the background.

Saturday morning, Grace stood at her kitchen window staring across the street, but she still didn't see TJ's truck. She had just finished unloading the dishwasher when the phone rang in the kitchen. Maybe it was TJ. Picking up the receiver, she heard Dawn Johnson's voice.

"Grace, I wouldn't bother you with this, but I simply didn't know who else to call. After our conversation the other day, I thought you might be able to help me out of a jam."

"Oh? I guess I can try. I have a lot of deadlines at the newspaper right now, but maybe I can help. What do you need?"

"I need someone to sit in on Evan Harrington's classes on Tuesday." She paused, letting her request sink in. "We've called off school Monday, but by Tuesday I think we need to be back in session again. It's short notice to try to find another chemistry teacher, and TJ Sweeney told me you were aware of the situation with Evan. What do you think? Could you help us? Me?"

Grace took a deep breath. This wasn't what she was expecting Johnson to ask. She suddenly realized the silence between them and thought about what she should say.

"Grace?"

"Uh, yes, I'm thinking about it. I didn't realize you would need me. The thing is, I have quite a few stories I need to get done for the newspaper. Spread a little thin these days. I don't know anything about chemistry." She walked around in a circle while she talked. "I mean, I can't imagine I could teach it." She thought about her cooking ability, figuring she would probably blow the third floor through the roof if she had to use some kind of Bunsen burner. Did they even use Bunsen burners anymore?

Her voice changed, confused. "Oh, you wouldn't have to teach. I'm sorry, Grace. I should have been clearer. I'm only looking for a warm body that can conduct a study hall, keeping it quiet and sane. I'll be on the phone all morning trying to find someone who is certified to teach chemistry. I imagine Endurance College might be able to give me leads. It's just past the semester mark, so maybe they could suggest a graduate who finished at mid-year."

"Would you be all right with me typing on my laptop if the kids are studying?"

"Absolutely. Like I said, I need an experienced person that I know can handle the situation. No chemistry knowledge needed. You're a known quantity. What do you think? Can you help me?"

She smiled for the first time. "It's the least I can do for Evan. Sure. Tuesday morning at 7:30. I can do it."

"Oh, Grace, thanks so much." She paused, and then added, "Grace, I don't mean to sound institutional, you know, so cold about this. I liked Evan and I know you taught with him for a few years." Grace heard her clear her throat and take a deep breath. "I'm sorry this has happened, but the law says I must have someone in that room Tuesday." Then Grace heard a sigh. "Well, I guess Sweeney will get it figured out. I hope she does so soon before anything else goes wrong. I'm already fielding calls from anxious and upset parents. Thank you, Grace. I'll see you on the fourteenth. You're a lifesaver."

When she hung up the phone, Grace had a grim thought. Watch your back, Johnson. The last person who said that to me is over at Woodbury on a slab, waiting for the medical examiner.

As Grace was putting some leftovers in the microwave to reheat that evening, TJ came dragging in the kitchen door. She glanced at Grace for encouragement, but Grace did not comply; her day had been long also.

She gave the detective a half-hearted shrug. "Hope you're not expecting any of Lettie's amazing creations. Just a few leftovers tonight, TJ."

"Nah, it's fine. I have to go back in anyway. I'm taking an hour off to get my head on straight. Can't even drink any wine. Got coffee?"

"Sure."

TJ took off her coat, hanging it over a chair. Then she sat down at the table and silently watched Grace make coffee.

"So, what's the story? Know any more about Evan?" said Grace.

"Yes. The video from the camera on the stairwell shows some arms in dark sleeves and gloves pushing him down the stairs. Just as Evan was turning the corner from the third floor to the second, the killer must have come through the door at the landing. Would have been a total surprise."

"Can you tell who it is?" She put a cup of coffee in front of TJ, who looked like she could use about ten hours of sleep. Her glossy black hair was hanging in tendrils, having escaped the rubber band in the back, and her eyes were rimmed with dark circles.

"No such luck, of course. Whoever it was must have known where the camera was. That's one more reason to think it's someone quite familiar with the building."

"Meaning, it wasn't an accident."

"No." She leaned over the table, looking down at her coffee cup. "You were right, Grace."

"What about cameras at the other building entrances? Would they show who was in the building before Evan's death?"

"Checked them. Nothing. But two doors at the west end have no cameras."

"The district probably ran out of money. Poor Evan," Grace said, sitting down across from TJ.

The detective looked up, stirring some sugar into her coffee. "Tell me once again what he said when you talked to him on the phone last night."

Grace repeated their conversation, trying to fit in every detail.

"And you had no indication of what he wanted to tell you?"

"No," said Grace, thinking about it. "But I felt like it was something he remembered. You know, we talked at the funeral, and I told him to let me know if he remembered anything that might help get him off the hook. And now—now he's dead because of the advice I gave him."

"Nah, Grace. Not your fault. You gave him good advice. We just couldn't keep him safe until he could relay what he knew." She shook her head slowly. "Damn. I wish he'd called me." The detective blew out a noisy breath. "I had to be hard on him. All the evidence was pointing in his direction." She stretched her arms and put her elbows on the table, rubbing her eyes with her fingers.

"Perhaps someone wanted you to think that, TJ."

She sighed. Then she drank her coffee to the bottom of the cup. "Could be right. Unfortunately, Evan's death shows how little I can do to keep people safe. On a different note, I talked with your old colleague, Marilyn Atkins."

"She appears to be terribly broken up over Hardy's death."

"She has reason to be. Her fingerprints were in Hardy's office."

"Oh, surely you don't suspect Marilyn, TJ."

"Let's just say she is mixed up in this mess more than we realize, and she's not telling me all she knows."

"What did she tell you?" asked Grace, a quizzical look on her face.

"Well, we know she was in the building during the time of the murder. Claims she was in the basement and had no idea. Left early because of the storm."

"Isn't that what Del Novak said?"

"More or less. The lampshade placed precariously on Hardy's head came from Marilyn Atkins' closet in her classroom."

"What?"

"Says she doesn't keep the closet locked since there's no key for it. She uses the lampshade in her classroom somehow. She also told me she lost her school keys Saturday morning. Searched high and low, dumped her purse, and nothing."

"Did they show up eventually?"

"Not before she was feeling desperate since she couldn't get into the school without them."

"Where were they?" asked Grace.

"Later that afternoon, they were in her purse."

"What? How?"

"I don't have a rational explanation, nor does she, and things like that always make me suspicious. The lady definitely knows more than she's telling, but eventually the truth will out, right?"

"I suppose you're right, TJ. It usually does come out. The school will be closed Monday. After the past week, I think the superintendent figures she needs to give you some time to work on all of this," Grace said.

"And you know about the superintendent's mind because? Don't tell me. Lettie again."

"No. I talked with Dawn Johnson this morning. She asked me to sit in on Evan's classes Tuesday while she tries to find a full-time chemistry teacher."

"What?" TJ said, standing up so suddenly she nearly knocked her coffee cup over. She leaned across the table, flustered, her face near Grace. "Why would she do that? You didn't say yes, did you?"

"But TJ—"

She pushed her chair back, stood up, and paced around the kitchen. "Grace, we don't know if the killer knew who Evan was talking to before he left the building Sunday night. Evan's cell phone is gone. If the killer has it, and he probably does, he would have the number of the last person Evan called. Guess who that is? This is a cold-blooded, evil person, Grace. Whoever it is doesn't care if you are beloved by your former students if he thinks you know something. This killer doesn't know for sure what you know from your conversation with Harrington. For once in your life, listen to me. You could be in real danger here."

"Oh." Grace thought for a moment before her face brightened. "Well, don't you see? It's even more reason I should go in Tuesday and act like I know nothing. It's just one day. The building will be full of people. I'm surely safer there than alone in my house. Anything you want me to check on while I'm in the building, or anyone I should watch?"

TJ turned away, but not before Grace saw how angry she was. Then she faced Grace and slowly said, "Leave the investigation to us, Grace. I don't want to find you run off the road or shot or poisoned." She stopped, taking a breath. "Why? Why, for the love of Pete, would you agree to this when you saw what happened to Evan Harrington? It looks like the killer is someone familiar with the building. I don't want to give you paranoia, but it's likely that someone you know is doing this. I may not be able to keep you safe if you insist on going back in that building."

"But I don't know anything, TJ. It's only for one day."

The detective shook her head and picked up her coat from the kitchen chair.

Grace walked over and grabbed TJ's arm. "TJ, it's the least I can do for Evan."

Then the detective put her hand on the kitchen doorknob, turned, and smiled briefly. "Somehow, I knew those would be the next words out of your mouth, Grace Kimball." She shook her head. "We'll have police in the building, but I can't be everywhere, so watch your back."

Chapter Twelve

GRACE WAS WORKING on the story about the feed store at the *Register* on Monday, but she couldn't stay focused. She kept thinking about Evan Harrington, wondering about his phone call. When she worked at the high school, she enjoyed conversations with him because he was well-read, his interests extending to books and writers. They'd discussed Tolkien since he loved fantasy and science fiction, but they also talked about Mark Twain, an author Grace loved. She remembered one time Evan told her how much he admired Twain because the author was ahead of his time. In *Pudd'nhead Wilson*, Twain used fingerprints to find a murderer. That novel was published sometime in the early 1880s, Grace thought, but fingerprinting by police departments didn't come to America until the 1900s.

She needed to get back to her story, but just as she examined her notes again, someone knocked on her door. Rick Enslow, the sales manager, stuck his head in her office doorway. "Grace, you have a visitor. She wants to talk to you, rather than me, about advertising." Then he rolled his eyes, whispering, "I can't explain. Strange-looking person. You'd better come out here." Grace stared at him a moment, waiting for him to continue, but he'd already retreated down the hallway.

"Well, great," she said out loud, slamming her pencil on the desk. "Writer, semi-editor, copy checker, and now advertising salesperson.

If Jeff doesn't get back soon, I'll be delivering papers too." She strode out to the main lobby area and saw the back of someone standing by the counter. How strange. Grace couldn't tell if this person was male or female. Whoever it was wore a man's hat over long, brown hair, laced with hot pink strands. The person was large-ish, covered in an ankle-length coat of black wool and a winter scarf made with various shades of orange hanging over the wool shoulder. The hem of the coat was dragging below the black wool in several spots, while below the hem were dark shoes which appeared to be a man's work boots. Then the person turned around. Grace was intrigued—it was a woman.

"Oh, you must be Grace Kimball," she said, extending her hand to Grace. "You're a legend at the high school."

Grace shook her hand, feeling her fingers go numb at the strength in the woman's grip. She stared at the person who now stood full-front: bushy eyebrows, a ring in the right side of her aquiline nose, full lips with no lipstick, dangling gold earrings that reached out from under her hat, along with the other end of the multicolored orange scarf. She remembered seeing Ellen Terry at the faculty meeting, but hadn't paid much attention to her. At the time, the drama teacher was sitting down, and she was more conservatively dressed. Her hair wasn't yet pink.

Then Ellen Terry, seeing Grace's expression, said, "Oh, I am so sorry. I fear I have the advantage of you. My name is Ellen Terry, the director of *dramatis personae* at the high school now." She spread both arms out as if to say, "This is me."

Grace recovered from her surprise just as Terry added, "I am looking for help with an advertisement for the play I am directing at the high school in a couple of weeks. This young man"—she turned toward Rick Enslow—"has kindly offered to help me, but I explained to him your reputation—of mythical proportions—precedes you, so I believe I must finally meet you personally. You know, as the great Southern dramatist once said, 'I must depend on the kindness of strangers,' or something to that effect." Grace glanced beyond Ellen Terry and saw Rick make a pushing hand gesture as if to say, "Take her to your office! Get her out of here—please!" She tried not to laugh at Rick, instead turning her attention to the drama teacher.

"Of course. You're the new play director at the high school. My neighbor, Ginger Grant, is one of your actors. She is so excited about being in your play."

"Yes, little Ginger," said Terry, in an ingratiating tone. "Such a clever girl, and so well-cast in the part of Abby Brewster."

"Come on back to my office," said Grace, smiling politely. "I'll see what I can do to help you."

The woman flung out her arms and pulled the layers of her scarf from her neck. "Lead on, Oh Teacher Extraordinaire!" Fortunately, with Grace in the lead, Ellen Terry couldn't see her rolling her eyes.

Once she arranged herself in Grace's office chair, Ellen Terry unbuttoned her coat while Grace took a moment to study her out the corner of her eye. She could see the edges of dark blue tattoos peeking out from under the cuffs of her wool sweater. The woman had on a stark gray jumper over the sweater, and when she was seated, it hung down to the tops of her scuffed boots. The boot laces had been knotted in several places, as if Terry didn't have time to pick up some new laces. Grace looked at her face, judging her to be in her early thirties. Head to foot, she was like no other teacher Grace had ever seen at the high school. What an amusing character, thought Grace.

"So, what brought you to our little town?" asked Grace, as she searched for an ad paper and a pencil.

"Well," Terry began, "even though I have such celebrated ancestral connections to those who trod the boards—meaning the stage, you know—I must also earn my living, alas, often the bitter plight of those of us who follow the muse. The superintendent, out of the kindness of her heart—and here she placed both hands in the vicinity of her right shoulder—signed me up at the very last moment, on the edge of utter defeat. School, you see, had already begun, so she was desperately in need of my talents. I'm now teaching a class of speech, one of drama, and directing the dear little ones in their class play. I have, you see, utterly saved the day." She sat back in her chair, re-arranging the ends of her orange scarf on her lap.

Grace wasn't quite sure what to say after this long speech. She decided it might be best to stick with the obvious. "Where did you teach before, Ms. Terry?"

"Oh, my dear, you may call me Ellen. Everyone does. I am a direct descendent, you see, of that great actress who once was the most famous Portia in the history of the theatre. Theatre is 'theatre,' of course, with an 're,' not an 'er.' Dame Ellen Terry—she who toured the British provinces and once had a sonnet to her beauty written by Oscar Wilde—is my great-grandmother. I am also a distant cousin of the late John Gielgud, whose Shakespearian talents were prodigious. My acclaimed great-grandmother toured the colonial provinces, including far-flung America, and made her debut in the colonies in 1883 at the tender age of thirty-six. *The New York Times* wrote she was 'all that was pure and lovable in womanhood.' " This last sentence was accompanied by dramatic hand gestures.

Grace was at a loss for words. When she did find her voice, she attempted to be positive. "My," said Grace, "you must come highly recommended with that kind of pedigree."

Terry stared at her a moment, trying to decide if Grace was making fun of her. "I assure you, my dear, her blood flows in my veins, and, as with an acorn, I did not fall far from the proverbial tree."

What funny, affected speech, thought Grace, trying not to laugh. Filled with clichés of every kind. She took a deep breath and considered how she might go about changing the conversation. "How do you feel about coming here with two murders on the faculty in a short space of time?" She began filling out the dates and information, glancing discreetly at this strange creature.

Terry pulled a tattered handkerchief from her purse, fastidiously dabbing both of her eyes. "I could feel the vibrations, you know, from the first day I stepped into the pedagogical fray, so to speak. A darkness, a terrible perverse atmosphere enveloped the building, and my soul knew a dreadful tragedy would occur here. It was horrifying, like those wraiths who chased the little hobbits in the—uh—hobbit story."

Vibrations, Grace thought. How ridiculous. But still, she smiled. "What did you think of Mr. Hardy? Such a sad situation."

She lifted an eyebrow, giving Grace a rather quizzical look. "Is this an interrogation, then? I had nothing to do with the death of Mr. Hardy. I would say he was the most wonderful man. He took me under his wing, giving me advice that added positively to my daily employment. The principal at my last school—not so much."

"Where was that?"

Ellen Terry looked up at her as if to measure Grace's intent. She paused for a moment, considering her reply. "I arrived from a small town in Nebraska, one of those dreary outposts where you could blink once and be through the outskirts of civilization. One stop-light." She shook her head slowly.

Grace wondered, from Terry's voice, if this was some kind of canned speech.

"The establishment where I taught was filled with young women who did not know a participle from a pronoun. Silly, giggling little nothings, they were."

"And now you're teaching in a building that has seen two deaths. I was shocked and so sorry to see John Hardy was murdered," said Grace. "He was a good man. Then to add Evan Harrington . . . I can't understand what's going on at that building."

Terry worried some knots in the fringe of her scarf, not looking up at Grace. "I didn't really know the chemistry teacher. Frankly, our paths would cross occasionally in the faculty lounge, but I spent little time there. Such stupidity when you have people together with a chance to complain bitterly of their plight. Best to stay away. I do hear, however, he had stores of chemicals in his laboratory, and I believe the constabulary would consider those highly suspicious. I had also heard he was not in the good graces of Mr. Hardy."

Grace thought about replying to that rumor, but decided instead to change the subject. She picked up her pen and said, "Well, I know Ginger is excited about your play, but I keep wondering if it's appropriate after the recent deaths."

Now Terry drew herself up, looking Grace dead in the eyes. "Appropriate? Evan Harrington said the same thing after Mr. Hardy died. What did he know? What does a chemistry teacher know about the drama? It is patently true that no publicity is bad publicity, in which case, the play will be the thing! Two weeks. We are counting on a large crowd, but I still believe luck is made, not hoped for. This means we need to place an advertisement in your somewhat daily tabloid to spread the word near and far."

"That I can do," said Grace, trying not to wince at the woman's grammar. She took down the information Terry gave her, along with the dates of the ad publication. "I know Ginger is so excited, so happy about this play."

"Ah, yes. I gave her a plum part, the dramatic Endurance debut of Abby Brewster, poisoner extraordinaire. She should have fun with it. I keep telling her to have fun. It's not every day you can poison several people just playing pretend." Then she smiled broadly.

"I suppose you're right," said Grace, thinking about John Hardy's death and how inappropriate the woman's remark was. She handed the pen to Ms. Terry so she could sign.

After scribbling an illegible name, the woman dragged herself out of the chair while digging in the huge pocket of her black coat to find something. "My coat is like my mind, presently . . . a bit crowded, unorganized, but dependable. Here, I found them." She pulled out her hand, along with several other objects that fell to the floor, and handed Grace two tickets. "These are for you."

Disorganized, thought Grace. "Thank you. I'll be sure to come. I promised Ginger I would."

"Excellent. I think you will find our little production quite . . . professional." She reached down, with some effort, picking up the objects that had fallen from her coat pocket, and then stood up.

She smiled with a look that made Grace uncomfortable. Suddenly, she was glad Rick Enslow was in the building.

After Ellen Terry departed, Grace went back to her writing. But she couldn't focus any more now than when she first came into the office. With her elbow on the desk, she rested her chin on her hand. What an unorthodox person Ellen Terry was, but after all, maybe she was one of those creative geniuses who was a bit odd. She must remember to ask Ginger about her. Then, with her typical Grace Kimball moral filter, she scolded herself. Stop being so judgmental. Maybe the high school kids do love her. She looked down at her computer screen, but her focus wandered from the feed store article to Evan Harrington.

Chapter Thirteen

SITTING IN THE living room in her favorite comfy armchair, blanket over her lap, with a cup of steaming green tea, Grace stared out the window, reviewing her day. She was still thinking about her visit from Ellen Terry long after dinner that evening. It was all very odd.

Even so, TJ didn't mention Terry as one of the teachers whose folder was flagged in John Hardy's office. Grace found that unusual, knowing John Hardy. He was a stickler for order rather than chaos, respect rather than incivility, and professionalism rather than shoddiness. Ellen Terry seemed to have a life with the latter qualities if Grace were to judge from her first impression. But perhaps she was being unfair. She had never seen her teach in a classroom.

Her mind wandered to Evan Harrington. Why would he get a bad review from John Hardy? It didn't make any sense. She must remember to mention it to TJ Sweeney. Thinking about her friend, Grace realized TJ hadn't said anything about either murder case lately. She had, however, taken the time to chastise Grace for going in the building tomorrow to watch Evan Harrington's classes. Well, she would show TJ. The murders always occurred at night or on the weekend when the murderer could get safely away. That, of course, assumes one person did both murders. Grace figured she would be safe on a Tuesday in broad daylight. Wouldn't she?

As if TJ knew her thoughts, Grace's phone played "Wanted Dead or Alive." She reached over on the table and unplugged it from its charging cord.

"Hi, TJ. I was just thinking about you."

"Kind thoughts, I'm sure, after I yelled at you."

"You know it, my friend. I realize you're only looking out for me. Besides, you're under a lot of pressure at work. What's up?"

"Working on the murders. Got some extra help coming in to-morrow from Woodbury. You may even see me in the building. I'll be the one lending an air of authority and gravitas to these murder cases we still haven't solved."

"Gravitas? I'm impressed."

"Trying to show you I'm not as illiterate as you think, Grace. But I do notice, since writing police reports, that I am losing words. Must be because I have no time whatsoever to read these days. And yes, I remember, in the olden days when I was in your class, you always preached that reading would expand my vocabulary. You didn't ex-plain what to do about getting an education and a job, leaving no time to read."

"That's a 'you' problem," Grace said, laughing.

TJ's voice paused, and then Grace could hear her sigh.

"So," said Grace, trying to make her voice sound encouraging. "Latest developments?"

"Things are . . . moving along. The autopsy on Evan Harrington showed he died of a cervical fracture, not unexpected after seeing the scene. The video from the hallway camera makes it unclear whether the killer was male or female. The arms were covered and the hands were gloved." She paused a minute as if thinking about that last statement. "Then I have the updates on John Hardy. Unfortunately, the tox screen on Hardy won't be back for two more weeks. That's how jammed up the lab is. We're proceeding with the theory he was poisoned somehow. The weird thing is the poison was not in the cof-fee cup with Harrington's fingerprints on it. Of course, someone could have moved the cup there from the teacher's lounge any time. That makes more sense than to leave it at a murder scene without poison. Finally, we have a time of death on John Hardy: between eleven in the morning and one or two. That doesn't leave many people in the building. However, Liz Hardy was there in the time frame."

"Oh. Do you know why she was there on Sunday?"

"She says to have it out with Hardy about his affair. Her visit fits in the time frame of his murder."

"And who else?"

"Marilyn Atkins. She hadn't left yet."

"Oh, yes . . . Marilyn."

"Grace, I may as well tell you what everyone else seems to know. Marilyn and John Hardy were having an affair. As a matter of interesting timing, we know he called it off the Friday before the murder."

Grace almost dropped her phone. "What? I can't believe it."

"That's why I am going to start calling you 'Pollyanna.' I have it on good information that Marilyn and John Hardy were having a fling. It also appears her husband and his wife had just become aware of it. Terrible timing."

Grace swallowed.

"Grace? You still there?"

"Yes, TJ."

"I'm sorry. I know it's always a shock when you learn some information that rocks your world. I don't remember the two of you being exactly chummy."

"Marilyn and I didn't always agree on a lot of policy issues, and this led to heated debates in the department meetings. She has a hard edge on her . . . brittle."

"The second set of prints on the vase in Hardy's office was hers."

Grace considered what she'd seen of Marilyn in the recent past. At both the faculty meeting and at the funeral, her eyes were red-rimmed, and Grace thought it looked like she hadn't slept in days. At

Hardy's funeral, Grace expected to see Marilyn's husband, Seth, but now she recalled he wasn't there, and she had thought it odd at the time, but figured they had some explanation. Now she knew why.

"What can you tell me about Ms. Atkins?"

Grace thought quickly about how she might describe Marilyn without her own prejudices filtering her words. "Marilyn is probably in her late thirties, has no children, and is married to Seth, who is a pharmaceutical salesman. She's a strong teacher, really drives the kids hard, and spends a huge number of hours at school grading on the weekends."

"So why do I detect a little reluctance in your voice?"

"We disagreed a lot about school issues. I felt sorry for her at times. Her husband wouldn't be easy to live with."

"Why?"

"Alcohol. Sometimes I think that's why she's in the building so much—to get away."

"Is he abusive?"

"I don't know her well enough to say."

"What do the kids think of her?" asked TJ.

"The really smart ones mostly like her because she pushes so hard. She came up through the school of hard knocks, a past she often mentions. Sometimes I think she resents kids who come from—shall we say more 'privileged' backgrounds. She was a favorite until Evan Harrington came along and stole their hearts. Kids can be fickle. Teaching isn't about popularity."

"This husband Seth. Do you think he might be angry enough to kill John Hardy, especially if he's been drinking?"

"Again, I don't know."

"Sounds like a couple I should interview."

"Just don't cross her," said Grace, putting some amusement in her tone.

"I'll tell her I came up poor and aced your Shakespeare exam."

They both laughed because Grace's Shakespeare exam used to divide the brilliant from the smart.

TJ paused a moment. "I've decided I'm over being ticked about you going into the high school. Besides, you might hear interesting gossip in the faculty lounge, something I wouldn't learn because everyone would shut up fast if I walked in."

Grace took a deep breath, thinking how she wanted to phrase her reply. "TJ, this is all hitting a little too close to home. These are people I know, or thought I knew, and no one appears to be as he or she seems." She paused, taking a deep breath. "The principal whom I believed to be a morally upright man was actually having an adulterous affair and he was murdered. Evan Harrington, whom I thought was a great teacher, was evaluated as bad and murdered. Then we have huge changes in the way teachers are evaluated. What has happened, TJ? Everything is upside down, and I've been gone not quite a year."

"That was a lot of 'whoms,' Grace." TJ's voice softened. "I don't think everything has changed, but I can see how this is an almost endless series of changes in the life you thought you knew. You are undoubtedly feeling this is like an avalanche of dominoes falling. Some of these events were caused by other situations, and unexpected death often makes the big picture appear uncertain. You've told me yourself everything always changes in education, especially since the laws are ever-changing, and the legislature is always upsetting the whole system. Remember? That was the Grace I remembered practically swearing at all of this and saying, 'Why can't they leave me alone and just let me teach?' It will come back to stasis again. You'll see."

"Just the fact that you are trying to impress me with your big words is helpful, TJ. It seems like stasis." She found herself smiling, despite her frustration. "Tomorrow when I go to the high school, I'll look for things that are the same. Maybe I'm only focusing on the bad."

"I also think you should watch for odd stuff, stuff which is out of the norm."

Grace giggled. "Like Ellen Terry?"

"She's out of the norm all right, all the time. Yeah, look for anything that doesn't seem quite right."

"I can do that, TJ. Thanks. I'm going to lay out my teaching clothes, take a shower, and try to dream happy dreams."

"Sounds like a plan. I may run into you tomorrow, but, of course, you know I'm going to say, 'watch your back.' "

"Absolutely. I will. I promise. Thanks, TJ. You've made me feel a little better."

"We aim to serve. Good night, Grace. Check your door locks."

Grace tapped off her cell phone and laughed at TJ's typical comment about door-locking. Then she began picking up piles of clothes, magazines, and other items which had accumulated during the day. On the way upstairs to take a shower, she thought John Hardy was really stupid. Grace shook her head, remembering the old adage that you should never sleep with someone who has less to lose than you. In a conservative town like Endurance, Hardy put his entire career on the line. And, worse still, Liz Hardy was not a forgiving woman.

The water and lather felt so good in the shower that she stayed an extra-long time, feeling its soothing warmth, trying to wash away all the negative events that had happened lately in Endurance. She laid out a blouse, sweater, and skirt to wear to school. It seemed like old times—so comforting. Her clock said it was eleven when she climbed into bed, but she realized she needed to go back downstairs, take a pill, and bring a glass of water up to bed. Must have had too much on my mind, she thought.

As she left the kitchen, Grace noticed the landline answering machine was blinking. At this time of night? Someone must have called when she was in the shower. She punched the button and heard, at first, a silence. Then Jeff Maitlin's voice, faltering, came on the machine.

"Grace . . . I know it's late. I'm—I'm sorry I'm calling so late." Then he paused, and when his voice began again, he was a little surer of himself. "I know, I know, you've been trying to reach me and left messages. I don't know what to say about that. I didn't want . . . I mean . . . I wasn't trying to hurt you. I just didn't know what to say, Grace. Please, believe me. Things here—well, they're a lot worse than I thought. Sometimes when you learn the truth about the past you thought was over and done with, it hurts more than you could ever imagine. Remember the old saying about 'the truth will set you free'? Well, it isn't true. It only makes you realize your life has been a lie, your past has been a lie, and you sure aren't worthy of starting over again, nor are you capable of having the life you thought you deserved. I found out . . . information, Grace. Some terrible things . . ." Here Grace heard his voice falter, as if he were trying to keep his composure.

Silence briefly. She listened, biting the knuckles of her hand. Then his voice began again. "I've made a decision, Grace. I'm having work stopped on the house. I'll figure out what to do about all of that, or my lawyer will. I thought I could have what I wanted: you and the house and a life in a small town where people know who you are and respect you. It can't happen now. It . . . can't. I'm sorry, Grace. I don't know what else to say. I don't want to hurt you." Then it was silent again.

Grace held her breath, tears streaming down her face.

His voice paused and she thought she heard a tiny sob. Then he seemed to get himself back together.

"Grace, I don't deserve your forgiveness. I'm not coming back to Endurance. Live your life. Love someone who will make you happy."

Then she heard a click as the machine stopped.

Chapter Fourteen

GRACE GLANCED AT the wall clock as she sat in Evan Harrington's late-morning class. She studied the tops of the heads of twenty students who were either reading or writing. The warm familiarity of being at the teacher's desk swept over her as she watched the students work. Earlier this morning, each class had been perfectly quiet, working, and cooperative. Shocking! She suppressed a giggle. Perhaps it was because of their teacher's unexpected death. Two deaths to deal with over a short period of time—that's a heavy load to process when you're a teenager. She'd only been gone a year, so she knew quite a few of the students. They were thrilled to see her when they came into the room each hour, as if a familiar face helped their shock and sorrow. After a few preliminaries, they got down to work.

She kept her fingers on her laptop keys and every so often she typed a paragraph or two, using her notes about her most recent historical column. But then her mind would drift back to last night; she would see herself replaying Jeff's message over and over again. The demons from his past were too deep, too dark, and too heavy for him to escape. Perhaps he has too much pride, she thought. Doesn't he know it doesn't matter who his parents were, or where he came from, or who his family was in the past? She only cared about him today, and she knew what kind of man he was. Grace realized he had no idea she even knew about the death of his parents.

After listening to the message multiple times, she finally went up to bed. But it wasn't much use sleeping. She tossed and turned, unable to rid herself of his words. Where was he now? Grace knew him well enough to realize he was feeling heartsick at leaving that message. She should be angry, but instead she was despondent, aching with pity for him and wishing she could tell him she loved him. Her thoughts were not intense like the roller-coaster ride of grief after Roger died. She—

"Ms. Kimball?" Grace heard a voice and looked up. It was Jim Blender.

"Yes, Jim," she said quietly. He sat in the front row. She could see the other students around him were pretending to read, but Grace could tell they were listening in, wondering where this conversation would go.

"Do you think they will find out who killed Mr. Harrington?"

The others looked up.

"Yes, Jim, I do. Also Mr. Hardy. It will just take some time."

He sat back in his chair. She could see his slumping shoulders relax, and he let out a deep breath. Then his eyes narrowed and he trained them intensely on Grace. "Why? Why do you think that?"

"Because TJ Sweeney, the lead detective at the police department, will figure it out. She's an expert at her job, and I have total confidence in her. She used to be a student of mine right here in this school—a highly smart and determined one."

"Well," he said, squirming a bit in his seat, "I also wonder if they will find someone to take Mr. Harrington's place."

"Yeah," said the girl who was sitting next to him. "It isn't that we're insensitive to Mr. Harrington's death, Ms. Kimball. We really, really like—liked him. But, you see, some of us are at the end of our search for colleges, and we want to make sure we get this chemistry information. We don't want to get behind." She took a deep breath, shaking her head. "I'm planning to be pre-med. It takes a lot of chemistry."

Grace smiled. She wished all her students had been this conscientious.

"Mr. Harrington seemed nervous that Friday before, uh, before his death," added a third student. "Distracted. He'd never been distracted before. He was always right on focus, with questions you'd have to think about."

"Really? Did you notice anything else unusual that day?"

"I did," said a fourth student, a boy sitting behind the girl who had talked first. "He kept looking at his watch. His prep period is next hour, so we figured maybe he had something important to do then, because he seemed nervous about it. He was usually laid back, calm, into the chemistry stuff."

Grace looked at the clock, realizing she only had about three minutes until the bell. Students were putting their belongings into their book bags. She hated to end this conversation since they noticed quite a bit.

She picked up the pace, speaking clearly. "To answer your question, yes. I think they will find a replacement for Mr. Harrington. I know you liked him. I taught with him for a time, and I know he was a good man, and he was special. You shouldn't worry. The superintendent has assured me she is working on it right now. If you happen to think of anything else that would be helpful to the police, you'll be able to tell them when you see them around the building. I know they're over here today, working."

The bell rang, they all scooted out of their seats, and shuffled out the door to their next classes. Jim Blender turned around, coming back to see Grace.

"Maybe this isn't important, Ms. Kimball, but I'm his lab assistant, er, was his lab assistant. Mr. Harrington's. A week ago, he asked me about the key to the cabinet where he keeps some of his chemicals. He always left it in his office desk, so if he needed to have me get something, I knew I could go in and get it. But I always remembered to put it back. You see, he trusted me."

"That's a good thing to know, Jim. Did he ever find it?"

"Yeah, he must have. A few days later I asked him about it. He said he had found it in a pocket of his lab coat. It seemed kind of strange to me because he was careful about putting it back in the desk. It shouldn't have taken a few days to find it. He acted as if he didn't really want to talk about it, like he was, you know, distracted."

"Great. Thanks, Jim. I'll mention what you said to Detective Sweeney. That's helpful. If you think of any other details that come to mind, let her know. She's in the building quite a bit this week, I believe."

"Sure thing!" He turned and walked out the door, joining the throng of other kids in the hallway. Grace closed the program on the unfinished story on her computer. She decided she'd head down to the teacher's lounge and see if she could pick up anything of interest. It was Evan's prep period.

Walking through the hallways amid the crowds of students was so familiar Grace could hardly believe she'd been gone. Occasionally, during the time she was in the halls, she'd catch a glimpse of TJ Sweeney or Jake Williams talking to various teachers. She looked at the line of students coming toward her. Every so often one of them would say, "Hi, Ms. Kimball," and smile. As she reached the teacher's lounge, she stopped, standing near the wall, watching the faces of familiar high school kids. She was reminded of her sojourn to her classroom at the basketball game. While she felt somewhat like an observer looking out over the hallway and its thinning student groups, she realized how much she missed it. Could her doldrums have something to do with the loss of Jeff Maitlin? Was she hanging on to these memories because her teaching years had helped her loneliness? She saw Alex Reid coming toward her, motioning her into the teacher's lounge.

"Grace," he said, moving toward the coffeepot. "How have things gone this morning?"

"Fine, Alex. Kids have been good as gold and very cooperative."

He filled a coffee cup, turning around. "I'm sure that's why Johnson wanted you in that classroom. You can sigh with relief, however, because she now has a teacher signed up to finish the semester . . . some woman who just graduated from the college."

"I can get back to my other job then," said Grace, not knowing whether she felt relief or a tinge of sadness.

"Sure can. Thanks for filling in for us, Grace. Let me know if you need anything this afternoon," said Reid. Then he was out the door with his coffee.

Alan Gladley, a PE teacher and coach, was sitting in a chair looking through his mail. Grace wasn't sure she'd ever seen him in anything but shorts, a T-shirt, and a whistle. The only exception was John Hardy's funeral. Alan was in in his mid-forties and in great shape; she could remember when he first came, taking the place of a football coach who retired.

"Hi, Grace."

"Alan. Good to see you again. I'm sitting in for Evan Harrington's classes. You probably knew that already. Very little's changed." She reconsidered, blinking her eyes. "Well, except for the awful deaths. The kids, by the way, told me Evan appeared distracted the last day he taught. Did you notice? I figure you're in here when he has his prep period. Notice anything unusual?"

"Ah, Grace," he said. "I liked Evan, and I'm sure you did too. I didn't see anything unusual, but, to tell you the truth, I come down here to check my mail during this hour. Then I go back to my office at the gym. I'd hardly seen him before all that happened. Sorry."

Grace wriggled her nose as if to say, "It's all right." He brushed past her and was gone as quickly as he'd arrived. She looked around. The lounge hadn't changed much since she'd been here, but, after all, that was not quite a year ago. No one really cared about the place the teachers gathered during their prep periods; it was furnished in cast-offs from various people and places. Somehow it appeared dingier than she remembered. Same coffee stains on the top of the microwave, same refrigerator which probably needed cleaning, same Xerox machine with packages of paper on the shelf under it. Long tables sat in the middle of the room, some of them covered with various papers people had left, dropped, or forgotten. A worn sofa and two unmatched chairs occupied the south end of the room, their covers frayed and worn. A loveseat was over by the door on the east wall, its arms threadbare, and the rose pattern barely visible against the rest of the shabby material.

Grace sat down on the loveseat and put her computer on her lap, thinking to finish the story she'd been working on all morning. She had barely started when a business teacher, Sally Wenstrom, walked in to check her mail. The mailboxes were wooden cubbyholes lining the north wall of the room. Sally was preoccupied and didn't see Grace until she turned around. Then she visibly jumped.

"Grace," she said. "You scared me. I didn't see you there when I came in."

"Sorry. Everyone's a bit jumpy around here these days. I can see why."

Sally said, "Yes, you're right. We're going to miss Evan and John. I don't know what this world is coming to." She shrugged her shoulders. "I think I'm still in shock."

"Did you spend much time in the lounge with Evan this hour?"

"Oh, some days. Yes. You know, he was an easy person to like, and we all had interesting conversations. Evan was into so many different topics."

"The kids in his class mentioned he was distracted or nervous shortly before his death. Did you notice that?"

"Hmmm," she said, thinking about Grace's idea. "I don't remember. No. But I do remember, late last week, he was looking in his mailbox. Suddenly, he turned around and said, almost as if to himself, 'that's it.' He dropped his mail back into the cubbyhole and left. At the time, I didn't ask him what he was talking about. He hurried out of the room right afterward."

"Well, that is something," said Grace, almost absentmindedly.

"It was after John Hardy's funeral, I think. You know, Grace, so much has happened lately that I'm a bit mixed up on what went on when."

"I can understand. Does Ellen Terry come down here much? I know this is her prep period too."

Sally shook her head. "Not really. Of course, I usually go back upstairs and grade papers after I look at my mail. Can't help you much." She glanced at her watch, grabbed her mail tightly, and started for the door. "Actually, I need to get up and do that now. Nice seeing you, Grace. We miss you up here."

"Thanks," said Grace, smiling again. She watched the business teacher close the door. Then she sidled over to the mailboxes. They were in alphabetical order so it didn't take long to find Evan's. She grabbed the papers out of it and looked through them. In the pile were all-school announcements from the week before his death, two ads from textbook companies, a circular announcing the play, a request for homework for a student, and a note from Marilyn Atkins about a curriculum committee meeting. The usual stuff. Then, as if thinking Marilyn's name in her head could summon spirits, Grace saw the door open and Marilyn Atkins came in, her pale skin accentuating the dark circles under her eyes.

"Marilyn. Are you all right?"

Seemingly without stopping to think, she said, "Please, Grace. Much you care about how I feel."

"Of course I care. Come over here. Sit down." She guided Marilyn to the sofa and leaned in to listen. "Can I do something to help?"

Marilyn fiddled with her purse, put her books and papers on the floor, and pulled out a tissue. She wiped her damp face off with the tissue. "Weird things keep happening. My lampshade disappears and ends up in John Hardy's office."

Grace tried to look genuinely surprised. "Your lampshade?"

"You remember I have a little area in my classroom with an easy chair, a lamp, and a table, so a student can sit down, relax, and read? It's kind of a symbolic, cozy reading corner. Often a student will even come in after school and sit there, reading quietly while I'm working."

"And?"

"Well, I just heard. Lots of details are leaking, some of them true, some, I'm sure, not." She put both of her hands in the air, shaking her head. "This time I heard Mr. Hardy was found with a lampshade on his head." She visibly blanched, her hands becoming shaky. "Grace, is it true? Do you know if that's true?" She touched Grace's arm, accentuating the desperation in her voice.

"I—I don't know. I suppose it's possible."

"I'm afraid I did something terrible. I've been trying to hide it from people ever since."

Grace said slowly, her voice warm and gentle, "You mean your affair with John Hardy?"

Marilyn began tearing the tissue into small pieces, the picture of anxiety. "Who else knows?"

"I have no idea, Marilyn."

Marilyn bit the cuticle on one of her fingernails. "We grew close working on a project involving the curriculum. One thing led to another. His wife—she, she doesn't understand him."

Grace wanted to shake her. How many men—and women—had fallen for the same set of words from the lips of a spouse on the prowl for opportunities? She quickly chastised herself for being so judgmental. John Hardy wasn't like that. "Marilyn, did Liz Hardy know about your affair? How long did it last?"

"Not long. A few weeks. She found out just before his death. So, I'm afraid, did Seth."

"How did they find out?"

"Someone sent her an anonymous note. It was all done up like the movies where a person cuts out letters, pasting them on a paper.

She got it in the mail. Then, she was so angry and vindictive she called Seth."

"Oh, no."

"He's been on a rampage, arguing with me, yelling at me since the Friday before John's death."

Grace saw Alex Reid open the door, take one look at Marilyn's face, and back out.

"Start at the beginning. Calmly. Just concentrate on the facts. What time did you come to grade papers?"

Marilyn gathered up the tissue pieces, squeezing them into a ball with her hand. "I came around ten o'clock that morning. I parked in the lot across the street and saw John's car parked behind the building when I arrived." She took a deep breath. "He had called me the day before to tell me it was over. I don't know what I felt—anger, sadness, or relief. So, I stayed down in the basement in my room, knowing he was upstairs, but not wanting to talk to him about it. I didn't—didn't want to see him.

"Around eleven, I saw Liz Hardy's car park next to his behind the building. I know it was eleven because I looked at my watch. She got out of her car with a small sack and a large purse in her hand and went into the building. I assume she has a key since no one let her in. My room, you know, looks out on the parking area behind the school. I was curious, so I waited until I knew she would be inside, and then I crept up the back hallway to the office. I had papers in my hand as if I were going to use the copier." She put the palms of her hands out. "I don't know why. I guess I figured if either of them confronted me, I'd look like I was on a mission.

"Anyway, I could hear them with the outer door closed. The door to his office was slightly open. They were having a huge argument. She was saying something about not confronting him at home because of the children, and his voice was quiet. I don't know everything they said because some of it was muffled. Sometimes her voice was loud and clear. She threatened him with divorce, saying he wouldn't want anyone to know what a despicable person he was." Marilyn turned to Grace, squeezing her arm tightly. "She is a dreadful person, Grace. The things he's told me about his marriage . . . just a dreadful person."

"Did you hear her threaten him specifically?"

"At one point, she said she wanted to kill him. But people say words in anger." She turned away and leaned over, putting her face in her hands.

Grace sat perfectly still, considering the disaster this was going to be. Then she pulled herself up on the edge of the sofa, asking, "What happened after that?"

Marilyn swallowed. "I saw Liz Hardy go back to her car around—oh, it must have been around 12:30. I didn't go back upstairs."

"Did she still have the sack she'd carried in?"

"Let me think a minute." She closed her eyes as if trying to picture the scene. "No. No, I'm not sure."

"And then?"

"I talked to Del Novak sometime later. Maybe an hour or two later. I left early because I was so upset I needed to get in my car, drive around a bit."

"Whose car or cars did you see when you left?"

"Del's truck was in the parking lot a few spaces down from mine. When I left, John's was still behind the building."

"Did he know you were there?"

"He had to have seen my car out in the parking lot. It's visible from his office windows."

"Did he come downstairs at all?"

"No. The only other person I saw was Del. Then I left." She took several long breaths, and then she said, "Grace, that isn't all of it."

"What do you mean?"

Marilyn stood up and glanced at the door, but no one came in. She walked around the room as she talked. "It's Seth."

"Seth? Your husband?"

"Yes. I don't think you know this, but he has a—an alcohol problem."

Grace started to say something like, "You don't have to tell me, Marilyn," but instead she shut her mouth and listened.

"Like I said, Seth's on the road a lot. He sells"—she took a breath—"he sells drugs for a pharmaceutical company. He hasn't been happy for some time, and particularly on the weekends he drinks too much." She stopped walking and sat down in a chair across from Grace.

"That must be really hard."

"Oh, Grace, it's horrible. He scares me so. It's not as if he has ever hurt me—he hasn't—but he threatens to. Sometimes I just need to come over here to the building to get away."

"I'm so sorry, Marilyn. I didn't know."

"Why would you? This job is the only thing that keeps me sane." She shook her head. "I don't know where he was on Sunday, Grace. He had been drinking steadily since that Friday night when Liz—she is such a bitch—called and spilled it all. She said, probably in her nastiest voice, that 'in the interest of community morality, she wanted him to know what a slut he'd married.' "

Grace watched as Marilyn's hands balled up into fists. "I hate her, and Seth was so angry. I've never seen him so out of control. He swore he'd kill John and then come back and take care of me.

"Sunday morning he was on the phone, and when I walked into the room, he looked really guilty. Whoever he was calling was someone he didn't want me to know about. We had a huge argument and I left for school. He taunted me all the way out the door, saying he'd deal with John Hardy, I'd better believe it. I don't know what he did all that morning, and he wasn't home when I got home from school because of the storm. He didn't come home all that night."

"Have you talked to him since about it?"

"No. He's not talking. He comes home late at night and doesn't speak to me. Just leaves the next morning. I'm so worried that he might be involved in all of this—this—John's death."

"Why? How could he be involved?"

"He's been in the pharmaceutical world for twenty years. I know he has all kinds of contacts with drug companies and pharmacists. Don't you see?"

"No, I'm not sure I do, Marilyn."

"Drug companies. Pharmacists. If anyone can find out how to get his hands on poisons, Seth could."

Chapter Fifteen

GRACE GLANCED OVER at Deb O'Hara, who was busy entering data into the computer at the Endurance Historical Society. Twenty years earlier, the town had converted an empty grocery store into an archive for the history of their area, and a group of residents started a foundation, buying the old brick building and manning it with volunteers. Now it was filled throughout several rooms with local newspapers, microfiche, city directories, census records, genealogy magazines, files, and folders. The *Stark County Newsletter*, the *Woodbury Sentinel*, and the *Endurance Register* were amply represented in its databases.

In the research room where Grace was working, old yearbooks from area school districts took up one wall. They weren't worth much these days, but people who were looking for genealogy records sometimes glanced through them. Grace was thumbing through various copies from the last thirty years, checking on which plays had been done at the high school. Since she was preparing an article about the current dramatic effort, she thought it would be interesting to research some background history of the theater at the high school. She kept coming upon pages with intriguing photographs, and she felt compelled to read every caption and article. After subbing all day, she was tired, but her curiosity kept her going.

Her interest was rewarded when she came across renovation information she didn't know about, since she hadn't been teaching yet at the school. It was intriguing, and even though she was researching for background on the play article, this looked like she might want to use it for a future history column for the newspaper. In the 1975 yearbook, she perused an article about burying part of the school building. The work was done in the late spring and all summer so it didn't disturb the school year any longer than necessary, but the yearbook staff evidently could go in and take photos.

The reason for the work was not one hundred percent clear to Grace, but it sounded like engineers had been concerned that this part of the school had foundational problems. At that time, the high school stage was raised considerably. This put what today would be the theater director's office a few steps below the new wing area backstage and between the lower level and the main floor of the building.

Then they constructed a new floor that covered the old auditorium seating and an orchestra pit that had been in front of the old, lower stage. This had the effect of lifting the stage and its wings—the areas in the back and on the sides of the stage which couldn't be seen by the audience. In 1975, two dressing rooms and storage rooms were under the stage, but they were sealed up by the engineers and workers after putting in structural supports. It looked like a door to that whole area was placed in the director's office, with stairs leading down to the old auditorium. Grace assumed that the door was currently sealed up. Now, the actors used classrooms for dressing rooms, putting dark paper over the door windows.

Grace examined the photos with a magnifying glass, enthralled by the old lighting fixtures, probably from the very early 1900s when the building was constructed. The black-and-white photos hinted at some of the original early 1900s architecture. Workers in blue jeans and work pants with lights on their helmets stood at various angles with tools while several others held boards and boxes. These little hallways and rooms must still exist beneath the current stage, but because of the way the construction was done, no one today really knew about them, well, unless they were around back then.

In a later yearbook from 1990, Grace saw the work they commissioned at a time she was teaching at the school. A new system of flies—a space above the stage to suspend, lower, and raise scenery—was put in, and the catwalk over the top of the stage was made more structurally sound. But it appeared to be a very small job compared to all the work from earlier.

So on to her real research. *Arsenic and Old Lace* had been done twice before at the high school, once in 1949 and a second time in 1972. Grace had seen the play in other theaters on a couple of occasions, and knew it had been made into a movie. It was the story of the two elderly Brewster sisters, Martha and Abby, who lived in Brooklyn with their nephew Teddy, their brother's son. Because the Brewster sisters came from a long line of mentally ill ancestors, they indulged in poisoning older men who were alone in the world and stopped at their house to rent a room. Their nephew, Teddy, believed himself to be Teddy Roosevelt, so not only did he dash up and down the stairs yelling "Charge!", but he also buried "victims of the yellow fever" in the Canal, which translated loosely to poison victims in the basement. Boy, thought Grace, this is a comedy? Strange what people thought was funny in the 1940s.

She was jarred from her research by Deb O'Hara's voice. "Hey, what's TJ doing today?"

Grace decided to take a break, and she stood up and walked around, bending and stretching, feeling the creaks and stiffness. Remembering Deb's question, she said, "I'm not sure. She's been so busy it's hard for me to keep track of her. I know she's interviewed Marilyn Atkins and Liz Hardy."

"Liz Hardy. Now that's a tough nut to crack," said Deb. "Funny how marriages go, isn't it? No one seems to be able to figure how they ever fit together. He was so kind and patient, and she's so nasty and distant. I hear people in town are putting their money on Liz Hardy as the black widow killer."

Grace hesitated, pondering what she should say. "Oh, I don't know, Deb. Who really knows what goes on in other people's marriages?"

"I suppose you're right. Poor Marilyn Atkins. She looks terrible these days. I hear Seth has moved out, and they're doing a trial separation. He took the affair pretty hard. I guess I can't blame him."

"You are beginning to sound more and more like Lettie. How do you come up with all this information about what's going on?"

"You never know what women—or men—will do for love or revenge. You read about it—all these passionate crimes, but you don't connect them with people you know."

Grace had been standing by the window looking out at the traffic slowly wending its way down the street. Now she turned and said, "Not sure I'd call that love."

Deb sighed. "You and I were lucky, Grace. We didn't have to worry about John or Roger cheating. They were those 'till death do us part' people, raised with that value and willing to commit to it for life. Of course, your Roger didn't get a very long life, but I'd put my money on his staying faithful to you even if he were still with us."

She slowly nodded her head. "True. I don't see either of us having affairs. We were both people who believed we made our vows before God, and we certainly thought of those vows as a lifetime commitment, come hell or high water."

"I think Jeff Maitlin would have been the same. Listen to me, speaking in the past tense. He is conservative in his personal life, people like him, and every so often I hear of some act of kindness he's done, especially in his work at the newspaper. I wish you knew what was going on there. When you told me about his phone message, I was shocked."

"Me too, Deb. Me too. Sometimes I almost pick up the phone to call him, but I know it won't do any good. He thinks his father's bad decisions resulted in him being tarnished too. It just isn't so." She paused for a moment, thinking. "You know, in some ways his ideas about his parents are like the crazy play about arsenic. People then believed that mental illness was passed on, just like the actions of parents passed down to their children. But we know better today. I've been thinking about what to do. Maybe I'll text him."

"Really? And say what?"

Grace knew Deb was a romantic soul, so her excited voice made Grace smile. "Just that I know about his parents, and it doesn't matter."

"In this age you'd think he would realize you have the entire Internet at your disposal, and he can't keep much secret for long."

Grace glanced at her phone lying on the table next to her laptop. "I don't believe it would ever occur to him that I would check him out." She sat down again. "However, I know someone I should research, and that's Ellen Terry. I think when I go back to the office I'll do that. She is really unusual for someone who has completed all the hoops you have to jump through in teacher prep."

"Before you do that, I think you should text Jeff Maitlin." She rubbed her hands together, watching Grace.

"And say what?"

"Just say something like, 'I know about your parents' deaths, and I still love you.' Or, let's see. I should be able to do better than that. How about, 'I love you Jeff, and I don't care about the past.' No, then he won't know you already know about his parents. I think that is key to his deciding to get back to you." She crossed her arms and Grace noticed a frown on her face. "It can't be any worse than his leaving you a good-bye message on your answering machine."

"I know that sounds awful, Deb, but if you could have heard his voice. He is really going through agony, and I don't know exactly what's caused that. I feel so awful." She considered her friend's plan and thought maybe Deb was right.

"All right. I will . . . text Jeff. Much good it will do me, but at least it will give him something to think about. Right now, in fact."

She picked up her phone, typed his name in the address, and wrote, "I no @ yr parents' deaths, and I still love you. Come home." Then she paused before touching the send button. "I don't know." She let out a deep breath. "He hasn't answered me in two weeks. I'm beginning to forget what his voice sounds like."

Deb walked over and put a hand on her shoulder. "Now or never. Send it off. He can't possibly ignore you after this. Now. Go. Send it!"

Grace hesitated, so Deb reached over her shoulder and touched the send button.

"Whoopee! Sometimes you just gotta go for it, Grace."

Chapter Sixteen

GRACE WAS EXHAUSTED after subbing for Evan Harrington and then researching. She didn't understand why since the day had been rather uneventful except for Marilyn's story. That added to her energy drain too. On the other hand, she loved the familiar feeling of being back in a classroom and seeing students she had missed. As she pulled into her driveway on Sweetbriar Court, she saw Ginger once again walking Stella for Ms. Brantley. She waved, rolled down her window, and invited Ginger to stop in after her dog-walking.

Taking off her coat, she checked the mail, all the while listening to Lettie whistling in the kitchen as she cooked. A few minutes later, Ginger was at the front door.

"I didn't see you at school today, even though I watched for you," said Grace.

Ginger, her face flushed from the February cold, said she had been quite busy since she had play rehearsals again after school. It was important that she get her homework done during her study hall because it was sometimes late when she got home from play rehearsals.

"So how did you like being back at the school, Ms. Kimball?"

Grace sat down across from Ginger. She wrinkled her forehead, considering the question. "It seemed strange, like I should be there, but it wasn't quite the same. I could tell time had elapsed since I left, and other people were around, people I didn't know."

Ginger nodded her head, a serious look on her face. "All the fun has been taken out of school lately. I keep hearing crazy rumors."

"Grace, is that you?" Lettie's voice came from the kitchen. Then the rest of her body came through the hallway, observing Ginger and Grace. "Oh, didn't know we had company. How about some hot chocolate?"

"Oh, yes, please," said Ginger.

"Sure, Lettie. That sounds good. Ginger stopped in with a school play report."

After Lettie left, Ginger said, "The kids at school are talking all the time about Mr. Hardy and Mr. Harrington. They say Mr. Harrington killed Mr. Hardy because he was afraid he might lose his job. Then Cecelia Lucas said Mr. Harrington wasn't married, so he was probably gay. Now, that's just dumb stuff. Third hour in PE, I heard Mr. Harrington was having an affair with a student, and she pushed him down the stairs. She leaned forward, her eyebrows furrowed. Where do these ideas come from, Ms. Kimball?"

"I think they are making things up to try to sound important, like they have the inside track."

"I always thought Mr. Harrington was a nice man, so it seems unkind to say such stuff."

"You're right, Ginger. Maybe it's like people long ago who didn't understand why volcanoes erupted, so they made up stories to explain what didn't make sense."

"You're being too kind, Ms. K. I have my own theory."

"Oh? And it is?"

"I think one murder caused the other. I think Mr. Harrington knew something, something that got him killed."

"Not a bad theory, Ginger."

"Jim Blender told me Mr. Harrington's chemical cabinet key was missing. What would TJ Sweeney make of that?" She raised an eyebrow, a quizzical look on her face.

"Perhaps she already knows. I think she's working on all of this, but she's been so busy I haven't seen her lately."

Lettie came back into the living room with a tray carrying two steaming cups of hot chocolate and a plate of cookies. When she left to finish cooking dinner, Grace changed the subject.

"How's the play going?"

"It's fun." She reached for an oatmeal cookie. "I think you should come to a rehearsal and take pictures for the newspaper. Could you?"

"If Ms. Terry says I can."

"We have all the blocking done and are supposed to have our lines memorized in two days. I've got a lot of lines, but so far I'm in good shape."

"How are you getting along with Ms. Terry? She stopped in at the newspaper to put some ads in for the play. She is quite a character, isn't she?"

Ginger laughed. "Boy, you can say that again. One of the boys on the scene construction group swears he could smell weed—you know, pot—when he got to practice the other night. Ms. Terry was very silly and giggly at rehearsal. She was running around in her bare feet making strange jokes, expecting us to laugh. Really weird, Ms. Kimball. It's hard to think of you and her both being teachers. You're so different."

Grace took a sip of her hot chocolate, thinking carefully about what she should say. "Maybe it would be a good idea to come take pictures of a rehearsal. Then I could see your director in action."

"Oh, would you?" She grinned widely and then glanced at the clock on Grace's fireplace mantel. "Gee, I have to get moving." She walked over toward the hallway, calling out to Lettie to thank her for the hot chocolate and cookies.

After Ginger left, Grace walked out to the kitchen. Weed! Grace shook her head. Maybe Bob Godina was right about standards slipping.

"Well, how'd it go?" asked Lettie.

Grace took a deep breath, counting to five in her head. "School? It was fine. Not really like being there as a teacher, but Alex Reid says they have someone to replace Evan, so I can get back to my newspaper writing." She decided it was for the best, but it would be difficult.

"Lots of people talking about the murders."

"I can imagine, Lettie. The high school kids are all speculating too. Getting hard to tell what's true and what's wild rumor. I had a chance to talk to Marilyn Atkins today. She seems to be in the thick of it all."

Lettie's eyes widened, and she sounded skeptical. "Marilyn? She's kind of nasty, but she doesn't seem like she'd hurt a fly."

"Oh, no. It isn't that anyone is accusing her of murder, but she knows a great deal."

Lettie stared at her, waiting for her to continue. When Grace didn't, Lettie filled the void in the conversation. "Gladys at the coffee shop says she's heard the grieving widow is spending the inheritance before her husband's body is even cold. Humph! Sounds like Liz Hardy. She always did put on airs. I thought them an odd couple: he was so likable, and she was so cold and uppity."

"Is this Gladys' assessment or yours?"

"Quite a few people were talking about it at the coffee shop. Seems like the merry widow was in Woodbury buying a new car, loaded with lots of those blue-in-the-teeth things."

"Bluetooth?"

"Is that what you call it when you can talk to the car?"

"Yes. What else did your jungle network tell you?"

Lettie put her hand up, pointing at nothing. "Rumors Hardy was having an affair with someone on the high school staff, and Liz, the Frost Queen, found out about it and took him out."

"I think people have been watching too much reality television. Eventually it rots the brain."

"I told you I hate having my Del work there. Whoever killed John Hardy was right in the building before Del arrived. People saw

Liz Hardy's car behind the building about the time of the murder. It's a wonder Del didn't walk right in on it. Liz Hardy has no idea what dealing with me would be like." She crossed both her arms in a final sign of finishing the job if Del were to become a third victim.

"To tell you the truth, Lettie, I'm beginning to wonder what's true and what isn't."

Lettie looked at Grace's face, worn out from not sleeping the night before, and her eyes narrowed. "What is going on with you, Grace? You usually come home in a chipper mood when you're at the school. What's happened today?"

"I'm feeling a bit down, that's all."

Immediately, Lettie pulled out a kitchen chair, plopped Grace on it, and went around the table to sit across from her. "Does this have something to do with Jeff Maitlin? What is this about work stopping at his humongous mansion? I talked to Mildred, who heard it from Charlie Sims, who was talking to Camilla Sites, who got it at The Depot from one of Todd Janicke's workers. Did Jeff run out of credit at the bank?"

Grace looked at her sister-in-law, her lower lip beginning to quiver. Then she got ahold of herself. "I got a message on my answering machine. Jeff isn't coming back."

"What? What do you mean?" Her mouth twisted and her eyes narrowed.

"He's not coming back."

"I knew it! That scoundrel." She waved her arms, stood up, and walked around the table. "He's a no-good, crummy, black-hearted, miserable son of a gun. He can't do this. How can he do this to you?"

"I don't know, Lettie. I thought we had something special going."

She turned to Grace and sputtered in disbelief. "He—he left a message on your answering machine? The dirty coward. Only one step higher than sending you one of those text-y things. Wait till I get my hands on him. He'd better not show his face back here again. My iron skillet isn't good enough for the likes of him. I might have to get out my turkey roaster."

This made Grace laugh through her tears. "Oh, Lettie. Maybe it's for the best."

" 'For the best?' No. You don't deserve this kind of treatment, Grace Kimball. For once in your life, I thought you'd found someone who was at least close to the equal of our Roger. Then he goes and does this. If he comes around, Endurance is likely to have a third murder . . . I'd get off with any jury in this town. Justifiable homicide."

Grace laughed again despite her misery. "Oh, Lettie. I didn't realize you even liked him enough to be so angry."

"Who says I liked him? I just thought he was perfect for you."

Grace looked at her sister-in-law's indignant face. "It will be all right. I'll manage to get through this."

"Humph. It's a good thing I made you a chocolate cake. Figure maybe TJ will show up and help you eat it."

"What would I do without you to cheer me up, Lettie?" She considered briefly. "Probably gain less weight."

"Dinner's on the stove. Cake is on the counter. I'll be back in the morning. Don't do anything drastic for love, please."

"I'm fine, Lettie."

Lettie left her there with the fragrance from a pork roast sitting on top of the stove and a pot of broccoli waiting to be eaten. Grace didn't have much of an appetite, but she decided she'd change clothes and eat while she watched the evening news. Passing the bulletin board by the kitchen phone, she glanced at the calendar tacked up next to various notes.

Suddenly it hit her. February 14th is coming up. Great timing, Jeff.

Chapter Seventeen

GRACE WAS FINISHING her coffee and cereal on Saturday morning when Lettie arrived, laden with sacks of groceries. Saturdays were a good time to sleep in, sit in the kitchen in her bathrobe drinking coffee, reading the newspaper, and considering what to do about Jeff Maitlin. The first three she had covered. Grace closed the *Endurance Register* she'd been reading and looked up at her sister-in-law.

"What's the good news, Lettie?"

"Good news? You want good news, go join a corporation—or better yet, a drug company—then make millions from the rest of us suckers. No, make it billions."

"Oh. I see. We're going to have that kind of day." Grace took a long sip of coffee.

Lettie pulled off her coat, hung it in the closet, and came back to the kitchen, eyeing the groceries that needed to be put away. She began opening cupboards and the refrigerator, sending food efficiently to storage as she talked to Grace. "Two murders in town. No solutions yet. My legion doesn't have much information, because it seems like everyone is keeping his mouth shut." Grace was aware Lettie's legion was a loosely formed group of contacts who kept their eyes and ears peeled for what was going on around town. Usually they heard details before TJ Sweeney did.

"What *have* they heard?" asked Grace, as she unwrapped the paper from another oat bran muffin.

Lettie stood over the kitchen table so she could use her finger to tap on the table, emphasizing her points. "Mildred at The Bread Box Bakery heard Marilyn Atkins's fingerprints were all over John Hardy's office. Wouldn't be surprised if they'd—well, that's a story for another day."

Grace frowned at Lettie. "I'd hate to think Marilyn would be involved in murders. I've known her for fifteen years, Lettie. She just isn't the type."

"According to you, Grace, no one's the type. But I have my theory."

"A theory? Have you shared it with TJ or Jake Williams?"

"Not yet." Lettie looked off into the back yard, distracted by a squirrel getting into the bird feeder. "I'm gonna get that sucker. I'm so tired of him taking the bird feed. A pellet gun. That would do it. One shot right in the—"

"Theory?"

"Theory? Oh, yeah." Lettie looked at the bananas in her hand for a moment, and then remembered what she had been saying. "Both of those women—Hardy's wife and mistress—were at the high school Sunday." She leaned over, lowering her voice for some reason. "I heard they were there during the prime time when the murder happened. Maybe it was both. Couldn't you see that, Grace? The betrayed wife plus the home-wrecker mistress, teaming up to kill the philandering husband."

Grace shook her head slightly. "Lettie, you read too many tabloids. This is little Endurance. We don't have that kind of drama here."

"We don't? Two more murders? What would you call that?"

"An unfortunate coincidence. What else has your local jungle telegraph heard?"

"A red lampshade with red feathers. Heard that from Gladys at the coffee shop. It was in Hardy's office, dangling from his foot. A red light bulb was in it, as if someone was sending a message about straying from your spouse."

Grace started laughing, almost choking on her muffin. Lettie glared at her.

"Lettie, you are so far off on the details this time."

"How do you know? Did TJ talk?"

"Occasionally, I hear a little from her, but no red lampshade, no red light, no foot, and no teaming up by two women. You have to stop listening to all this garbage."

"Garbage? Usually I'm way ahead of Sweeney, but this time people are keeping their lips zipped. I don't quite understand it."

Grace simply shook her head.

"Oh, I also heard the toxicology report showed he had been poisoned by arsenic, just like the title of the play Looney Tunes is putting on next weekend at the high school."

"Don't think so. I know for a fact the tox report is not back yet." But I won't mention it's probably coming later this week, Grace thought. She decided to move Lettie away from that topic. "Speaking of Ellen Terry, I plan to do a little checking up on her at the newspaper today. I think a bit of research is called for. I'm doing a feature article on the play."

"Hmm," said Lettie, and she pulled out a cookbook, opening it to the index. Moving her finger down the page, she said, "Ah ha!" and thumbed through pages to find a recipe. Then she looked up at Grace saying, "I think something is not quite right about that woman."

"You think?"

"I think. Del says her room at the high school is always total chaos. I thought teachers had to be organized. All of mine were."

"How long ago has it been?"

"It wasn't a one-room schoolhouse. That play woman isn't like other teachers, Del says. He'll be so glad when the weekend is over.

He finds it almost impossible to clean around the stage area or in her room. Stuff everywhere." ———

"Maybe being organized isn't her style."

"I'll say it's not."

"I'm curious about her too, so when I find something out, I'll let you know. Right now, I'm headed upstairs to get dressed and go down to work at the newspaper."

"How about beef stroganoff for dinner tonight?"

"Sounds lovely," said Grace as she went upstairs.

Grace spent most of the afternoon at the *Register* office, but each time she thought she would look up information on Ellen Terry, someone came in, asked her a question, needed something, or just wanted to talk. Bucky Carmical stopped in to place a want ad for his mom just as Grace was taking some papers to the social page desk. She had to grin and greet him because he'd been one of her favorite students. *Two years ago, he'd organized an alarm clock brigade: ten students hid alarm clocks around the building, set to go off at various times. Sure kept the assistant principal busy tracking them all down.* She chuckled as she walked back to her office. By the time she glanced at the clock, it was already five.

"Oh, bother," she said. The thought of beef stroganoff settled into her brain, and she thought she would go home, eat dinner, and come back in the evening. No one would be in the office so she could work undisturbed.

Once home, she decided her house was unusually warm and cozy for a February night. Maybe she wouldn't go back to work this evening. Then she remembered the play was the following weekend, and she really needed to get a bit of background on Ellen Terry. Besides, she was curious about the unusual woman. So, after arguing with herself, work won out.

At the office, a light at the front of the building in the public lounge was on, left on during the night hours. Also, a flood light covered the sidewalk at the main door, but the deserted parking lot had only a couple of lights on tall poles. After some of the events which had happened recently, Grace felt a little unsettled about being in the building alone, but then she decided that was silly. The front door was locked, as it should be, and she locked it carefully behind her. As she walked through the building, she turned on lights so she wouldn't be anxious.

She unlocked her own office, hit the power button on her computer, and took off her coat and winter things. Then she settled in for something she loved to do: research. She found it exciting to start on a new project, because research on the Internet was intriguing. One idea led to another, which led to another, and so on. As she brought up her browser, she thought about what Bob Godina had said about teachers as professionals. A love of learning, as well as intellectual curiosity, were musts for teachers. How could a person inspire students to learn if she didn't love to find out about ideas herself?

Let's see, she thought. Nebraska. Small schools. Private schools. How many could you find in small towns in Nebraska? She found fifteen using a filtering program, and once she began to settle in on those, she looked for the names of faculty from 2011. The first seven schools were dead ends. The eighth one was Our Lady of Perpetual Sorrows, a Catholic school in Millage, Nebraska. What a depressing name for a school. The town had seven thousand people, a public high school, and this private school.

And then, there she was—Ellen Terry was listed as a drama teacher, English teacher, and play director. Grace was about to look for a photo when she heard a noise. She paused and listened, her head cocked to the side. Nothing. She licked her dry lips, took a swallow of bottled water, and looked up several times at the window of her office door.

Now, where were we, she thought. Oh, yes. No photo. Ellen Terry had been there for two years as a full-time teacher. English, drama, play directing. A newspaper article about the school board meeting listed her as resigning in the late summer of 2011, and the board replaced her the following month. Hmm. I wonder why she would leave a full-time job at a private school for a part-time job at a public school in a small town in Illinois. Obviously, she likes small towns, but why leave a full-time job?

Again, Grace thought she heard a noise. Maybe it was just the furnace kicking on. She left her desk and stuck her head out the office door. She couldn't see anyone or anything moving in the hallway or the visible part of the main lounge. All the lights were on. She walked out quietly, her nerves on full alert. No one in the lounge and Jeff Maitlin's office door was closed. Walking over to the front door, she checked it to make sure it was locked. It was. My nerves, said Grace to herself. Frowning, she crept back to her office.

She continued to look through the newspapers for the little Nebraska town, theorizing the school plays would probably be in the fall and the spring. April was always a good month for a play. She began looking through the archived newspapers for the month of April, concentrating on the days leading up to each weekend. Then she found it. In April 2011, the spring before she came here, Ellen Terry had put on *Arsenic and Old Lace* at her former school. The newspaper carried a picture of the student cast, including their names. A brief summary of the plot—enough to interest people—followed. Grace gazed at the photos of the students in their costumes. The girl who played Abby Brewster looked nothing like Ginger. The whole cast appeared excited, much like Grace remembered the faces of her own high school students.

She sat in her chair looking at the computer screen thoughtfully. Why would Ellen Terry repeat a play she'd just done the spring before she came to Endurance? Obviously, she must have chosen it again because she was familiar with it, and she would not have as much work to do since she'd know the play, the blocking, and the characters. That made sense. After all, it had been years since the play had been put on in Endurance. No one would know she had directed it recently at another school. Clever woman.

She scrolled through several more newspapers, thinking she might find a review of the play, but nothing. She was just about to look at the fall newspapers to see if Terry had put on an earlier play when she thought she heard the front door open. This is silly, she said to herself. I'm simply on edge because of the murders. But no, she was sure she heard the door close, latching with a click.

Her heart pounded and her shoulders tensed as she reached for her purse to find her cell phone so she could call 9-1-1 if she needed to. Who would be coming in at this time of night? The next paper didn't come out until Monday, so no one would be in on a Saturday night. Thinking about a weapon, she looked around, but the closest thing she had was a heavy dictionary. Right, like that would help, she thought. Slowly, she rose from her chair, praying its familiar squeak wouldn't happen this time. It didn't.

Creeping softly to her door, she touched the handle, pulling it open far enough to go through the space between the door and the doorframe. Holding her breath, she made sure she moved the door carefully because it sometimes squeaked too. With excruciating nerves, Grace stuck her head out, inches at a time, straining to look down the hallway. She didn't see anyone. But she could hear something. She couldn't identify the noise. It was soft, furtive, like someone searching for something.

What should she do? She thought. Can't call 9-1-1 or whoever it is will hear me. Turn out my office lights and hide? Maybe he won't come down the hallway. No, it wouldn't work because he would see her light go off through her office door's window since that light reflected into the hallway. Nothing for it. She needed to check out the noise.

She took a deep swallow, put her hand on the doorframe, and tentatively stuck one trembling foot into the hall. Nothing unusual happened. No gunshots down the hall, no shouts of "Who is it?"

She pulled her whole body out into the hallway but plastered herself up against the wall. Inching her way down the wall, she tried to stay as flat as she could. If someone was out there, at least she had the element of surprise, and it was darker in the hallway once she left her office door. Maybe she could make it to the front door and run out before they caught her. Just a few more inches and she could see beyond the hallway, out into the main room of the front office, the place where people came in to see Rick Enslow, who managed the ads . . . Rick, who was not here tonight when she needed him.

Another inch or two. She leaned forward slightly with her head so she could see into the office. A man stood at the counter with his back to her, looking at some pieces of paper. Suddenly, Grace got her nerve back, feeling the anger rise through her back to her shoulders and neck. She stood up straight, moved forward, and demanded in the strongest voice she could find, "Who are you? What are you doing here?"

Whoever it was put his hands up in the air and turned slowly around. She braced herself and punched in 9-1-1, but didn't actually send it. One punch on "send" and it would go flying off to the dispatcher and then to TJ. Glancing between her phone and the stranger, she watched him turn the rest of the way around to face her.

Jeff Maitlin.

For a moment her whole body froze. Then she dropped her phone, raced across the remaining space, and folded him into her arms.

Chapter Eighteen

JEFF SAT BACK against the sofa cushions, his eyes closed momentarily. Then he felt Grace's concern. "I saw your car in the parking lot and was afraid if I just walked in, slamming the door, it would scare you. I was trying to be quiet."

They had both driven to her house and were sitting on her living room sofa, a bottle of wine open, glasses poured, and a fire providing warmth against the cold and darkness outside. She searched every inch of his face: the drawn look, the dark circles, the sadness about his eyes and mouth, the two-day stubble on his chin. He stared into the fire while she breathed in his scent, sitting in silence, waiting for him to speak.

"What did you mean—your text—my parents?" he asked, his eyes glued to the label on the wine bottle sitting on the coffee table.

Grace took his hand, put it up to her cheek, and kissed it before returning it to the sofa. "TJ. She saw a story about your parents' deaths."

He took another sip of wine, paused, and his stare shifted to the fire.

Grace said, quite simply, "Don't leave me and refuse to take my calls again, Jeff. These weeks have been so empty. I don't think I could stand it again."

He didn't answer her immediately. After a long pause, he slowly shook his head. "I'm sorry, Grace. What I've been through in the last few weeks—well, you have no idea. It was so much more than I—"

"Time you shared it with me," she said. "After all, I don't believe you can tell me anything that will change how I feel about you. Let's sweep away the secrets."

He squeezed her hand, leaned down, and kissed her.

"You know," she said softly, "the sins of the father are not visited on the son. What happened long ago was not your fault."

He poured more wine into each of their glasses. "I wish I could believe you, Grace. I am starting to, little by little, but it's so hard to justify what my father did . . . difficult to square it with the man I knew growing up."

She waited for him to go on, watching him look down at his hands as he spoke.

"It's been so hard not knowing all these years, feeling guilty because I wasn't there." He reached over and took his wine glass, swirling it in his hand, and setting it back down. "Well, here goes . . . the whole story. Maybe it will change the way you feel about me, but it's time you knew." He stood up and walked over toward the fireplace, eyeing the smoldering embers and the dancing sparks.

Grace thought, he can't look at me.

"I didn't know what my father did for a living other than he was a lawyer. I grew up in the Chicago suburbs in a huge, brick mansion. An only child. My mom didn't work, but she was heavily involved in charities. We lived a privileged life. I—I always thought it was because attorneys made lots of money. It was the early 1960s, so I didn't understand much that happened. Sometimes a man would come to the house, and Father would always take him to his office in the back of the house. It didn't happen much. Often the man—it was more than one specific man—would have a briefcase with him. I didn't know what was in it; I figured he was bringing my father papers, legal papers."

He returned to the sofa. "What did I know? I was just a dumb kid. I found out later my father was in court quite often, defending scum, killers, money launderers, pimps, and numbers racketeers. I guess it wasn't a secret to other people. Back in the early sixties, the mob was powerful in Chicago, as well as other big cities. I knew we had a wealthy lifestyle, lived in a conservative suburb, had a house-keeper, cook, and a gardener, and so forth. I didn't realize other people didn't live like we did."

"Jeff, you were only a kid then." He looked at her and she muttered, "All right, I'll stop making excuses. Go on."

"I know, I know. But still, looking back on those times, I think I just didn't notice anything." He held out both hands, considering how to explain. "I took it for granted life would always be that way. I went to a private academy, had lessons in tennis or horseback riding, and ran with other boys from fortunate families. Life was good."

"You see those things now because you're an adult."

"True. I understand. In the summer, I was always shuttled off to camp in Minnesota. I loved the summers too; the summer camp was like a second home." He reached over and picked up his wine glass, this time taking a long sip, prolonging the moment, Grace thought.

"However, one summer, this all ended. I was taken home by my grandfather. The summer of '61. I'll never forget it. I was eleven, about to start sixth grade. He came to the camp in his old, battered-up station wagon, and drove me back to their little town in western Indiana, where my grandmother was waiting. They had moved all my possessions to their home; when we arrived, they sat down to tell me both of my parents were dead. I can still remember every detail of the moment—the pattern of the drapes in their living room, the texture of the burgundy arm on the sofa, the doily my grandmother had cro-cheted lying on that sofa arm, the television console with my parents' wedding pictures on the wall behind it . . . school photos of me. Even now I can see their living room."

He frowned and looked straight ahead, avoiding her eyes, thought Grace.

"I can't remember exactly what my grandfather said. However, I'm sure it's mixed up with my better understanding from later years. My parents had been shot, execution-style, at night in their bedroom. If I'd been there, I would have died with them." He looked down at his hands, clenched in his lap. "Believe me, I had many moments over the years when I wished that had happened. I missed them so terribly, especially since I never got to say good-bye."

And now Grace felt tears in her eyes, thinking about Jeff as a boy, listening to the horrifying news that his parents were simply wiped out of his life in one stroke. She put her hand on his arm while he reached up, closing his hand over hers. Then he nodded, patting her hand.

"I'm fine, Grace. I've come to terms with my parents' deaths over the years. I've visited the cemetery where they were buried without me. Frankly, once I grew older, I loved the small town where we lived, especially since my grandparents gave me a cheerful, secure, and comfortable home. Not a rich home financially, by any means, but I was loved.

"During those early years, my grandfather was still working as the editor of the small newspaper in town, so I often went to his office after school, helping clean up and stack newspapers to tie them for delivery." He smiled, turning toward her. "My memories of those days were all so happy except, of course, for the absence of my mother and father. My grandparents—they were my father's parents—did everything they could to make me feel loved, wanted, cherished. My mother was an orphan, so I only had the one set of grandparents, plus a few distant cousins I didn't know.

"I always thought I'd live in a small town again." Now he leaned in toward Grace, taking both of her hands in his. His voice rose as he continued. "I was telling you the truth when I said I'd grown up in a small town and wanted to end my career in the same kind of place.

When it came time to go to college, I went to Northwestern, double majoring in journalism and history. I always loved history. Well, you know the rest about how I went from a small newspaper to much larger ones during my career, ending up in New York City."

Now his voice took a quieter tone. "Over those years I always took care of my grandparents, making sure they wanted for nothing. I visited whenever I could, but I know they worried that I didn't marry or have a family of my own. Nevertheless, I often went back to Indiana and made sure they were doing well." He shook his head slowly. "Going home—a welcome respite from the craziness of big cities. I could actually relax, sleep at night, go fishing with my grandfather, and eat my grandmother's rhubarb pies. Eventually they passed away, first my grandfather, then my grandmother. They're buried there in a small cemetery I visited, off and on, over the years. I was there last week."

"I suppose it was like a chapter of your life ending."

"Exactly. I owe them so much. It couldn't have been easy for people in their sixties and seventies to take care of a crazy teenager who had become an orphan overnight."

"After that, you were moving here, there, and everywhere?"

"Yes. I was always restless because my only roots were in my grandparents' small town. But I could never quite settle down. In a sense, I was married to my job, and I found it endlessly fascinating. Years went by. I suppose it became easier to simply keep moving."

"So, who called you when you left here a few weeks ago?"

He shifted in his seat, leaning back against a cushion. "I think I always wanted to know what happened exactly, and who had killed my parents. I knew the why. As my grandfather explained years later, my father's 'clients' put more pressure on him to work expressly for them. He didn't want to do it, but it became easier as time went by since it assuaged the guilt he felt when he considered a more secure life financially for my mother and me. While their money might have been illegally obtained, I'm sure they paid my father well. But I imagine they also made some threats." He shook his head slowly, pausing for a deep breath. "My grandparents, you see, never approved of his work with organized crime, so it was a source of friction between them. A few weeks before my parents' deaths, my father talked to my grandfather, telling him he was going to turn state's evidence. In his thinking, it was the only way to keep us safe."

"Obviously, someone else found out about his plan."

He pulled back, drawing his hands into his lap. "Yes. Not knowing who killed them, ripping them from me, has been on my mind ever since I was a teenager. I've felt guilty because I wasn't there. I kept thinking I might somehow have stopped it. Of course, that's crazy; what could a kid do?"

"But Jeff, they would have killed you too."

"I realize that. I also found out, much later, that over the years before his death, my father had given money to my grandparents to put in a trust fund for me. It's a great deal of money. Thinking it was dirty money, money laundered from illegal businesses, my grandfather didn't want to take it. My father assured him it wasn't; it was money earned from people who had nothing to do with the mob. My grandfather invested it wisely, so by the time I was ready to go to college, I could pay for my education, leaving the rest as financial security down the road. I left the remaining money, after college, in investments, and used the money I made working to pay my own expenses. This means I will never have to worry about having enough to live on. It's even made it possible to renovate Lockwood House." He gazed down at his hands. "Of course, the government confiscated my parents' other assets."

"It explains a great deal. But you still haven't told me who called you, sending you off on this wild-goose chase."

"It wasn't . . . a wild-goose chase, Grace." He stopped speaking, glanced at the fire, and turned toward her, looking into her eyes. "It was the final chapter and it was so dark compared to living in this lovely little town of Endurance. Now I understand my parents wanting to protect me from this. I talked to the hit man who killed them."

"You what?"

"I talked to the hit man. I met him. I sat across a table from the man who killed both of my parents."

"Oh, Jeff. How awful." She wanted to put her arms around him, but she saw him flinch out of the corner of her eye.

He put his face in his hands momentarily and paused. "It was the most horrific thing I've ever done. He was simply hired to kill three people he didn't know, two of whom meant—meant everything to me. You see, over the years I wanted to find out about what had happened that night. I hired an investigator—the man who called me; he's found various leads through the years. Mostly, they've been dead ends, so after a while I stopped getting my hopes up. But recently his contacts gave him information about a prisoner who had turned in another inmate for confessing to the hit. The killer was twenty-nine when he shot my parents; now he is eighty, in prison for a life sentence because of another crime where they caught him."

"But why? Why would he confess now?"

"Precisely what I wondered. I went with Ben Throwdin, the investigator, to the federal penitentiary in Terre Haute, Indiana. We interviewed the hit man—Ziggy Einstein—I doubt that was his real name. Grace, he was just an old, broken man—I'd never notice him if I passed him on the street. He said he knew he had nothing to lose because he was going to spend his life in prison anyway. Believe it or not, his conscience was why he agreed to talk to me. The murder had haunted him over all those years. You'll never guess why."

Grace shook her head. "Why, when he so obviously had killed other people too?"

"My mother was the first woman he ever killed. It haunted him. He'd never been hired to kill a woman before; he was also told to kill me, leaving no witnesses." He rubbed his hand over his forehead and paused. "Turned out, of course, he didn't have to kill me, so I lived because I happened to be away at camp."

The last words came out with bitterness, and Grace reached over, taking his hand again.

"Makes a great essay for what I did on my summer vacation," Jeff said.

"Jeff, how do you know this guy is even telling the truth?"

"I thought about that myself. First, he didn't have anything to lose by telling the truth, but I had already considered how I might check his honesty. I asked him some detailed questions about our house. I'd lived in that house my whole life up to age eleven. I knew every nook and cranny, every color combination, every fabric in our house. He passed my questions with flying colors. He was definitely in our house."

Grace stared at him thoughtfully for several seconds. "Did he have any kind of evidence other than the description of the house? After all, he might have been in the house for some other reason: painting rooms or changing the electrical wiring or fixing the television or something."

"I know he was the killer because he did have something else. Over all those years he had left something with his sister, an older sister, who, remarkably, was still alive in Naperville, Illinois. This Einstein gave us her address, had the warden call her to let her know we were coming, and . . . we went."

"How odd he would have kept something."

"I think it isn't unusual for killers to keep what they call a 'trophy' of some sort. In this case, the murder of my mother had shaken him up considerably. We drove to his sister's house, a small, eyesore of a place at the end of a street in a much older part of Naperville. The porch steps were rickety and the front doorbell didn't work. I knocked on the door, and in a moment I saw an elderly woman peer out from a window, holding back a curtain. She came to the door, opened it a few inches with a chain lock, and asked my name. Once I had satisfied her with my driver's license, she went over to a table, pulling a small, sealed envelope out of a drawer, and handed it to me silently."

"She didn't say she was sorry for what her brother did or anything?"

"No, she said nothing. After giving it to me, she did speak. She told me it would be better if I left, that the envelope was the last thing she had of her brother's. She was relieved to get it out of her house."

"Amazing."

"I set it on the dashboard of my rental car when Ben and I left. I thought I would open it when I got back to the hotel, but curiosity got the best of me. A few blocks away, I found a place to pull over because I wanted to see what was in the envelope. I didn't know what to expect, and my hands were shaking. I managed to tear a small corner, then a little larger hole. Turning it upside down, I watched a necklace fall out and slide through my fingers."

"Your mother's?"

He slowly nodded his head, slipping his hand into his jacket pocket. "Here."

Grace took the small envelope, turned it upside down, and felt the slithering metal chain of a necklace slide into her palm. She sorted out the chain and saw that while the necklace was badly tarnished, it was a silver chain with a heart locket. Opening the locket, she saw a tiny, black-and-white photo with a toddler who had Jeff's eyes. About an inch of links in the chain was darkly stained, a grim reminder of where it had been.

Jeff looked at the necklace, saying, "My mother's, of course. I remember this necklace because she often wore it." And then his voice faltered. "She said—she used to tell me it was her favorite."

Grace saw the stricken look in his eyes. Tears were sitting on the edge of his lower lids, threatening to fall. She wondered if this buried story would set him free, as he ironically said, or make it more difficult for him to forget.

A log in the fireplace shifted, sparks flew up the chimney, and Grace realized the fire had burned down to embers during their talk. She looked at the clock over the mantel, startled to see it was almost midnight.

"Have you slept at all?" she asked, quietly.

He shook his head. "I haven't been able to sleep. I'm exhausted. I keep seeing my parents, their faces, their smiles, the house, and the hooded eyes of their killer."

Grace stood up, closing the glass fireplace screen. As Jeff watched, she began turning off the lights in the living room. She went out to the kitchen, turning off lights and checking the lock on the door.

Jeff stood up. "I guess it's time for me to get going. I need to turn in the rental car in the morning so I can clear some things up and try to get back to the paper."

Grace walked over to him, taking his face in her hands. Then she put her arms around him and kissed him. "I've missed you, Jeff Maitlin." She pulled back, considering his cornflower-blue eyes. "I love you. It's as simple as that. Tonight you'll stay here, and I'll hold you in my arms all night long, keeping you safe and warm."

He looked back at her and gently cupped her face with his hands. "Are you sure?"

"Yes." She pulled his hands down from her cheeks, softly kissing the palm of each one, and led him slowly up the stairs, turning off the lower stairway light from the landing.

A few minutes later, her cell phone lit up. "Strange car in yr driveway. You OK?" TJ Sweeney must have been at her house across the street and seen Grace's lights go out.

She returned the text, hitting "send" before she turned off the phone. She could imagine TJ smiling as she read it.

All is well.

Jeff Maitlin is home.

Chapter Nineteen

"GIN!" GRACE SHOUTED, a huge smile on her face. "Another Sunday, another withering defeat for you." She had invited TJ over for lunch—Lettie had made scrumptious chicken pot pies—and told her much of Jeff's story.

"Wipe that smile off your face, Grace Kimball. You are in way too good a mood today for a woman who was boohooing just last week about the missing Jeff Maitlin."

Grace collected all the toothpicks once again, and pushed the cards to TJ to shuffle. "It so happens Jeff is home to stay. He has plans to write a story about his past, thinking the simple act of writing may destroy some of his ghosts. He might or might not publish it. Also, he's going to start work again on Lockwood House."

"You seriously don't have to look so smug. I know I had my doubts, but if he turns out to be legit, I'm good with it. By the way, it's hilarious to see you're blushing, Ms. Kimball, because it's about time someone else on Sweetbrier Court had a strange car parked in her driveway all night. Thanks for taking the pressure off me. What will the neighbors say?"

Grace shuffled the deck of cards, considering how to reply. "If anyone asks, I'll explain my cousin was visiting from Minnesota. It was a rental car."

"That should work for last night." She looked at Grace, grinning. "How many cousins do you have?"

"Oh, TJ, come on. It's the twenty-first century, not the 1950s. Anyway, since he's back now, you won't have to worry so much about my being alone at the newspaper at night, at least the few nights I work late."

"I'll give you that." TJ shuffled the cards, cut the deck and turned up the queen of spades. "What do you know about this Ellen Terry? There she is!" She pointed at the playing card.

"Why? I know she's kind of strange, but what would she have to do with John's death or Evan's? She's only been in town since last August."

"She's doing a play next weekend called *Arsenic and Old Lace*. Quite a coincidence, wouldn't you say? And, for some reason, she's involved in this teacher evaluation question. I'm getting differing opinions on her teaching abilities." TJ flipped the queen of spades over, putting it back in the deck.

"Circumstantial at best. What were her means, motive, opportunity, or alibi, Madame Detective?"

"Very good questions, Grace. Let's see. I'm not sure about her opportunity or alibi. She does have a key to the building—"

"—like everyone else who works there, and who knows how many other people? You'll have to do better than that, TJ."

"For her alibi, she says she was at home working on the blocking and the prompt book, whatever those are."

Grace pointed at the deck of cards. "Deal the cards. A prompt book is what the director uses to record and diagram the stage movement, which is called blocking. Can anyone verify she was home?"

"No. She says she was alone. So, no alibi."

"What motive could she possibly have? You said it yourself: her evaluation was quite positive."

TJ picked up her cards, looking at them with a smile. "Didn't you say you did some Internet searching on her last school?"

"Yes. I thought detectives were supposed to have poker faces. After that tell, maybe we should play for cash." Grace took a card off the deck and threw one away. "I checked her old school in Nebraska. She put the same play on last year."

"Is that usual?"

"Well, it means she wouldn't have as much work to do if she repeated it. She would already have the prompt book to use as a guide. It does seem strange she left a full-time job at a private school for a part-time job here," said Grace.

"Wouldn't the pay be better?"

"Private versus public? Yes. But full-time versus part-time? Maybe she thought she could parlay this job into full-time over the next year or two."

"Anything else interesting in your little research project?" asked TJ.

"Not much to report. The cast for the play was pictured in the local newspaper. That's about it." She discarded with a sour look on her face.

"I wonder how she found out about this job?" said TJ.

"My guess would be she saw it online on a database of available jobs since most teachers check on jobs that way, especially if they're in another state. Maybe she wanted to stay in a small town. She seems like quite a character compared to the other, more conservative people on the faculty. But the kids like her."

TJ examined her cards, then glanced at Grace, a speculative look on her face. "You know, I think I'll have a little talk with Superintendent Johnson about her this week."

"Why? You said yourself she doesn't have a motive or the means. Why would she kill either of those guys?"

"Don't know, Grace."

"I think I'd go back to Liz Hardy. She's got great possibilities as a suspect."

"That she does. I have several things to check out this week, plus a number of people to interview, including Seth Atkins after what you told me from talking with Marilyn. I found out a couple of interesting bits of information." She studied Grace. "Oh, stop smiling at your hand. How can I play cards and think about murder strategy too?"

Silence followed, broken by Grace's phone playing the theme from "Jaws."

"I thought you were going to change that," said TJ.

Grace studied her cards. "I can't think of a more appropriate ringtone for Lettie. I'll call her back in a bit."

"Anyway, after that story about Marilyn losing her school key that Saturday, I checked with some hardware stores. No one recognized a customer asking for a key that looked like the high school key. But I hit pay dirt in Woodbury with a store owner who recognized the key and a photo of Seth Atkins. He had a spare key made from Marilyn's."

"Really? Oh, TJ. Do you think he did it?"

"I can put him at the scene with the building key."

"How?" asked Grace.

"I remembered Del Novak telling me he saw a dark sedan in front of the building Sunday afternoon. The license plate started with 'SAM.' Sure enough, Seth's plate is 'SAMA2.' Seth Atkins plus Marilyn Atkins. Always a good idea *not* to get vanity plates, especially if you're going to commit a crime."

"You give me such good pointers, TJ."

"Darn right."

"So, you're going to see him."

"Absolutely. Next on my list."

"Do you really think a sales rep would murder someone?"

"Human passions know no boundaries as far as day jobs, Grace. It could just as easily be a sales rep as a buttoned-down accountant—"

"Gin!"

"—or a police detective who lost once too often at cards." She reached across the table, putting her hands lightly around Grace's neck.

"Okay, okay, I get the picture!" shouted Grace, removing TJ's hands. "Liz Hardy. I'm putting my money on Liz Hardy."

TJ looked at her watch. "Gotta go. Jake is meeting me at work to go over the evidence and consider follow-up interviews."

"I think I'm going to take photos of a play rehearsal at the high school this week. Ellen Terry thought it might be a good spread for the newspaper so they'd get some decent audiences. I'll keep my eyes and ears open." She put her finger on her lips, thinking for a moment. "You know, TJ, I think I'll talk with Bob Godina about those teacher evaluations. I'd like to know more about what they're doing these days when it comes to evaluating personnel."

"Just be careful," said TJ.

Later that afternoon Grace drove to Lockwood House to meet Jeff. As she left Sweetbriar Court, she realized the snow was melting considerably. She could see the bricks on the street, a sight she hadn't seen in months.

"Amazing!" she said to herself. "Finally, a sign the weather won't be like this forever." She smiled at the thought that the first brick streets in Endurance were laid down in the late 1800s from Judge Lockwood's brickyard. She had researched the subject when she looked up information on the judge and his second wife, Olivia Havelock. The town fathers began the brick paving at the public square, moving outward down Main Street. Before that, the streets were simply dirt or—after it rained—mud, and the sidewalks were dirt or a series of wooden planks set down to save the dress hems and leather shoes of the town's feminine population. Since Grace could see brick pavement, she considered how comfortable it was to live in a small town where history was all around her.

She passed a candy store that occupied two floors of an old brick building near the square. The building used to be the Lenox Hotel and Dining Room, a town institution during Judge Lockwood's time—white linen tablecloths, waiters in starched shirts over sharply creased pants, and cuisine unrivaled all the way to Chicago. Driving slowly around the square, she passed the southeast quadrant, which was formerly a huge department store owned by the judge. The store had extended an entire block. Simon Barclay, an attorney who handled Olivia Havelock's finances, had an office in the upper floor of the bank building that was owned by the Folger family for a great many decades of the town's history. She glided past the Second National Bank, whose ownership was no longer in the Folger family, although the family still had a presence in the town. Once again, Grace reminded herself she needed to check on Emily Folger and her children.

Rounding the square, she turned onto Endurance Avenue, heading toward the college district. This was an area of Victorian houses, including Jeff Maitlin's. Driving north on Second Street, she thought about how much easier it was to get there now that the streets were reappearing from under the winter's snow. She glanced at two huge Victorians, one of which was the home of the president of Endurance College. Two people, plus a third person on a ladder, were taking down Christmas decorations, now that the weather was a bit more conducive to outside work. The second Victorian belonged to a local businessman who had renovated it ten years earlier. According to Grace's research, it was said to be haunted.

Turning left onto Grove Street, she smiled as she saw Jeff's car sitting in the driveway of Lockwood House. "Right where it should be," she said out loud. Although the outside still looked in shambles, she was excited to think Todd would be back working on the inside once again. She parked her car and sat staring at the house in the lowering, late afternoon light. What a magnificent place this once was, she thought. Grace could picture it: the carriages pulling up to the front of the house, passengers alighting and moving across a path to the huge front door, and horses tied to a hitching post, patiently waiting, like sentinels. Now, the house still looked dark, she thought, but spring and front porch lights would brighten it up significantly.

She finally turned off her car, lifting a picnic hamper of food Lettie had made to take to Jeff's. Even Grace's sister-in-law was glad to have him back and still happier to see Grace no longer moping around the house. This would be a perfect afternoon to catch him up on the current history of recent weeks. We had too many other things to talk about in the wee hours of this morning, she thought with a smile. Hitting her door lock, she tripped across the street, turned around in a circle swinging Lettie's basket, and danced at the thought that Jeff was back. She would make him forget his sadness and his memories of the past few weeks.

Chapter Twenty

THE FOLLOWING DAY, Grace parked her car at Endurance High School. Stepping out into the slush and muddy water reminded her spring was somewhere out there.

She had called Bob Godina and he said he'd be glad to talk to her during his prep period. After checking in at the office, Grace climbed the stairs to the second floor. She shuddered briefly, remembering her trip up these stairs with TJ the night of Evan Harrington's death.

Passing Evan's classroom, she glanced in and saw a young woman at the white board, pointing to a formula. Gee, thought Grace, they seem younger every year. She walked toward Bob's earth science room, farther down the hallway, and turned into his doorway.

Bob got up from his desk saying, "Come on in. I don't have students for another forty minutes. It's really nice to see you again, Grace."

Glancing at the huge stack of papers on Bob's desk, Grace felt her shoulders relax at the one thing she didn't miss: grading. She set her purse down on the floor and sat down in a desk across from Godina. Glancing around, she noted all the displays on a table by his desk and charts on the walls detailing types of rocks and periods of geologic time. He sat quietly waiting for her to speak.

"I was hoping, Bob, you could fill in some answers for me about the new teacher evaluation system," she said.

"The teacher evaluations? Hadn't expected that request. Why on earth for?"

"I'm interested in how the new system works. I know it hasn't been long since I was here teaching, but these new evaluations were never something I knew about. I understand the percentages of classroom instruction plus student test scores add up to a total evaluation, but the test scores are less important—thank goodness—than the classroom observations."

"Yes. The district decides on a combination of test scores. Some are standardized tests like the ACT test, while others are made by the district, and still others are individual teacher-made tests."

"I think I'm most interested in the last one. I'm looking for places where people could cheat."

Bob's face became more serious, and he cocked his head slightly sideways. "You're following up on that rumor I heard?"

"Maybe. I'm trying to check out every possible angle. People like you make up a test for students to take early in the year; but then they have a follow-up test later after you've taught the material, right?"

"You're right," said Bob. "Four of us teach freshman general science, so we share the same curriculum and the same test. We made up the test together."

"Do you grade the tests your own students take?"

"We do. We've already given a first semester pre-test, plus a follow-up test, and we'll repeat that this semester. I grade my own students' tests, as do each of the other teachers, and we report the scores to the office. Mr. Hardy—" He paused, closing his eyes a moment. "Alex Reid will get the second-semester scores like John got the first-semester scores." He shook his head slightly. "Sorry. Seems such a habit to say 'Mr. Hardy'. "

"I'm curious. John said he was suspicious of a teacher cheating on those test evaluations, right?"

Bob thought for a moment, rubbing his hand over his mouth. "Yes. But he didn't tell me who. Maybe, a month ago. I remember he said he was going to check on it. He—" Suddenly he drew in his breath and looked at Grace with shock on his face. "You don't think someone killed him because of evaluations, do you? That's absurd."

"I'm not sure. I know the evaluation controversy seems to be a thorn in everyone's side; the timing makes me wonder because the personnel reports to the board are due almost momentarily. This is the time of year for that. Before the March board meeting, the superintendent was supposed to hear from John about his recommendations. That's coming up soon. The timing seems curious."

"Makes sense," Bob said, nodding his head. "I've been thinking about the rumor that Evan was going to get a poor evaluation. I can't believe it for a minute. John had nothing but good things to say about Evan, and I had a prep period with him. I think I'd know if he was in trouble. He wasn't, Grace. He was certain he'd be rehired, that his evaluations would continue to be positive."

Grace thought about this idea, which had been repeated by several people now. If Bob were correct, someone had switched copies of Evan's true evaluation for a false one. "Bob, who else has a prep period with you besides Ellen Terry, Evan, Alan Gladley, and Sally Wenstrom?"

"Oh," Bob looked off over Grace's shoulder, considering the answer. "I can think of two other people—Marilyn Atkins, Ginny Shadley."

"Ginny is up on the science floor, isn't she? She teaches biology. Another person with third-floor cabinet keys." She paused in thought. Then she said, "Bob, I need to ask you something else about the evaluations before I forget."

"Sure. Anything."

"How did Hardy conduct classroom evaluations?"

Bob opened a drawer in his desk and took out a paperback book. "This is a description of how the system works. Evaluations aren't like they were when you were here, Grace. I'll lend you this book so you can see it in detail. The principal, or whoever is a certified evaluator, looks at four domains: Planning and Preparation, Classroom Environment, Instruction, and Professional Responsibilities."

Grace took the proffered book and examined the page Bob had bookmarked. She scanned the page quickly. "You're right. This is much more formal than I remember."

Godina nodded. "At the beginning of the year, John put out a schedule of who would be evaluated and approximately when. He uses four standards: excellent, proficient, needs improvement, or unsatisfactory. If someone received unsatisfactory in two or more areas, he would have to have a meeting. A whole lot of paperwork would result and a plan for improvement would be drawn up. Or, with a first-year teacher, if he were deficient enough, John might let him go. Fire him. He could do it only if he thought the teacher had no chance of improving. Obviously, that doesn't happen often."

"And he had to do this for everyone?"

"Not all teachers. Evaluation would be on a two-year cycle, and people who were here the shortest amount of time, like Ellen Terry or your replacement, Jaski, would be seen more often." He blinked several times, remembering something. "Oh, sometimes John would even do an informal walk-through."

"So, if a teacher was disorganized or didn't get his test scores in on time, he might get an unsatisfactory on Planning and Preparation," Grace said.

"Correct. But Instruction is the most important of the domains. A teacher getting an unsatisfactory on Instruction is in deep trouble."

Grace pursed her lips and leaned forward. "This may be breaking a confidence, but since John has passed away, could I ask you if he ever talked to you about unsatisfactory teachers?"

"Not really. The only person he ever said anything about, because he was frustrated, was Ellen Terry."

"Why? What frustrated him about her?"

"It's more like 'what didn't?' Oh, you remember John." He raised his eyebrows. "Mr. Organization. Ellen isn't exactly what anyone would call your typical teacher. Organization is not her strong point. Sometimes she would ask questions in the lounge, and one of us would try to help her. What that woman didn't know would—" Suddenly, Bob stopped talking, a shocked expression on his face.

"What's wrong, Bob? Are you all right?"

"Yes. But I remembered something," he said, looking at Grace in a most peculiar way.

"What? You remember what?"

"A conversation that happened in the lounge a few weeks ago. Ginny Shadley is rarely in the teacher's lounge, but she happened to be there that day. Evan was also and Ellen Terry and me and—no, I think that's all."

"A conversation? About what?"

He stared at her, a stricken look on his face. "Poison."

"What?"

"Yes. At the time, I didn't think much about it because Ellen Terry was talking about putting on *Arsenic and Old Lace*. I think that's how the subject came up."

Grace tried not to let her excitement show. She calmed herself down, took a deep breath, and worked hard not to reveal her interest. "What do you remember about this discussion?"

"Let me think," Bob said, rubbing his forehead. "I don't know who started the conversation. I was running some assignments off on the copier, so I didn't hear the first part of the discussion. By the time I was done and walked over there, Ellen Terry was asking Evan a question about arsenic, since it was in her play. I think Evan said something about his CSI unit, and Ginny Shadley asked him a couple of questions about the kinds of poisons he had upstairs. Evan said

166

something about Ginny coming over to his lab. He'd show her what chemicals he had, and how he set up this unit for the chemistry students. To tell you the truth, I didn't talk, and I don't remember the entire conversation. Frankly, I don't know much about poisons, so I kind of sat, listening, as I was grading papers."

"Do you remember how people reacted?"

"I remember Ginny was really intrigued because she's been teaching at least ten years now, and she suggested they might think about a one-semester forensics class where they could team teach. I recall Ellen Terry joking about it, saying she could learn just as much on television or the Internet. She tends to have unusual reactions to things anyway. You never quite know what she's thinking. Keep that book, Grace, if it will help you."

"Thanks. It gives me more to think about. I hope you have a good year-and-a-half, Bob."

Bob smiled. "I plan to." He glanced at the wall clock. "You might want to slip out before the hallways are crowded."

The bell rang and Grace grabbed her coat, scooting out of Bob's room before teenagers began filling the doorway. She said hello to several she knew and went down the stairs, past the office, and down again to the front door and her car. Trudging through the slush and water in the thawing February day, she almost slipped, but caught herself by grabbing the hood of her car. That's when she noticed the envelope under her windshield wiper.

What's this? she thought. She looked around, grabbed the envelope, unlocked her car, and got inside. Opening the corner at the short end of the envelope, she pulled out a piece of typing paper, unfolding it. Someone had cut out magazine letters, just like the missing note Liz Hardy claimed she'd received. Holding it by the corner in case TJ might be able to get fingerprints from it, Grace read the note. Her face grim, she reread the note, shaking her head. A killer is still out there, she thought, and now I may have a target on my back.

She climbed back out of her car and looked down the row of three other cars in the parking area. Grace knew Alex Reid's on the end and Ann Cummings' car right next to Grace's. But she didn't recognize the black car in between them. She walked along the back of the row. The black car's license plate said, "Liz."

How easy it would be to slip this under my windshield wiper on the way into the school, she thought.

Chapter Twenty-One

THAT SAME MORNING, TJ Sweeney decided she would call Ellen Terry's last school before she went to talk with Superintendent Johnson. Might be a good idea to find out what they had to say about her and why she left.

The secretary at Our Lady of Perpetual Sorrows explained that Principal Kay Bailey was in a meeting, but would call her back. TJ fiddled around with some paperwork, waiting for the call. She went through a mental checklist of questions she needed to ask the principal, and followed it with a written list of possible questions for Johnson.

Her mind wandered back to Grace. Her friend was talking with Bob Godina this morning about evaluations, figuring she and TJ would touch base around lunchtime or after. Grace said Jeff Maitlin had called Todd Janicke to start on Lockwood House again; fortunately, Janicke hadn't started another huge project in the past week. He was probably too busy still swearing from Jeff's call telling him to stop work, TJ thought.

Jeff Maitlin. TJ knew his return would cut down on her coffee and pie sessions with Grace. She sat in silence for a few minutes, staring at the wall. She'd never really known Grace when she had a man in her life. Roger Kimball died years ago, so Grace had been alone all this time. She'd been busy for years raising her three children, and had always been pleasant and happy, but more so lately since Maitlin had returned. She had a blush to her face, a gleam in her eyes which TJ hadn't seen before. Part of her thought it was about time Grace had some love in her life.

Well, she'd check on Grace's mood if she stopped by later. She dropped her feet from their perch on the desk drawer and pawed through some papers on her desk. Still, introducing Maitlin into their lives on a more permanent basis would change the time Grace had to spend with TJ. Well, she thought, we'll have to deal with it. I—I will have to deal with it.

When her phone rang, Myers told her he had the principal on the line from Nebraska.

"Hello, Principal Bailey," TJ said. "Thanks so much for returning my call."

The female voice at the other end of the phone sounded professional, no nonsense, to the point. "Detective Sweeney. My secretary said you wanted to talk with me about Ellen Terry. What can I help you with? She isn't in trouble, is she?"

TJ paused. "Would you think she might be?"

"Not at all, but you are a police detective. Let's see what I can tell you. I still have some records for her here. I'm curious about why you're asking about her."

"We've had some problems back here at the high school in Endurance, Illinois, so I'm checking on everyone who is new to the faculty in the last year. I am aware she left your school and came here right at the start of the school year."

"Yes. It was kind of unusual. She made a lot of friends here, and she did a great job. The faculty embraced her because she had no family; her parents had been killed in a plane accident when she was only a young teenager, so I gather she'd been raised in foster homes. The kids were drawn to her also, and her play productions were first rate."

TJ waited a moment for her to go on, but when she didn't, the detective asked, "Did you find her at all strange or unusual?"

"Hmm. No, not really. Despite being in her thirties, I think this was her first teaching job. She'd graduated as a nontraditional student from the University of Minnesota a year earlier."

"Did she give any reason why she left your school? She came here for a part-time job, but I gather she had worked full-time at your private school."

Bailey thought a moment. "I wish I could answer your question, Detective. The thing is, you asked if she was strange or unusual. She wasn't strange at all, but her leaving was."

"How do you mean?"

"She turned in her letter of resignation through the mail rather than coming in to talk about it. Surprised all of us. I can't tell you how difficult it was since her decision was just before the start of our school year. Because she had talked with her students about play selections for the following year, they were devastated when she left. We had no idea she was even considering leaving. Late summer is a terrible time to try to find a quality person to take a teaching job. You know, most of those positions have been filled much earlier in the spring or summer. At the time, I thought it wasn't like her to leave us hanging. I walked down to check her room, thinking she might have left some of her files and property there. But it was completely cleaned out, and I have no idea when she did that. Ellen simply was gone, leaving her keys in her desk drawer. I received a fax from her new school in Endurance, requesting her information, so I sent it right away."

"It does seem strange, like she left very quickly. Nothing disastrous happened, or she wasn't angry or upset about something? What else can you tell me about Ms. Terry? Did she have good evaluations?"

"The best. As I said, everyone really liked her; for a first-year teacher, she was quite good. Of course, a nontraditional, beginning teacher has a real advantage. Maturity makes a profound difference. Your gain is our loss, I'm afraid."

TJ nodded her head, furrowing her eyebrows as she thought about Grace's description of Terry. "Thank you very much, Ms. Bailey. I appreciate your help, especially since I realize how busy working people are these days."

"You're welcome, Detective Sweeney. Call anytime."

TJ put the receiver down thoughtfully, going over the conversation in her head while she looked down at the notes she'd written. She'd ask Dawn Johnson about Terry's quick departure from the Nebraska school since she had interviewed her. Maybe she would know why Terry left her last position.

Fifteen minutes later, she was sitting in Johnson's office, thinking she had not talked to so many school administrators in one day since she'd been caught putting a box of toads in the air shaft leading into the principal's office when she was in junior high. Watching people come and go, TJ quietly observed the superintendent's outer office. Several parents came in with forms for various programs, while one of the two secretaries appeared to be fielding phone calls about transportation issues with the bus driver. She sat back in a leather chair, checked her phone, and stuck it back into her inside coat pocket. A large fish tank sat on one side of the room, water bubbling constantly, fish darting in and out between fronds of moss, and a fat scavenger trolling the bottom. All in all, TJ thought, it seemed like a quiet, orderly place to work, hardly a workplace which had seen two murders recently.

When the door to Johnson's office opened, TJ heard the superintendent's voice ushering out whoever had the appointment before her. It was Alex Reid, probably stopping in for a pep talk since he'd been bumped upstairs. Everyone knew he was in over his head, but perhaps Johnson had him in to discuss his replacement for the remainder of the year. The superintendent eyed TJ, and as Alex left, Johnson came over, a smile on her face.

"Come on in, Sweeney," she said, gesturing for the detective to go ahead of her. She indicated a chair in front of her desk; then, instead of sitting behind the desk, she took the other chair and turned it toward TJ. Pointing to a huge pile of folders on her desk, she said, "This is what education has come to these days. Testing, grant money, paperwork listing facts and figures which must go into the state board, booklets filled with new laws and mandates that must be applied, changes to programs you just put in place which now must be redrawn, and . . . well, I don't have to tell you, Sweeney, what we already know since you work in law enforcement. Now we have all this information that has to go in about the new evaluations."

Johnson put her hands in the air and shook her head, a look of disgust on her face. "John Hardy had a good handle on the evaluation situation, but now I have Alex Reid." She gave Sweeney a pained look, saying, "That was off the record . . . the remark about Alex." She once again shook her head back and forth. "So now, now we have two murders, one an administrator and the other a teacher. Tell me you've made progress on figuring this out because I have parents on my back daily."

TJ chuckled and said, "Me too. You sound like the police chief. You know, I spent a lot of time in the principal's office when I was in school, so I'm used to being in trouble around here." They both laughed. "The problem with a murder investigation is you have to put all the pieces into the puzzle very carefully, making sure you dot each 'i' and cross each 't.' However," said TJ, a smile on her face, "I can assure you we are about to put the last few pieces into the puzzle. I'm positive, Ms. Superintendent, we are going to solve this fairly soon."

"Dawn, call me Dawn. Ah, what a relief to hear. You came here to ask me more questions, I'd imagine. What can I do to help now that I'm done ranting about all the uglier parts of my job?"

"I need to ask you first about fingerprinting. You fingerprint everyone who works in the school, right?"

She nodded. "Even myself. Cooks, aides, janitors, teachers, administrators . . . everyone."

"Good answer. I was hoping you would affirm that. I also need to ask you some questions about teacher evaluations."

"Okay, what do you need to know?"

"Is it true Hardy was supposed to give you recommendations for two groups: personnel he recommended you should keep, and personnel he'd carefully followed and was recommending for remediation or firing?"

"Yes, to both. We have to send the information to the state"—she pointed to the piles of paper—"and we need to discuss it in closed session at the next school board meeting, which is approaching."

"Had Hardy given you this information yet?"

"No. We were planning to meet on the Monday afternoon following the day he was murdered."

"Does this mean you have no idea what he was going to tell you about those personnel issues, or had you discussed it more informally before?"

"We had discussed it briefly from time to time, yes," said Johnson, nodding.

"Tell me about the late Evan Harrington. Had he mentioned to you that Harrington had a negative evaluation, so he was going to recommend remediation?"

Dawn Johnson looked confused. "Evan? Absolutely not. He was one of the shining young stars of the faculty."

"Would it surprise you to learn Hardy's recommendation, both in his files and a copy in Harrington's desk drawer, was negative, and Hardy signed the papers saying Harrington should be remediated? What does that mean, by the way?"

"Seriously? It makes no sense. He spoke to me on several occasions about Evan Harrington." She drew a deep breath, thinking about the interpretation of this news. "I can't explain why you would see such findings in his personnel folder. Remediation, by the way, means the principal goes over a list of areas where the teacher needs to improve and suggests ways for him to do so. The following semester, he increases his supervision to see if he has improved. But Evan Harrington would never have been on his probation list."

"Curiouser and curiouser," said TJ. "Did Hardy mention any of the teachers he was going to recommend for remediation, people who needed to either be let go or helped with improvement?"

"We hadn't reached that point yet."

"Hmm . . . Too bad."

"Detective, do you think this has something to do with why they were killed?"

"It's one of the pieces of the puzzle, D-Dawn." TJ stumbled a bit on the "Dawn" moniker since she was used to school administrators calling her mother, who'd give a much worse punishment than the school. "I just talked with the former principal of Ellen Terry, your high school drama teacher. She gave a glowing report about Terry's work at their school, but I hear bits and pieces from people at our high school about unprofessional behavior and unusual attitudes on Terry's part. Perhaps they're rumors, but it does seem like a bit of smoke that needs to be checked out. I have the impression she and John Hardy locked horns occasionally, yet her own personnel record was spotless at her last school and positive in Hardy's file cabinet."

"I wish I could help you. He did mention once to me, much earlier in the year, he was concerned about her, but then I didn't hear anything else. That's John, however; he usually solved his own problems before he said anything to worry me. He wasn't one of those administrators who came running to my office with every little thing. I can tell you we hired her at the last moment. In fact, we had to fill in the position with an emergency person before we found her. She actually started the second week of school, relieving John considerably when she showed up with her credentials."

TJ nodded her head. "Sounds like the person I need to talk with is John Hardy, unfortunately, so I believe I will keep pushing on. But

I can assure you, Dawn, we are getting close to solving this. I know this sounds strange, but large chunks of my job involve thinking about the pieces and how they match. I can feel the end coming, and the pieces are beginning to fit together."

Johnson smiled. "I will be so relieved. Can't tell you how it's weighed on my mind, much more than all these piles of paper. Thanks, TJ. Anything else I can do or help you with, just call."

"I will," said TJ as she moved to leave. She pulled one of her business cards out of her jacket saying, "Here's my number if you think of anything else." Walking into the outer office, she retrieved her phone from her pocket, turning the volume back up. She had felt it vibrate while she was talking to Johnson. Checking the phone, she saw a voicemail from Grace.

"TJ. It's me. I'm going to head up to the police station. Right now, it's 11:35, so I'll meet you there or give the information I have to Myers. I got a warning note stuck on my car windshield. Could have fingerprints. Don't worry, I was careful. See you soon."

Chapter Twenty-Two

GRACE WAS TALKING to Myers at the front desk of the police station when TJ walked in. Myers was mildly flirting with her, and had given her coffee and doughnuts. Grace was laughing at something Myers had just said when TJ approached.

"Oh, there you are. Get my message?" Grace asked.

TJ nodded, saying, "What's this about a warning?"

Myers handed the detective an evidence bag with the envelope and paper Grace had found on her windshield. "Here it is, TJ." He sat back, winked at Grace, and waited for orders.

"Grace, I let you out of my sight for just a day or two and this is what happens," said TJ, smiling. "All right. Come back to my office so you can tell me about this." Myers looked moderately disappointed, a situation Grace remedied by waving at him over her shoulder.

She followed TJ, still thinking about her talk with Bob Godina. TJ unlocked her office door, pointing to a chair, and Grace sat down, leaving her coat on.

"Now," said TJ, leaning back in her chair with her feet up on her favorite desk drawer footrest, "what's happening at the high school? Where did this come from?" she asked, holding up the letter in the plastic evidence case.

"I talked to Bob Godina." Her face was flushed and she pulled her chair closer to the desk. "Oh, TJ, he remembered a conversation Evan Harrington might have been thinking of when he called me. A group of people in his prep period discussed poisons. Poisons, TJ!" Grace related the details of Godina's story, ending with the teacher's opinion that Evan Harrington could never have received a bad evaluation.

"Actually," said TJ, thoughtfully, "the evaluations are puzzling. Not certain yet exactly how they fit in. The evaluation process simply keeps coming up."

"Remember Liz Hardy said she'd received some note about her husband's infidelity? Well, this note to me could be like the one she described. It has letters cut from a magazine like the one Liz received, warning her of her husband's affair. I thought it might have fingerprints."

TJ smiled. "Good thinking."

Grace beamed.

"I'll send it in to AFIS."

"Which is?"

"The Automated Fingerprint Identification System. Fingerprints are sent in to the state's software database, called AFIS; then the software checks any prints against their system. First, though, I need to have one of our guys pull up the prints from your note."

"And TJ—"

"Yes? What else?"

"You never really saw the note Liz claims to have received, right?"

"Correct. Do you think, in this small town, she might have figured the affair out without the note? Something had to precipitate her call to Seth Atkins."

"True. Or she got the note and it gave her the idea for this one."

TJ thought for a moment. "Do you think this was Liz?'" She held up the evidence bag.

"Her car was not parked in the lot when I went into the school. But when I came out it was. How simple it would be to stick it under my windshield wiper. If only one person is responsible for this mayhem, my note may contain the identifying print. The message on this paper is just your standard, 'Shut up. Keep away from the high school' kind of warning. Do you think you might be dealing with two killers—one, like Liz, on the spot—to kill her cheating husband, and another to kill Evan for—oh, whatever reason?"

TJ didn't answer. Then she said, "Perhaps you should actually heed the warning."

It was quiet for a moment as Grace thought about this. TJ took her feet down from her desk drawer and leaned over toward Grace. "Before I talked to Superintendent Johnson, I had a little discussion with Seth Atkins. He has anger issues and had a school key, which I now have."

"I told you what Marilyn said."

"That's precisely why I needed to see him at home. I saw his car in the driveway. It was a dark sedan with the correct license plate that was parked at the school lot the afternoon of the murder."

"Oh, the one Del saw."

"Seth's a mess. Not the clean-shaven, well-dressed pharmaceutical rep you see at the doctors' offices. He was sloppy, unshaven, and obviously had been drinking."

Grace thought for a moment. "But Hardy's murder was more than two weeks ago."

"Exactly. Between his wife's affair and possibly killing two people, he's a mess."

"How do you see that?"

"Think about it, Grace. He'd just found out about his wife's affair. He was drinking from Friday on. Stealing her school keys, he copied them Saturday morning, and his car was spotted in the school parking lot. He says he changed his mind and didn't go into the building. When I talked with Marilyn, I realized she was genuinely afraid of him—said she'd never seen him so angry at her or John Hardy."

"Are you going to arrest him?"

"I'm debating it. We don't have his fingerprints in Hardy's office. Marilyn would never have seen his car that day because her room is in the back of the building. He could have gotten in and done the deed while Del was cleaning elsewhere, or even talking to Marilyn. It would have been gutsy or stupid of Seth Atkins."

"But why would Hardy drink something the husband of his lover gave him?"

"I'm working on that one."

"And where would he get the poison?"

"That too. He is, you know, connected to lots of pharmacies and chemical companies."

"Why would he kill Evan Harrington?" Grace asked.

TJ stopped to think a moment. "Remember I told you I thought Evan was lying to me about something?"

"Yes."

"And remember you told me he'd been in the school the day of Hardy's death?"

"Yes," said Grace. "But he told me he was only there a few minutes."

"Maybe that isn't completely true. What if he saw either Seth's car or Seth himself in the building? He might have assumed Seth was there to pick up Marilyn or talk to her. He'd even assume she let Seth in. Then later he put two and two together."

"Could be that's what he remembered and wanted to tell me. If Seth had a key, he might have come into the building at any time starting that day, even the night Evan was pushed down the stairs."

"So," said TJ. "Now you see where I'm headed."

Grace nodded her head slowly.

TJ continued, staring up over Grace's shoulder as she thought. "So, we have Liz Hardy with a two million-dollar motive, anger at being betrayed, on the spot during her husband's murder, with a knowledge of pharmaceuticals. And boy, was she angry at him!"

"She may also have a new boyfriend in just two weeks."

"What?"

"Her lawyer."

"Hmm. That's interesting too. She's a perfect suspect."

"Then we have a nutsy drama teacher who left her last job quickly for some reason, maybe had problems with Hardy, has great evaluations despite that, and a glowing recommendation from her last school. She seems odd and eccentric, but she doesn't really have any motive or opportunity or means. She's just spreading silliness and maybe smoking a little illegal weed, according to my neighbor."

"Yes, I agree, Grace. Everything checked out on her last school and credentials. Finally, we have Seth Atkins, the other part of the betrayed duo. Big motive, anger issues, possible drug supply connections, a key to the building, on the spot when Hardy was murdered, and certainly smart enough to make it happen. But no fingerprints. I checked. He's in the system because of his job, but we didn't find his prints in Hardy's office."

"Maybe he wore gloves?"

"Maybe."

Grace leaned back, using her hands to gesture. TJ would not be happy. "I'm going over there tonight to take photographs of the technical rehearsal for the play this weekend. No one will be at the rehearsal but Ellen Terry and the play cast. Should be safe enough. Lots of people around."

TJ shook her head, letting out a deep breath. "Grace, if you have to do this, call me before you go and call me again when you leave the school. Got it? No texting. Other people could do that with your phone. I want to hear your voice."

Grace lowered her eyes and sighed. "Yes, TJ. No problem." She picked up her purse. "Now, I'm going to meet Jeff for lunch. Would you like to come along?"

"Nah. I think I'll stay here while they work on this print. Could come back quickly. But, Grace, I'm glad to see you smile again. I thought you'd lost it."

"Lost what?"

"Your smile."

"It's back. I'll call you before I go tonight."

Grace sat across from Jeff Maitlin at The Depot. She had ordered a Santa Fe salad while Jeff, after much deliberation, ordered a Porter's Delight. She watched him check out the décor, every so often saying hello or waving at someone. Her heart warmed. Their food arrived on the arm of Annette Callahan. *Grace remembered the day Annette came to school with short, green hair, the product of a late-night attempt to bleach it blond. It must have grown out quickly, just in time to not be green for St. Patrick's Day.*

Grace moved her fork through the salad, checking on the ingredients.

"What's in the salad?" asked Jeff. "Looks good."

"It appears to be three different kinds of beans, red pepper, olives, a little onion, chilies, cheese, maybe sour cream, and some seasonings," Grace said. She lifted a salad-filled fork to her mouth, tentatively chewed it, swallowed, and pronounced it good. "How is yours?"

The Porter's Delight was a French dip sandwich on sourdough bread with beef broth for a dipping sauce. Jeff took a bite off the end, thought about it, swallowed it, and looked at Grace. "Great! This beef is so tender. Good thing your students decided to start this place. The food is amazing."

Grace examined his face, deciding the dark circles and drawn cheeks were somewhat better, more relaxed than when he'd suddenly appeared at the *Register*. He'd been home for almost two days and had spent much of his time catching up at the newspaper. She thought they had an unspoken agreement to talk about serious topics once he was more rested. Despite his reticence before he left, Grace hoped he was going to be more forthcoming about his past.

"So, how do the past issues of the newspaper look? Have you had time to see what we've done while you've been gone?" she asked.

Jeff wiped his mouth with his napkin, swallowed, and said, "I think you all don't need me. It appears you have a well-oiled machine going, because I studied the coverage of the murders, which was amazing, especially when you realize you were in the thick of it. Do you think TJ is any closer to wrapping it up?"

Grace thought for a moment, a quizzical look on her face. "TJ doesn't always confide in me, but lately I've noticed she's been humming again."

"Humming?"

"Yes, humming," she said, smiling. "It's what she does when she is about to put the pieces together to catch the bad guy. Listening to her, she has only days to go before she makes an arrest."

Jeff smiled, putting his hand over Grace's on the table. "You and TJ are awfully good friends. In fact, you can practically read each other's minds. I know you need time to be with your pals. I'm not saying I won't be a little jealous—oh, double negative. Let me start over. I'll always be a little jealous of your friend time, but I also know, after being alone so long, that I, too, need a bit of space. We aren't exactly teenagers in love, so I think we read ourselves quite well. We can figure it all out. I know we can, Grace."

"Maybe make it up as we go along?"

"Exactly." He stopped watching her so earnestly, took his hand back, and attacked the bowl of salad sitting next to his plate. "I get this feeling TJ doesn't quite trust me. I understand. Over time, maybe I can earn her confidence. You know, while I was gone I had time to think about us. I've never made a long-term commitment to anyone, although I was close once. Years ago."

"What scared you off?" Grace asked, her voice skeptical.

"Oh, I don't know now. It's been a long time ago. I think our goals weren't really the same. It's what I love about you, Grace. I'd be perfectly happy to settle down in this little town for the rest of my life. It's exactly the existence I want. To think I found you here in the same place is just—well, it's just perfect." The last he said slowly, but Grace could see the emotion and sincerity on his face and in his eyes.

"We don't know each other very well," she said. "Maybe, given time, we can fix that."

He smiled, "Well, maybe we know each other a little better after the other night."

Grace felt her face get hot and realized she was blushing. Geez, she was a grown woman, fifty-seven. This was ridiculous. She looked up at him, saying, "Yes, you're right. Frankly"—she gazed around at the other tables of people who were ignoring their conversation—"I wasn't sure after all this time I could remember anything about making love. It's been such a long time."

"I think it came back quite well," he replied, making her blush all over again.

"I'm sure that practice makes perfect."

"I believe you're right. We'll have to see if it's true."

She looked down at her salad, poking at the olives in the bowl. "Might be better to change the subject, since we're sitting around a lot of people, people who know me."

"That's what's so fun," he said, "watching you get all squirmy." He placed a finger under her chin to lift her blushing face. "What else should we talk about?"

Grace glanced over his shoulder, thinking about an answer. "My neighbor, Ginger Grant, is going to be one of the leads in the class play this weekend. Want to go?"

"Oh," he said, "you mean like a real date?"

She smiled and said, "Yes, Mr. Maitlin. Is it fine, in this day and age, for me to ask you?"

"I believe so. Sure. Friday night?"

"I have two tickets."

"It's not going to cost me anything? That's even better."

Grace looked up pensively, rubbing her lips together. "Well, I didn't exactly say that."

Jeff chuckled. "I thought we changed the subject."

"Oh, you're right. How about dinner at my house, the play, and then . . . we'll figure out the last act."

"Sounds like a perfect plan." He laid his napkin beside his plate. Grace thought he was wrestling with what he did or didn't want to say. "Grace, I can't tell you all the emotions going through my head when you sent your text."

"Deb sent it."

"What?" His face and voice both reflected his astonishment.

"In the interests of total disclosure, yes, Deb sent it. I wrote it, however. I meant to send it. Before I could hit the button, she reached over my shoulder. I think this means you've officially been voted in."

Jeff Maitlin sat back, laughter erupting from his usually calm face. "I can see I may have underestimated how difficult it's going to be to court only one woman. I obviously have to win over the entire group."

"Shouldn't be too hard. Jill might be the most difficult nut to crack. If you can talk numbers to her or go jogging with her in the morning, she might crack."

"I'll keep it in mind. Let's go on Friday night to the play, but I might have to meet you there."

"That would work. I want to watch Ellen Terry, the drama coach, in action. She's a strange character herself. And then—"

"—after the play?" He smiled. "I've already talked to Janicke about temporarily halting the downstairs repairs while stepping up the front bedroom so I can move in officially. We'll see how soon it happens. I'd like to move in, despite the work. I'm gone most of the time during the day, anyway. It seems silly to pay rent at my apartment when I own a small piece of this huge house. At this point, the bank owns all but a board or two."

Grace picked up his hand. "I'll take that as a nightcap at my house."

"What was it you said? Oh, yes. 'We'll make it up as we go along.' "

Chapter Twenty-Three

"SO? WHAT DID he say about where he's been?" Lettie asked, while she placed a plate with a sandwich on the kitchen table. It was Monday afternoon, and Grace figured she was in for an interrogation.

"Seriously? You haven't already heard from your network of spies?" Grace took the bottle of milk from the refrigerator, filled a glass, and sat down at the kitchen table while Lettie ate.

"My network occasionally has a problem when no one is talking. Was I right? FBI? CIA? Witness protection?"

Grace laughed. "What can I tell you? He's from New York."

Lettie gave a huge "Humph!" holding out her hands. "Nothing. You tell me nothing I don't know," Lettie said, sitting down across from Grace. "The man is mysteriously missing for three weeks with—nothing!" She picked up her sandwich, but before she took a bite she added, "But I do notice Todd Janicke is back at Maitlin's future bankruptcy asset on Grove Street with several additional trucks of guys. Do I assume Maitlin is back to stay? Or are they taking it all apart again?"

"Back to stay."

"Does this mean you're moving out of here sometime soon?" Lettie blurted this out without thinking.

Grace saw the anxious look in Lettie's eyes. "Why? Are you worried? I thought we'd had this discussion before when I explained I was sticking right here."

"Well," Lettie paused. "Let's say I noticed two breakfast plates in the dishwasher from sometime this weekend, and I didn't figure one belonged to TJ. See, if you'd followed my advice, leaving the dishwasher out of the kitchen remodeling, you would have washed them yourself, and I'd be none the wiser."

Grace watched her sister-in-law with amusement. "Lettie, how many years have I spent all alone since the children left?"

"You know," Lettie said, her brain taking off in a different direction, "the drug companies have some kind of new drug out for women which is supposed to help their—their drive. Mildred at the bakery says Florence Tilderson tried it and almost had a heart attack."

"What?" She gave Lettie an incredulous look. "Florence Tilderson is eighty-nine if she's a day. What was she thinking, for goodness' sake?"

"Well, you know," said Lettie, thoughtfully, "your body may age, but your brain still thinks you're young."

"Florence Tilderson." Grace put her hands over her eyes. "I don't even want to think about it, let alone imagine it." She paused, then studied Lettie's face. "How is Del doing? Is he over his scare at the high school?"

"I think so. He's thankful he isn't there during this week, at least on the weekdays, in the evening. The crazy woman has her play rehearsals at night now." She picked up a plate from the dish drainer in the sink and began wiping it. "He still thinks it's such a shame John Hardy and Evan Harrington were killed because Del admired them so. He reminds me quite often they were good people, then he simply shakes his head. This makes me think he's dwelling on the morbid topic."

"Well," said Grace, taking her plate to the sink. "You know I love reading Ben Franklin's wisdom. One of his epigrams is 'Death takes no bribes.' Even good people die, and sometimes they don't die in peaceful ways. I certainly understand how Del feels—I worked with both and I share his opinion." She paused, stacking her plate in the dishwasher. "Lettie, the world has become such an uncertain place. Lately, it seems to me it's more the case now than it was when I was growing up. I'm almost afraid to watch the evening news these days. TJ would say, 'People fall through the cracks and often they create chaos.' "

"I know what you mean," Lettie said, a serious look on her face. "Danielle Baker was pulling out of her drive last week when she accidently hit her neighbor's pet rooster. No more 'cock-a-doodle-doo' in that neighborhood. Opinion's divided on whether she did it on purpose because the darn thing woke everyone on the block at dawn. I think, after a while, that would get quite old." She shook her head. "You're right. The world has become a violent place. You can't even wake people up in the morning without becoming chicken stew."

Sometimes Grace had to examine her sister-in-law's face to see if she was being serious. This was one of those times. She was. "I need to get down to the newspaper. I'm not going to be here for dinner, Lettie. Have to go to the high school play rehearsal so I can take pictures."

"With the nutsy play director?"

"Absolutely. Quite a few people will be at the rehearsal since the whole cast plus the technical people have to practice."

Lettie stretched her arms wide. "They've carried two bodies out of the building, I tell you and Del to stay away from there, and people kill roosters, but no one listens to the voice of common sense."

"I don't look or sound like a rooster, Lettie, so I'll be safe."

Lettie had left the house an hour earlier, telling Grace to be careful when going back into that "scary death trap" for the play rehearsal. Grace was halfway up the stairs, planning to change her clothes, when she heard the doorbell ring. Now who could that be? she thought. As she turned around to walk back down the stairs and answer the doorbell, she saw a dark sedan parked out in front of the house. Then she heard loud pounding on the door before she even reached the bottom of the stairs.

"Good grief! Whatever could this be about?" she said out loud. She opened the door and came face to face with a towering, angry Seth Atkins, surrounded by a cloud of alcoholic vapors. His coat was half-buttoned, his face unwashed and covered with at least a week's stubble of beard, and he was balanced precariously on legs that were not at all steady. She could smell his body odor, and she was close enough to see beads of sweat on his forehead. One of his arms was braced on the doorframe, and his movements seemed jerky and uncontrolled. She was so close to him she thought she'd pass out from the fumes. It all happened so quickly that Grace felt her heart race. She opened her mouth to scream, but nothing came out.

He looked down at her through dark eyes, and his voice came out in a shrill cacophony of confusion. "Grace . . . Kim . . . Kimbezel. You stay away from . . . from . . . from . . . my wife or you—" And here he stopped to get his bearings and seemed to look past her shoulder as if he weren't sure where he was. "And . . . and you stop filling her—her head with poison about me . . . or . . ." He paused for a moment, smiled in a suddenly lucid way, and whispered in a moment of complete candor, "You'll get what that bastard Hardy got."

Grace started to say something, but he put his huge paw over her mouth and shoved her backward a few steps. Then, his body filling the entire doorframe, he literally fell through the doorway and moved toward her. He grabbed her arms, his foul breath hitting her face. Grace gasped, her eyes wide with fear, and she felt as if she were going to pass out.

"I warned that Har—Har—Hardy to stay away from her." He swallowed and kept his face right in front of hers. He was so close Grace could see spittle on the corners of his mouth, and his eyes seemed unfocused. She didn't have time to even consider what to do to get him off her. It was all happening so fast.

"Well, he got what he deserved, and if you don't—"

Suddenly, Grace felt the pressure released from her arms and saw two hands come over the top of Seth Atkins' shoulders. He was whipped around and away from her, and she fell to the floor in front of her stairway. When she looked up, TJ Sweeney had turned Atkins around and cuffed his hands behind his back. With her hands on his neck and in his back, TJ pushed him ahead of her out the door and marched him in a stumbling gait to her waiting squad car. Grace could see another officer standing by the door. They lowered him into the back seat and shut the door. Then TJ came back to the house.

"You all right, Grace?" She helped her up from the floor and sat her down on the stairs. Then she got down on one knee so she was even with Grace's face.

Grace took a deep breath and blinked her eyes several times, still feeling light-headed. She put her hand up to her forehead and took several deeper breaths.

"Yes, TJ. He caught me by surprise. He threatened me and said I'd get what John Hardy got if I didn't stop telling Marilyn lies about him." Then she had a new idea and looked at TJ asking, "How did you know he was here?"

"Marilyn called me when he left the house and said he had threatened to come over here. He's no one to mess with and probably outweighs you by eighty pounds. Even when he's sober he's scary because he's devious and smart enough to have killed Hardy, and he has plenty of connections as far as getting his hands on chemicals. From what I can tell and have heard, he was still relatively sober but angry on the day Hardy was murdered." She glanced back out at the squad car.

Grace sagged against the back of the step and pressed a hand to her forehead. "Thank you, TJ. I've never seen him like that before. It's as if he's a totally different person than the Seth I've met with . . . with Marilyn." She drew in a deep breath. "It's all right. I'm fine."

"You sure? Do you want to press charges?"

Grace smiled. "No. I'm all right. I'll be good as new in another minute. What will you do with him?"

"At this point, take him down to the jail, let him sober up in a cell, and then have a little 'come to Jesus' meeting with him. He's already lied to me about the day Hardy was killed, and this will give me a chance to have a lengthy conversation with him about his whereabouts in the last week or two." She turned to leave, but then remembered something. "You still planning to go to the play rehearsal tonight?"

Grace nodded her head thoughtfully.

"Don't forget to call me before you go and when you leave."

"Yes, I will, TJ."

Grace arrived at the play rehearsal well into the second act. Ellen Terry had told her on the phone they would be rehearsing in earnest, but she could stage some scenes for photos at the end. Grace thought it would be amusing to watch the rehearsal, so she arrived early. She sat in the back of the darkened auditorium thinking the theater hadn't changed any, but then she hadn't been gone very long. The heavy, velvet maroon curtains were still hanging across the stage front, and now, with them open, Grace could see the flats representing the Brewster house in Brooklyn. A window seat generally held random dead bodies on the left side of the stage, a fireplace mantelshelf—the repository for the poisoned elderberry wine—sat against the back wall, and a door to the supposed basement was on the right, near the bottom of the stairs.

Three high school students were on the stage when Grace arrived, saying their lines as Ellen Terry walked around, yelling commands to the lighting crew. At one point, Ginger Grant stared out at Terry, saying, "Aren't I supposed to have a dinner plate with pie in my hand?"

Terry called out, "Props!" They waited but nothing happened. She swore under her breath, saying, "Where is Andy?"

A few seconds later the door to the basement opened and Andy Pelvin came out, saying, "Oh, sorry. My bad. Here." He handed a plate to Ginger, a look of chagrin on his face. "Sorry, I ate the pie."

Ellen Terry clapped her hands. "People! People! We only have three more days to make this perfect. Your parents aren't coming on Friday to see a big mess. So, come on, get with it. Okay, Ginger, take it from your line after Martha Brewster's entrance. Remember, ladies, you are poisoning people to rid the world of useless human beings. Have fun with it!"

Grace winced at those directions, but watched for another half hour, as the play went smoothly, everyone remembering lines, cues, and entrances. The lights seemed to be the problem. "Obviously, they have a few things to iron out with the light crew," muttered Grace to herself. Ginger walked down the side aisle, plopping down next to Grace.

"What do you think so far, Ms. Kimball?"

"So far, it appears you have a few bumps to level, but I think, all in all, you're in a pretty good place. Three days isn't long, but all your lines are memorized."

"I have a spy report," said Ginger, whispering. "Ellen—she says we should call her that—has been in a really foul mood lately. We took a test for her class in the fall, a test we repeated about a month ago. She didn't hand them back, but I know the grades because I was in her office picking up her prompt book, and I saw them sitting on her desk. Everyone got A's, so when I told some of the other kids, no one complained. 'Why spoil a good thing?' Jason Tucker said."

Grace didn't reply, but her mind was racing. Then a new thought came into Grace's head. Maybe she could go down to the drama office and take a peek at those tests while Ellen Terry was up here working. She knew a restroom was near Ellen's office, so it would give her an excuse to be in that area. She waited until Ginger was called back to the stage; then she picked up her camera and quietly slipped out the back door.

Carefully glancing around, Grace saw no one in the hallway behind the auditorium. She tiptoed down the stairway as softly as possible, watching for Terry or any of the students. She could barely hear them still rehearsing. The stairway led to the second floor, including Terry's classroom, which was at the end of the hallway. Since the door was open, Grace could see the total chaos Del had complained about: costumes lying on top of pushed-together desks; makeup and hairspray sitting on tables, some of it spilled; empty soda cans and paper plates with food piled up on one desk; backpacks, scripts, and textbooks lying around on the floor; and an overflowing wastebasket. What a mess! But, thought Grace, it is a play rehearsal, so maybe it isn't always like this.

Passing the classroom, she walked softly down the hallway past the math wing. Then she turned the corner so she was behind the stage. Tiptoeing around in the old building, she remembered the article she'd read about the auditorium renovation. Grace knew the drama department had an office off stage left, so she reasoned if the workers back in the past had left an opening to the underground orchestra pit and storage rooms, it would be somewhere near this office. She'd kill two birds of curiosity with one stone: tests and the underground. She walked clear around the back wall of the stage and over to the left side, opening a door from the hallway. Steps went up to the backstage area or down to the theater office. She watched the students from the stage wing, all engrossed in their rehearsal; faintly, she could hear Terry's voice off in the distance. Then she turned, taking the stairs down. Maybe she could find out more about Ellen Terry, but she'd have to be quiet.

The door to the office was open, and Grace peeked in, checking to see if she was alone. She was. Walking into the room, she examined the desk, finding piles of papers from Terry's classes, publicity for the play, and homework. She quickly thumbed through them but found no tests. Suddenly, she heard Terry's voice coming toward the office. *What can I say to explain why I'm here?* She scanned the room to see if she had any options for hiding, but saw none. Then Terry's voice grew more distant. Grace breathed out a long breath.

Besides the hallway entrance, two doors came into the room. Grace realized one was a closet because she opened it, spying the coat she remembered from Terry's visit to the newspaper office. The other door, on the west wall, might be the door which went to the underground rooms they had sealed up. Its location would lead under all the seating area above in the auditorium. It was padlocked securely. Turning around the office three hundred and sixty degrees so she could see all the surfaces, Grace didn't notice any keys on tables, hanging from nails, or lying on chairs or the floor. She walked past Terry's desk, her eyes stopping on a pile of theater magazines with a pair of scissors lying on top of the pile. Something clicked in her head. The anonymous letter Liz Hardy supposedly received. It had words cut out of magazines. The warning Grace found on her windshield. She suspected Liz Hardy of her warning letter, but maybe she was wrong. She walked to the table, and just as she started to remove the scissors, she heard Terry's voice again, this time closer, coming toward the office. The scissors slid off the pile of magazines, clattering onto the floor before Grace could catch them. This time she had no time to recover the scissors or slip out the door. Terry was definitely coming to the office. She froze.

She heard loud, clumpy footsteps on the stairs and Terry came through the door and stopped short. She stared at Grace, a confused expression on her face. "Ms. Kimball? What are you doing here?"

"I—I thought maybe it would be better if I waited down here for you to finish the rehearsal. You did say we should take some photographs after you were done." Grace paused and added, "I didn't want to interrupt anything." Her knees locked and her shoulders tightened. She hoped the woman couldn't detect fear.

Terry's smiled thoughtfully as she studied Grace. "Where is your camera?"

"Oh, right there." Grace recovered, and starting to breathe again, walked past Terry to the door where she picked up the camera from a chair. Thank goodness I didn't leave it upstairs, she thought. Then she moved back toward the table.

Ellen Terry glanced at the table next to her, and Grace saw Terry's eyes settle briefly on the scissors. Then she looked back up with what, Grace thought, was a puzzled face.

"Well," Terry said, "the play is going fine; it actually runs itself. I'm a bit like a football coach. I make up the plays, the kids execute them, and I simply watch from the sidelines."

"Sounds good," Grace said, wishing she could get out of this space, but Terry was in front of the door. Then she thought of another idea. "By the way, when I was researching the high school, I ran across an article which mentioned some renovation done in this area back in the mid-seventies. I think it said a warren of storage rooms and an old orchestra pit were sealed up under the auditorium. I thought I might write a historical piece on it for the newspaper. Were you aware of that?"

Terry glanced at the padlocked door. "I believe the area behind this door is the pathway to which you are referring. I call it 'hell,' as in Shakespeare's theatre." She clasped her hands, rubbing them soundlessly. "I feel cold spirits from hell . . . Sometimes when I'm working here at night, I can hear fingernails scraping on the other side of the door. I've always been a person of the most delicate sensibilities, so naturally the spirits would attempt to contact me."

"Have you made contact with them?" Grace asked, lowering her voice, trying her best to sound serious.

"Sometimes I hear them whispering about me." Her face took on a wide-eyed look, and then she muttered under her breath, "Laying their plans. But I am stronger than they are."

Grace worked hard to keep her face a mask, but she was shocked. She cleared her throat and said, "Have you ever opened the door or checked out the underground area?"

"Once. It has passages, storage rooms, and old flats which were used years earlier. Nothing of any value, I believe. I keep it locked because the students must never go in there. I could not be responsible for their safety."

"Sounds intriguing to me," Grace said, hoping to win back the drama teacher's trust.

Terry took a step toward Grace, and Grace took a step back, bumping into the table.

"Ms. Kimball. Despite your eagerness to be back in this building, and even though you have a positive aura here, I would beg you to remember the old adage about the cat, including what killed it."

For the next forty-five minutes, Grace took pictures of scenes, writing down the names of the cast members, even though many of them she already knew. They were either exhausted, trying to balance their homework with their play schedule, or excited at the prospect of the play going on in three nights. She was always in the middle of a group of cast members, whose excited voices reminded Grace of her teaching days. Once again, her heart gave a tug about what she missed.

Finally, she finished the group photographs and turned to Ellen Terry, attempting to sound enthusiastic. "Now, let's get a photo of you with the two Brewster sisters and their nephew."

"No, I think we shall not," Terry said, crossing her arms and turning away from Grace.

"Oh, but it's your big production; you should get credit for turning out such a marvelous evening of entertainment." Grace poured it on. "One little photo. We can line you up right here in front of the window seat." She motioned Ginger and another girl over.

"No, no, I think not. I prefer to stay in the background. Let the kids get the credit."

"Just one? It won't take long."

"No. A definite no, Ms. Kimball. You may think I'm a bit of a diva, but I'm actually superstitious. Never like having my picture taken. Each time someone does that, I fear a bit of my soul leaves me."

"Oh, it's such a small thing, Ellen. I know people will want to see the mastermind behind this production. Maybe one little picture?" Grace couldn't understand why the drama coach was making such a protest about a photo.

"Ms. Kimball. What part of 'no' do you not understand?" Terry's voice had shifted into a deeper, angry tone, while Grace stayed calm, smiling politely.

Now Ginger and her friend moved away from the window seat, watching Grace to see what she'd say. Even Grace sensed a quiet tension in the students sitting out in the seats, watching. No sense to have a scene here in front of frightened students. She paused for a moment, then smiled and said, "Fine. We'll leave it as it is. I think I have enough to get a great spread. Thank you, one and all." In the back of her mind, Grace thought about how she could get this photo. Terry simply wasn't being rational about having her picture taken. Was there a good reason?

All the cast members began moving around, collecting their belongings, and getting ready to leave. Ellen Terry reminded them of their next rehearsal as Grace was putting on her coat. Her cell phone was in her right pocket, so she turned off the flash, taking a surreptitious photo of Ellen Terry on the brightly lighted stage. She checked on her cell screen to see if she got her. Then Grace offered Ginger a ride home, but the teenager had brought her mother's car.

Leaving the building, Grace felt uneasy about this woman teaching teenagers, but she patted her coat pocket, thinking about the photo she'd taken. It seemed as if Terry had a fear of having her photograph taken where others could see her. Could it be more than simply a body image problem? She'd ask TJ about it.

Chapter Twenty-Four

TJ LEANED BACK in her office chair Thursday afternoon going over the information she'd accumulated about both murders. She had told Dawn Johnson the truth when she said they were closing in on the murderer of both men. Information from Nebraska, from the crime lab, and from local interviews should be coming together today or tomorrow. Whenever she was close to the end of a case, her adrenaline kicked in, her senses were heightened, and her energy level went sky high. Already, her nervous system was telling her she would close the books on this one over the weekend. She could feel it, and the details of the puzzle were coming together. She heard a knock on her door, and Myers stuck his head in with a paper in his hand.

"Yeah, come on in, Myers," she said, looking up from the paperwork cluttering every square inch of her workspace. "What've you got?"

"Tox screen on John Hardy, TJ. Just came in." He walked over to her desk, laying it in the middle of the pile. "Anything else you need?"

"Yeah, Myers. An arrest warrant. Got any idea whose name to put on it?"

"Ah, not sure. Maybe Liz Hardy?"

"Hmmm. I'll think about that one. You are right, however. She doesn't have much of a fan club in town. What about the fingerprint we sent in to the Bureau of Investigation? Anything yet?"

"Not yet. I told them to put a rush on it since we already have two bodies, but I know it takes up to forty-eight hours with a rush. The guy told me they'd send it in to the AFIS database, so if this killer is in the system, we'll know. I'm hoping to hear something this afternoon. You'll be the next to know, TJ."

"Perfect. Thanks, Myers." She hardly heard the door close because she was back again to her evidence. She picked up the tox screen information from the tests done at the autopsy for Hardy. "Geez," she said. "Someone wasn't fooling around. Arsenic, strychnine, cyanide—quite a lethal cocktail. The question is, how was it administered?" She had done some research on strychnine since speaking with Martinez. Coffee would be the best bet because the strychnine would be bitter and the crystals hard to dissolve. The coffee cup had Harrington's fingerprints, but no trace of poison. The murderer carried the poison in and out. That's the only explanation for no container. Had to be someone he knew because, otherwise, why would he drink it? Liz Hardy carried a sack of some sort in, but I don't know what was in it. Could have been a coffee thermos and a cup. She put the paper down, picking up her phone.

"Myers, get me Liz Hardy on the phone, please." Finding a blank piece of paper on her desk, she grabbed a pencil, and began making doodles. Eventually her phone rang and Myers had Liz Hardy on the line.

"Hello, Ms. Hardy?"

She was guarded when her voice came on the phone.

"Officer Sweeney. What can I do for you this time? I can't imagine you have any questions I haven't already answered."

"Well, Ms. Hardy, I had a couple of questions I figured you might be able to help me with. You know, trying to tidy loose ends up."

"I've told you everything I know, Detective."

TJ sat back in her swivel chair, pulled out her desk drawer, and put her feet up. "This could well be the case, ma'am, but I have a couple of items I'm curious about. Only take a few minutes of your time."

TJ heard an irritable sigh at the other end of the phone. Then, "All right, fine. What now?"

"When you went to see your husband on Sunday afternoon, did you carry anything into his office with you?"

She heard a silence at the other end of the phone. Then Liz Hardy answered, "No. Well, my purse."

"Ms. Hardy, we have witnesses who saw you carry a bag other than your purse. Would you care to rephrase that answer?"

Silence once again. "This is silly, Detective Sweeney. It has nothing whatsoever to do with his death."

"You'll have to let me be the judge." She waited, counting to ten. On nine, Liz Hardy spoke again.

"Well, if you must know, I took him a few packages of condoms because I was angry. I—I wanted to pull his chain."

TJ didn't know if she believed this story or not. "What happened to them when you left? We didn't find any packages of condoms on the scene."

"I changed my mind when I talked with him. Decided it was childish. I put the bag in my purse and simply walked out with it."

"Would you have this paper bag at your house?"

"I went to the mall in Woodbury after I left, dropping it in a trash bin outside the store. It wouldn't do to have my children finding these somewhere. I didn't expect to stay long at the mall, so if your next question is about the storm that day, well, I missed it. I only had one thing to pick up, so I was in and out rather quickly."

"You destroyed the anonymous letter and now this bag witnesses saw." TJ looked down at her paper. She'd scribbled 'condoms?' 'trash bin Woodbury' on her doodle paper. She decided to switch the subject. Those trash bins were long emptied by now. "All right, Ms. Hardy." She paused, shifting the pencil in her fingers. "I have another question I need to ask."

"Yes."

"This is on a totally different subject. I'm wondering if John ever talked to you about teacher evaluations."

"Not really. I know he was concerned about some teachers, but mostly he didn't bring his work home."

"Did he keep any files or information at home, say, on a computer?"

Again, she heard silence on the other end of the phone. "I thought the police took his computer, but now that I think about it, one of the kids was playing with his electronic notepad while the police were here. They often did that—the children. I suppose the police might have assumed it was Jack's notepad since he was playing games on it. Just a minute. Let me check." TJ could hear her put the phone down, footsteps echoing across the room. Silence. Then he heard the footsteps return and shortly Liz Hardy picked up the phone. "I do still have his reader, Detective. Sometimes he used it, but mostly the children played games on it. He has a jump drive sticking out of a port, probably some work-related stuff."

"I'll be over shortly to pick it up, Ms. Hardy. Thanks."

The tone of the widow's voice lightened considerably. "Oh. Well, that was easy. I'll be here for one more hour. Then we have an ortho-dontist appointment. Fortunately, he has hours after school. Unfor-tunately, he'll have to wait for his bill to be paid since the insurance money is being held up until you finish your investigation." The last few words came across in a tart voice, causing TJ to smile.

"Should be soon, Ms. Hardy." TJ heard a sharp intake of breath on the other end of the phone, and silence. "Closing in on all kinds of possibilities. I'm sure I'll see you soon."

The detective had two more jobs on her list. She scribbled a quick note to the principal at Our Lady of Perpetual Sorrows. Then she paused, considered the photo Grace had taken, scanned it, and paper-clipped the scan to the fax. She added her cell phone number, hoping the woman would get back to her. She'd drop it with Myers on the way out.

TJ dropped her phone in her pocket, grabbed her gun out of the desk drawer, and put on her badge. She went out the back door of the station to her truck, noting the thawing snow. It had been a decent day, weather-wise. The temperatures were high enough to melt some of the snow, and the late February sun tried to peek through the clouds at the end of the afternoon. She was humming as she reached her truck.

Chapter Twenty-Five

GRACE DRESSED FOR the play Friday night, grimly considering her options for checking out Ellen Terry's office. She wanted to get a look at the magazines on the drama teacher's table, especially with the pair of scissors suspiciously close by. Reasoning that she might be able to sneak away while the play was going on, she slipped the theater tickets in her pocket, along with a small LED light she often used in situations where she had to look at an item—like a play program—in the dark. Her phone had gone off earlier, playing "A New York State of Mind," and making her grin. It was Jeff, saying he was almost done and would meet her at the high school rather than picking her up.

On the way to her garage, she noted the clean sidewalk. Spring was only a few weeks away, her roses would blossom again, and the seemingly endless, bleak Midwest winter would fold her white blanket and pack herself away, leaving room in the heartland for a new season of warmth and possibilities. Grace thought again about how much she loved the seasons, a concept her Arizona children couldn't understand. They had grown up in Illinois, but they hated the winters in the Midwest, leaving for a warmer climate as soon as they finished college.

She drove to Deb's house to pick her up since Deb's husband, John, would not go to any more Terry-produced plays. Then, thought Grace, after the play Jeff and I will have a leisurely wine-and-cheese after-party at my house—she started humming a melody she'd heard on the radio—and see what happens. She smiled at the thought. Having Jeff back was so much better than she could ever have imagined, even though they still had a great deal to talk about. At least he was willing to talk now.

She pulled up in front of Deb's house, watching her friend walk blithely down the clean steps onto the cement sidewalk. Ah, it would be comforting to have this winter over.

"Hi, Grace. I'm glad to be getting out of the house to go somewhere fun. It's one of the things I hate about winter—being cooped up or having events called off because of the weather. Well, this time we're on!"

"Climb aboard. Jeff's meeting us there. My neighbor, Ginger, says the play has come together, and they're quite confident. Hope she's right."

"Still doesn't make much sense to me to do this play after the deaths at the high school."

"We'll see. I have a feeling it's going to be a night to remember," Grace said, thinking about the small flashlight in her pocket.

When TJ's phone rang, Myers came on, telling her Principal Bailey was on the line for her.

"Hello, Ms. Bailey. You must be working late." She began doodling on a piece of paper and hastily moved the piles of paper on her desk, looking for her Bailey questions.

"Detective Sweeney. I'm sorry to get back to you so late. I was at a conference, but I stopped to check my messages once I came back this evening. I must say, your communication was quite cryptic, but when I looked at your photo of Ellen Terry I was truly puzzled."

TJ breathed deeply, having found her list, and then let out her breath, all nerves on edge. "That's exactly what I figured you would say. Is this picture the Ellen Terry who taught at your school?"

"No, not at all. Our Ellen Terry was in her early thirties, had blond hair, and was very slender."

TJ wanted to bang her hand on the desk, overjoyed at Bailey's reaction. She pulled back on her enthusiasm, telling herself to be calm. "Do you know the woman in the picture? Someone who knew Ellen Terry, perhaps?"

"Yes, yes, I do recognize this woman. Her name is Amy Deffly. She was a roommate to Ellen; as I remember, she often came to rehearsals to help her with plays. I thought she was a little . . . different looking, but she didn't cause any trouble, so from what I could tell, she followed Ellen around, watching her work and helping with the theater productions. Now I'm confused. Why would Amy Deffly say she is Ellen Terry?"

TJ shook her head quietly. "I don't have a good feeling about Terry's whereabouts, Ms. Bailey. Can you tell me anything else about this roommate, Amy Deffly?"

The other end of the phone was quiet for several seconds. Unexpectedly, the principal began to speak again.

"I only spoke to Amy Deffly on a couple of occasions when I had a few moments and went down to watch play rehearsals. At first, I was a bit concerned because she seemed . . . odd. You see, I had to consider she was coming into my school working with underage adolescents. Something about her made me apprehensive. Couldn't exactly put my finger on it." She paused for a moment, then began speaking again. "I had this feeling of suppressed anger or, well, I hesitate to say, violence. I never saw her say or do anything violent; it was just a feeling under the surface that she might be a bit scary. However, Ellen Terry was her friend and roommate, and I totally trusted her ability to make good decisions. Since nothing was reported by kids or parents, I thought maybe my concerns were pointless."

The detective took in another deep breath. "Ms. Bailey. I know you said at the end of the year you received a resignation from Ellen Terry. Did you see her after the last day of school?"

"No, I didn't. I remember telling you I was really surprised when she sent a resignation in by mail." She paused. "Oh. I see what you mean. This isn't good, is it?"

"No," said TJ. "Did Ellen Terry still have paychecks coming? I know teachers are paid throughout the summer."

"Yes, of course. They would have been direct-deposited to her bank account. Would you like me to check with our financial people to see if they went out? I don't deal much with the financial end of paying teachers. Since it is Friday night here, it will wait until Monday. Would you like me to check on that?"

"Yes, please do," said TJ. "And Ms. Bailey, thank you so much for your help. I hope to call you again after the weekend with good news. But I'm afraid I fear what I can already hear in your voice."

Again, TJ heard a silence at the other end of the phone. She heard Ms. Bailey's voice come on again, this time hesitant, almost on the edge of a sob. "You're welcome. I'll—I'll check with the financial people." Then TJ heard a long pause. She waited. "I'm afraid I can't—can't talk any more. Next week, Detective." TJ heard the phone connection click off.

"Well," TJ said out loud, "some of the pieces of the puzzle are clicking into place. Funny thing about institutions—unfortunately, people slipped through the cracks because the record keepers were too busy to follow through." Ellen Terry had been hired after school began, and Johnson admitted her records came through with her fingerprints from the earlier school. Because the beginning of the year was so busy, she hadn't had her re-printed, but figured she'd get around to it later. Later never came.

"This means," TJ continued out loud, "Amy Deffly sent Ellen Terry's credentials and fingerprints, along with her own photo, to the Endurance district, hoping time was on her side. It was. That, of course, leaves us with still another question: Where is the real Ellen Terry?"

She pushed in her desk drawer, grabbed her gun and badge, and pulled her coat off the hook just inside her door. Stuffing her cell in her pocket, she walked out to the main desk to tell Myers she was heading over to the high school.

"You might want to see this first, TJ," said Myers. "It's the fingerprint report. Came in a few minutes ago. They got a hit."

"Let me guess: the print on Grace Kimball's letter belonged to someone named Amy Deffly."

Myers looked down at the fax, checking the name, and said, "Wow! How did you know? Are you psychic or something?"

"Because I'm a genius, Myers, a freaking genius. I should have picked up on this sooner. Let me see the report."

She looked at the folder with a picture of Deffly from 2006 when she was arrested in Michigan on a homeless/vagrancy collar. Her last known address was in Minnesota.

So, thought TJ, she's kept her nose clean since 2006 as far as arrests. But it's only the tip of the iceberg. What lies beneath?

"Thanks, Myers. Call Jake Williams and have him get an arrest warrant for Amy Deffly signed by Judge Kollert . . . for now, on threatening Grace Kimball, based on the fingerprint on Grace's letter. We'll add more charges later. Send him to Endurance High School with the warrant. I'll be in the back of the auditorium."

"Right, TJ. You can be reached—"

"—on my cell. Myers, get on it quickly."

"Right. Got it!"

TJ grabbed the keys to the police car parked behind the station and left for the high school. On the way, she thought about how Amy Deffly and Ellen Terry might have met. She vaguely remembered the principal's comments about Ellen Terry being an orphan and something about foster homes. Deffly's profile mentioned foster homes and vagrancy. The two women were different, however. Of course, she'd never met the real Ellen Terry, but the principal's assessment caused TJ to wonder how these dissimilar people would have been rooming together. Well, she'd find out.

Chapter Twenty-Six

GRACE'S STOMACH HAD been a little queasy as she walked up the aisle, heading for the back door. TJ was coming to the play, but she hadn't seen her yet. Probably a good thing, she thought, because TJ would scold Grace about taking this step. Maybe her stomach was acting up a bit, too, because she thought about confronting Ellen Terry in her office. That would not be a pleasant experience.

She closed the back door of the auditorium softly, smiling at the young high school girl at her ticket-collecting station. Grace didn't know her, but she smiled and spoke to her, figuring she could be a freshman.

She looked down the second-floor hallway, trying to keep a low profile. In the distance, she could see several students in their costumes at the far end of the hallway, waiting to go on stage. Creeping down the next flight of stairs, she figured she wouldn't come across students on the first floor. She'd have to circle below the auditorium and go up the stairs and then down a small flight to Terry's office again. Lettie was right, she thought. This building is a little scary at night. Except for tiny night-lights, the entire lower hallway was dark and shadowy. It was cold, too. In an old building like this, the lower floor would be the coldest. She put her hand on her pocket, feeling the security of her LED light. Staying by the side of the hallway near the wall, Grace stopped every few yards, listening for anyone else in the vicinity. Nothing. Her stomach muscles were tight, a familiar symptom of high anxiety. She could vaguely hear the play going on above her.

The door to Terry's office was just ahead. Grace climbed up the stairs and could clearly hear the play going on. Stairs came down to the office from the upper floor, a possible flaw to Grace's plan. Someone could come down those steps quickly and enter the office behind her, just like Terry did at the rehearsal. Well, nothing for it, she thought. This is the best time to go in, check out those magazines, and see if Terry was the mad warning writer. She came up to the office door, stopping again to listen for footsteps behind her. Now the actors' voices were louder; occasionally Grace heard laughter from the audience.

She touched the doorknob, thinking it might be locked. It turned silently, but the door hinge could do with some oil. The minute she heard the creak of the door she stopped, waiting again for anyone who might have heard it too. Nothing. Then she opened the door in tiny increments, satisfied the screeching hinge stayed quiet. Quickly, she slipped through the door, closing it behind her, inch by inch.

She was alone in the darkness. Remembering how cluttered Terry's office was, Grace didn't move until she found her small flashlight and turned it on. The door had a window in the top half panel, so she couldn't let the light show to anyone in the hallway. She put her hand around it, shielding it from the window. Stealthily, she tiptoed to the table where she'd seen the magazines and scissors. She gasped. They were gone. Nothing. No magazines on the table, no scissors. Did Terry see them on the floor and figure out what Grace was doing? If that was the case, Terry would be on the lookout for Grace, keeping an eye on her every move.

Training the light on the floor, she recalculated her plan, circling around the desk. Softly, she opened each drawer, shining her light into numerous piles of papers and rubbish. She rifled through the papers with her spare hand. Nothing. When she reached the third drawer, her patience was rewarded. The magazines and scissors were hastily thrown into the drawer with two boxes of staples and a book on top. She pulled the top magazine out of the precarious pile, laying it on the floor. Keeping her light on the magazine, she opened it and found—nothing. No pages had holes where Terry might have cut out letters or words. She kept turning the pages until, finally, she came to places where entire words were cut out.

Grace sighed with relief. Not a wild-goose chase. Ellen Terry was the one who had sent her the warning, and possibly she had sent the letter to Liz Hardy about her husband's indiscretions. Finally, Grace had the goods. Should she take this with her? No. TJ's lectures about chain of evidence came pounding back into her head. Leave it here, but have TJ find it so she could use it to nab Terry. Grace could hardly believe it. The woman was a little eccentric, but a killer?

She put the magazine back, carefully laying it between the book and the other magazines in the drawer. Then she softly closed the drawer again. She realized, as she stood up, that her stomach was less tense now, and she only had to slip back out and up to the auditorium. TJ would be showing up any minute because she'd been working late at her office. Grace would tell her about the magazines. She cautiously walked around the desk, feeling her way and leaving the light off so no one would see it through the window.

Grace's stomach lurched and her legs trembled. The window. She stared at a black looming shape in the door window, the hall lights behind it. Ellen Terry. Flee or hold her ground? The door opened. Before Grace could even say a word or find a place to hide, Ellen Terry came through the door, flipped on the light switch, and faced Grace, a weird smile on her face. Grace looked down and saw a gun in her hand.

"Well, Grace Kimball, as I live and breathe. Hmmm. What might you be doing in my office?"

"I don't suppose you'd believe I'm searching for a lost earring," Grace said, forcing a smile on her face.

"No, Ms. Kimball, I wouldn't." Terry closed the door behind her, keeping her eyes, and the gun on Grace. "You have been the proverbial thorn in my side, Grace. I'm tired of your constant interference in my life. Right now I don't have time to deal with your silly detective playtime, but I will have to deal with you later. For now, I simply need a spot to put you in safekeeping until I'm not quite so busy."

Grace watched the drama teacher's eyes move to the padlocked door. Thinking quickly, Grace kept her hand away from the flashlight in her pocket. No reason to let Terry see she had anything in her pocket. Her cell phone? Had she brought it? She concentrated on the pockets of her slacks, feeling her phone on the left side. As she watched Terry walk over to her desk, Grace knew she couldn't turn on the cell phone or hit 9-1-1. That would be way too obvious. So, she waited.

Terry reached into her desk drawer and drew out a small key. "Here," she said, and tossed the key to Grace. "Over there." She used her head and the gun to gesture toward the door to what she had earlier called "hell." Then she motioned again to Grace repeating, "Over there. Open the padlock on that door."

Grace moved across the room, keeping an eye on Terry as she did. She didn't see any way to get past the woman to escape out the office door, so she walked over, turning the key in the padlock.

"Now, give me the key, Grace, and open the door."

"Please don't do this, Ellen. I don't like confined spaces. They give me claustrophobia."

"You won't be there for long. I have plans for you. I repeat, open the door."

Grace opened the door, feeling a cold draft encircle her legs. Oh, this is not good, she thought. She didn't make a move to go through the doorway because she could see it was pitch black.

"In," said Ellen Terry. "Be gone with you for now. Don't worry. No dead bodies down there, only spiders and probably some mice. I won't tell you again. Move!" She used the gun to point toward the door.

Grace stepped through the doorway, shaking, and could see stairs with just enough light from the office. As soon as she put her foot on the first step, Ellen Terry slammed the door shut, hitting her back and knocking her down the steps. She fell, head first, down maybe three or four steps, landing on a cement floor, and holding her hands out to slow her fall. Knocking the breath out of her, the fall scared her momentarily, but not as much as her fear when the light went off in the office. She was in total darkness.

Checking to see if anything was broken, she tried to get up slowly. Well, she thought, at least I have that going for me: nothing seems to be broken or sprained. Thank you, lots of milk and calcium supplements. She winced as she took in a breath. I take that back, she thought. Maybe a bruised rib. She felt a wet, sticky spot on the right side of her forehead where she had hit the floor. Taking in a deep breath, she put her hand in her pocket, and pulled out her flashlight. At least she'd have a little light. She switched it on. Nothing happened. Feeling the end of it with her fingers, she realized her fall had broken it.

Distant laughter revealed the play going on overhead. She realized, from having read the article in the high school yearbook, that the audience was sitting above the ceiling over her head. But no one would be able to hear her. All she could see was darkness, but she did have the wherewithal to check the door and see if it was locked. It was. The whole area smelled musty, closed for years with no light or activity. Standing in the dark, she couldn't figure out how to let anyone know where she was. Even if TJ, Deb, or Jeff realized she had been gone too long, they wouldn't know about this area below the stage. Did she tell Deb about it when she was reading the article at the Historical Society? She couldn't remember.

Then she realized she had her cell phone in her pocket. She could call 9-1-1. TJ, Deb, or Jeff would probably have their phones off if they were upstairs in the audience. She pulled out her phone, figuring she could raise Myers with a 9-1-1 call. Hitting the button brought some light, making her feel less afraid. She punched 9-1-1 but nothing happened. Checking the battery, she saw she had at least 45 percent left. It should work with that much juice. She looked at the bars at the left corner, suddenly felt sick, and couldn't stop herself from gasping. She was underground, after all—the bar area said "no service."

Her heart began to pound in her head. Oh please, she thought. Don't let me be buried alive here and die.

TJ was almost to the high school when she glanced at the clock on her dash. The play was supposed to start at 7:30. It was already 8:30, so it must be in high gear. Might be better to cuff Terry/Deffly after it was over rather than take her out in front of the kids. Well, we will see what is possible, thought TJ.

The parking lot of the high school was crowded. Lots of people here for *Arsenic and Old Lace*. She pulled her vehicle up in front of the school, parking near the door, but not right in front of it. If she had to take Terry out, it would be easier with the car parked in front. The audience might think she was there for crowd control.

Entering the school, she flashed her badge at the adolescent in the ticket office whose eyes got big, and then she wandered down the hallway to the auditorium. Quietly opening the back door, she slipped in, letting her eyes adjust to the darkness in the house. She knew her friends had tickets for seats down near the front because Grace wanted to be sure and see her neighbor, Ginger, after the show. Standing at the back, TJ scanned the front seats in all three sections. Then her eyes lighted on Jeff Maitlin, since he was tall enough to pick out in a crowd. She could see an empty seat next to him, then Deb O'Hara.

What the heck? she thought. Where is Grace?

Chapter Twenty-Seven

GRACE SAT ON the steps she had just fallen down. Calm, calm, she said to herself. She needed to catch her breath. Take deep breaths. Don't get anxious. Use your brain. Stop. Think. First, was she hurt?

She moved her hands up her legs. She had a tear in the right leg of her pants, but couldn't feel any blood under it. Her right knee also had a huge tear, and she could tell the knee was scraped, some loose skin hanging from where she had hit the edge of the stairs. Her right side must have taken the worst of the jolt. On her right side, she had a pain when she breathed, possibly a rib. Otherwise, she was un-broken. Listening for any movement like mice, she heard nothing and decided she was alone.

Why hadn't she brought a sweater? Her arms were cold, and she was feeling shaky, partly from the fall and partly from the cold. Tak-ing a deep breath of cold air, she decided she had taken stock of her injuries, a rational thing to do. So, what to do next? A plan. She would need a plan to get out of here before Ellen Terry showed up again, putting her out of commission forever.

The photographs she'd seen in the old yearbook article about the building renovation were still vaguely in her memory. She recalled two aisles leading to the back of the auditorium beyond the orchestra pit where she must be now. Some of the auditorium rows of seats were gone; still others were battered and heaped into piles. But even if she managed to find her way to the back of this underground maze, what guarantee did she have she could ever get out? Maybe the doors at the back were sealed shut. The workers had been cautious about having students get injured by ever coming down into this area. Even if she could get out of a door, where would it lead to on the other side?

She checked her time on her phone, being careful not to leave it on for long. It was stuck at forty-five percent. That's right, she thought. "No service." How long had she been away from the play? Maybe a half hour? Even if TJ was looking for her, she wouldn't have the slightest idea about this abandoned storage area. So, Grace thought, time to figure it out myself. Which aisle should I try first? Right-handed. Let's try the right side since I'm right-handed.

She turned her cell phone on again, using the light from the screen for a dim flashlight. Walking through the debris was a cautious job, and she hadn't charged her cell since she left work. Grace had no idea what she might find. She kept the light close to the floor, moving carefully up the aisle. It was dark, musty, and freezing. Occasionally, she came on some ice on the floor, evidently seeping up from wherever. No wonder she was shivering.

She thought she was making good progress, staying close to the floor, when suddenly she walked into something—she almost screamed, but then realized she needed to shut her mouth or swallow whatever it was. She dropped her phone. It must have landed screen-down, so now she was in total darkness. Grace decided she had walked into a giant spider web, reaching across the aisle from one pile of trash to another—it was all over her face, hair, and arms. And sticky . . . it was so sticky. Who knew what was in it? Ugh! Oh! This was awful! Probably lots of dead stuff. She tried to pull it off her face and hair, and then it got stuck on her fingers. Using her pants to wipe her hands, she managed to get part of the sticky stuff off, but she was still covered in it.

My phone, she thought. She got down on her haunches, feeling around for her cell phone. Touching the loose debris on the floor, Grace winced as she thought about what she might be touching—mouse feces, mildew, dirt, and who knew what else from decades ago? Finally, her left hand landed on her phone. Oh, thank God, she thought. Please let it not be broken. She pushed the button again, saying, "Let there be light," and a dim glow came on. Time to try to find the end of the aisle once more.

She estimated she had walked twenty yards at least. Let's see, how long might the auditorium be? Thirty? Forty yards? must be at least halfway there. Willing the battery to stay on, she kept her phone close to the floor. One foot in front of the other, she thought. Was the light in the phone screen dimmer? Oh, please, don't let me be left in the darkness, she thought. Then, since she was walking bent over with her eyes on the floor, her head hit the wall at the end of the vast space. "Ouch!" Geez, spider webs were bad enough; she didn't need a concussion too.

The door was in front of her; an old-fashioned metal bolt arm-lock reached across the door on the left side and through brackets. It felt like it was at least two inches wide, very long, and freezing metal. They must have put it in when they closed the area. How long had it been since anyone opened it, Grace wondered. She stuck her phone in her pocket, and using both hands to feel the metal, she tried to move the bolt to the left, hopefully unlocking the door. Of course, she thought, I have no idea what's on the other side. It wouldn't budge. She stopped, and gathered another deep breath, trying it again. She thought it moved slightly.

Then, what she had dreaded came to pass. She heard the door in Ellen Terry's office open. Terry's voice called out, "Grace, where are you?" in the tone of a children's game. It sounded as if she was saying, "Yoo-hoo." Grace's hands were shaking on the bolt, and she felt chills travel down her spine. Looking back, she could see the beam of a flashlight, maybe forty yards away. Her own cell phone was in her pocket, which meant Terry wouldn't see any light where she was. As the light came toward her, she felt her way behind a pile of trash and debris.

"Grace, I'm coming to find you," said Ellen Terry's voice, in a singsong, lilting tone.

Grace felt the wall to her left; it was smooth and, of course, covered with dust. Moving to her right, she found herself between a pile of trash and the back wall. Reasoning that Terry might shine her flashlight up the aisle, Grace stayed put, barely breathing. Once again, she heard the killer's voice, a light shining down the aisle where Grace had just been.

"Eenie, meenie, miney, mo, which way did our dear Grace go?" Then Grace saw the beam of light disappear. Terry had evidently gone down the left aisle, which gave Grace some camouflage with piles of old chairs and debris between them. Grace moved back over to the door and pulled once again on the locking bolt. In the distance, she could hear Ellen Terry's voice, but it was faint now. She must be down the other aisle, but when she didn't find Grace, she'd try this area next.

She had to get out of here. She whispered quietly, "Come on Grace, push that bolt!" The rest of her was shaking, trembling partly from the cold but mostly from the prospect of Terry shooting her and leaving her body buried under the school. This wasn't really where she wanted to end her life, as much as she'd loved her job. She put her hand in front of her mouth to keep from laughing hysterically. She bit her lower lip hard, and reached for the bolt again.

The bolt moved another precious inch as Terry's voice brought a wave of adrenaline to Grace. Taking another deep breath while holding the bolt handle as tightly as she could, she pushed it with both hands, hard enough to clear the bracket in the wall next to the door. Then she grabbed the handle below the bolt with both hands and the door slowly opened, screeching in protest.

Suddenly, Grace was hit by arctic air, nearly knocking the breath out of her.

Chapter Twenty-Eight

TJ LOOKED AT her phone, gauging when a break might come so she could walk down the aisle and find out Grace's whereabouts from Jeff. She hated to walk in during the play, but she couldn't wait. Just as she was about to start down the aisle, she heard something from the stage which startled her and stopped her in her tracks. The teenager playing Martha Brewster brought out her elderberry wine, explaining its contents: one teaspoon of arsenic, a half teaspoon of strychnine, and a pinch of cyanide.

TJ took in a deep breath. This cinches it, she thought to herself: Ellen Terry is turning art into reality. She hiked silently down the aisle and got Deb and Jeff's attention, motioning them out. Heads turned to see why a police detective was in the auditorium, but TJ simply walked back up the aisle, speaking to no one. Deb and Jeff followed her out the double doors.

"Where's Grace?"

"She left to go to the restroom, but it was maybe fifteen minutes ago. I was getting worried, but figured she might have run into you and the two of you were out here in the hall talking," said Jeff.

"You didn't see her, TJ?" asked Deb.

"Haven't seen her. I just got here. Knowing Grace, she decided to take things into her own hands." TJ's muscles tensed and she gave a disgusted sigh. Someone called out her name. Turning, she saw Jake Williams coming around the corner from the ticket office.

"Got the warrant?"

"Right here," Jake said, pulling a paper out of his coat pocket. "What's up?"

TJ turned to all three of them, saying "It's Ellen Terry. She's the killer. Can't give you all the details, but I'm afraid Grace decided to investigate herself. Where might she be? We need to split up and try to find them. Jake and I will look for Terry since we don't know if she's armed. We need to find Grace too." She looked at each of them, planting her feet, taking charge of whatever the plan would be. "What do we know for sure?"

"Terry has a director's office down below the stage. Grace might have gone down there," said Deb, quickly pointing in the direction of the left stage wing.

"Where else could she be?"

"Backstage?" said Jeff.

Deb shook her head. "No, I don't think so. My guess is she would search Terry's office. TJ, do you know where the theater office is?"

"I think I remember well enough to find it." She pointed to each of them, focused and direct. "Deb, you check backstage for Terry. If she is there, don't do anything except try to stay out of her range of sight. We don't want to spook her. Then find me in the theater director's office. If she isn't backstage, come down there anyway to let me know she's on the loose. Jake, you and Jeff come with me."

The three of them ran quickly through the hallway, moving around to the back of the stage. The lights were on throughout the hallway, and no one slowed their progress or even noticed. Closer to the office, they stopped. Then they moved more cautiously, using hand signals to communicate. Jeff prudently hung back a bit. Both detectives checked their guns, moving deliberately toward the door of the office. All the lights were on, but the office was empty. TJ cleared the main office while Jake pulled open the closet. Nothing. About that time, they heard footsteps running down the hallway outside. Jeff stuck his head in, saying, "Deb's back. No Terry backstage."

TJ glanced at Jake saying, "Great! Where would she have gone? Where could she have Grace?"

Deb pointed at a doorway. "Grace was examining articles on the high school and found one about an underground area they sealed off years ago. That padlock's hanging open. It's probably the opening, since I know the pictures showed that the area went under the new auditorium."

"You remember anything about the pictures?" TJ asked.

Deb thought for a moment. "I remember seeing storage rooms under the new, higher stage, and the old auditorium with two aisles and seats and debris. It's possible they could be down there."

TJ examined the open doorway, moaning, "Geez. Why did she have to go to ground, *underground*?" She shook her head, giving Jake a resigned look. "Okay, Jake. Let's do a quick check first. Deb, you and Jeff stay here. She could be armed."

TJ put her foot on the first step down, moving very slowly as she pulled out a flashlight. She held up the light, scanning the area, and returned, walking backward, up the steps. "Looks like aisles on either side. No lighting, probably been turned off for years, and definitely no heat. Which way you want to do this, Jake?"

"I was about to say, 'you take the left while I'll take the right.' However, stands to reason if she's armed, these flashlights will be a dead giveaway. Not sure I want to be a sitting duck."

"Another option is to smoke her out, so to speak. Hit those hallways with a smoke bomb or pepper spray. Don't think the smoke would set off detectors because this auditorium wouldn't have 'em."

"But what about Grace? If she's down there, she'll end up in the smoke or pepper spray, and you don't know if she's alive, conscious, unconscious, or what," said Jeff.

"Did I hear someone call my name?" Grace's voice came out of nowhere.

All four of them turned, staring at the strange being standing in the office door.

"Grace?" said Jeff. "Is that you?"

"In the flesh, although less of it than an hour earlier."

TJ looked out the doorway at her friend, her face registering shock. She figured Grace was in the thick of this mess, but it was hard to recognize her. She appeared to be a giant gray blob, covered with dust, dirt, soot, and what could be dirty, blackened spider webs. Her face was plastered with gray patches of dust, dried blood was visible on her forehead, and strands of gray webs with dead, dried bugs were everywhere. Her pants were torn, hanging in shreds near her knees.

TJ gave her one of her sternest looks. "I don't even want to know what you were doing. Are you alright? Where is Ellen Terry?"

"I think I may have bruised or fractured a rib falling down the stairs. It hurts to breathe. As for Terry, last time I heard her she was down in what she calls 'hell.' Down there." TJ watched Grace point to the stairway into the underground auditorium.

"Armed?"

"Yes. She had a gun earlier. I got out before she got to me. She's crazy, TJ. You should hear her singing childish songs. She was planning to make me victim number three."

"Jeff, you better get Grace to the ER and see what they can do for her. She may need to have her ribs checked or stitches in her forehead. On second thought, maybe she should go through the car wash first. Deb, you go too." Then she paused, adding, "Grace, how did you get out?"

"Magic," she said, smiling through the gross bugs and dust.

"Seriously?"

"They left doors to the outside at the end of the aisles. Locked on the inside, they lead to the outside in the back parking lot. Also, ridiculously hard bolts lock the doors, but it's amazing what fear can do for weak arms."

TJ wrestled with yelling at Grace or chiding her more softly. She settled for in between. "Okay, get her out of here. Soap, water, blankets, ribs." She shook her head. "You could have been killed here."

She watched her friend meekly turn, leaving with Deb and Jeff on either side of her.

TJ looked at Jake. "So, who's going to do outside duty, and who's going to go underground? Want to flip for it?"

"You can stay, TJ. I'll keep an eye on the outside doors. She should exit into the back lot. I can spot her, either door," said Jake, zipping up his jacket.

"Call the station for backup. I'll stay and see if she emerges."

"Got it." Jake left, hurrying out, and TJ settled in to keep an eye on the door. She decided to shut it to within four inches, leaving the lights on in the office. Then she positioned herself outside the office door, her eyes and gun on the opening to the underground. A voice startled her, and she turned her head.

"Whoa!" said Del Novak, backing away. "What are you doing here, TJ?"

"Watching for Ellen Terry. Need to keep my eyes on the door, Del. You might want to back out."

Del craned his neck to look around TJ. "She's down there?" Novak asked.

"Yeah. Jake's got the outside doors covered. We're waiting for her to emerge for air. Not good for you to be here, Del. She may be armed. We're waiting because it's too dark in the underground."

"They left lights in the underground area," Del said.

"Really? Where do they turn on?"

"They don't."

TJ gave him an exasperated look. "Why did you tell me about lights then?"

"They're on a breaker. It's turned off since we don't use that area. But I can flip the breaker so it will turn them on . . . well, only some of them since the bulbs are replaced occasionally for inspections by the fire chief and all. They're pretty dim. Want I should turn them on?"

"Yeah," said TJ.

"The bat-crazy play director down there?"

"She is, we think."

"She the one who killed John and Evan?"

"We think that too."

"You get her, TJ. Alive, if you can. I'd like to see her stand to judgment."

"I'll try."

"Anything I can do to help besides flipping the circuit breaker?"

"Nah. We have backup on the way, and Jake's here too."

"You got it," said Del, leaving to go to the breaker box, just down the hall.

TJ waited a few minutes until she saw dim lights go on down the stairway. She sent a text to Jake, telling him she was going in. Then she made sure she had extra ammunition within close reach.

Carefully, she took one step at a time down the stairs, her gun loaded and aimed ahead. Her eyes narrowed, scanning the huge area, noting hiding spots behind debris, and alerting her trigger finger to any possible movement. Figuring out which aisle to go up was another problem. The detective studied both, and seeing no one, figured Terry was hiding behind some of the debris piles. Could flip a coin to determine which aisle, she thought.

The lights were faint, as Del had said, and TJ's body was at full alert, moving cautiously, straining to listen for any noise. She stepped toward the left, careful to watch for sudden movements, peering into the dim wasteland of discarded chairs, wood, and debris. Adrenaline pumping, she heard her heartbeat racing, felt her muscles tense and her breath move quickly in and out.

She was only a few feet away from the stairs when she heard a shot and felt its impact on her left shoulder, spinning her around. Somewhere in the recesses of her mind she realized she was hit, fired a return shot, and felt her gun leave her hand. Dimly, she thought she heard a voice, and then she heard nothing.

Chapter Twenty-Nine

LETTIE OPENED GRACE'S kitchen door and backed in with two bags of groceries plus muffins from Mildred at The Bread Box Bakery. Grace was up making coffee, fully dressed and somewhat functioning, which seemed an odd situation for a Saturday.

"You're up?"

"Sure am. Ready to greet the day."

Lettie looked at her suspiciously. "It's Saturday, Grace. The last time you were up this early, the Civil Rights Act had just been passed by LBJ and you wanted to watch the signing." She walked over to Grace. "What's going on?"

She turned to Lettie after pushing the "on" button on her coffee-maker. "I had a rather long night. I'm surprised you don't already know."

"Oh, I know about TJ. Got shot in the shoulder by that crazy woman. She gonna be all right?"

"Yes, the prognosis for TJ is a full recovery. We'll have to feed her and help her recuperate."

"Sounds like I need to go back to the grocery store."

"I'll tackle the wine shop."

"What about Maitlin? Where's he?"

"He's been at the *Register* most of the night, writing the story about the capture of Ellen Terry by the intrepid detectives of Endurance. Should show up on the doorstep this morning."

"Humph! The crazy drama director. Well, I'll be. How come you weren't in the thick of it this time the way you usually are? In fact, I don't see any bullet holes or puncture wounds in you. No bandages. Just a tiny butterfly bandage on your forehead. Does this mean you finally decided to leave it up to the police for a change?"

Grace turned her head this way and that. "Well . . . I have a few scrapes, lacerations, and a bruised rib. I had to sleep in the recliner all night because it hurts to breathe or turn over in bed. I also have a huge pile of clothes which may have to be burned."

Lettie stopped, coffee cups in midair. "Burned? What are you talking about?"

"Open the muffins. I'll get the coffee and tell you what I know."

Lettie set down the coffee cups and rubbed her hands together. "Oh, good!" Then she stared at Grace, a strange look on her face. "Clothes? Burned? Grace, what did you get into this time?"

Later that afternoon, Grace was at the hospital sitting in a chair next to TJ's bed.

"Man, you didn't tell me it hurts to get shot, Grace," said TJ, lying in bed, surrounded by pillows. "Now we're tied for gunshot wounds."

"Going into an underground tunnel by yourself with minimal lighting does not seem to me like a smart thing to do."

"It was the only choice, Grace. It's my job."

"You could've had Jake back you up."

"He did. I should have waited for him before I went in. Didn't quite happen like I'd envisioned it. Jake and I managed to hit her with two bullets as she came to finish me. Terry's in the hospital too, under guard. She'll survive."

Grace's eyes widened. "So, has Jake had time to interrogate her? Is she talking?"

"All morning. She waived her right to counsel. I think she was interested in an audience. You know, she's quite the diva. We're working with the police in Nebraska, but they may never find the real Ellen Terry."

Grace could tell her friend was on pain pills; she talked far more than usual about her job.

"The 'real' Ellen Terry? You'd better start at the beginning. Why did these horrible things happen? Why would she kill two good men and almost kill you?"

"Me? I was collateral damage. But Ellen Terry and I have that in common. I guess, in a way, so does Amy Deffly."

"Amy Deffly? Who is she?"

"Ellen Terry. It's quite a winding story. She told Jake some of it—once we sort out the truth of the statement—we'll trace much of the rest in legal documents. Amy Deffly—who you know as Ellen Terry—was born in 1980 in Minnesota. Her father was a Viet Nam vet who had lots of mental problems both from his drug use and his war experiences, while her mother had a heroin dependency. They married—a lethal combination when you think about it—after he returned from the service in '75. They had a daughter, Amy, and two sons."

"She has brothers?"

We'll need to trace them. Once her father came back from the war, the family took up a nomadic life with the parents still involved in drugs and legal problems. The three children were eventually taken away from them by a court, split up, and placed in foster homes, none of which were nurturing or kind.

"Her own psychotic episodes began in her teens. She ended up in a series of mental hospitals, wandering off from the last one in 2005." She looked at Grace and held out her good hand. "Mind you, a lot of this still has to be checked. Somehow, she got from Michigan, where she was picked up for vagrancy, to Nebraska. As far as we can verify, she was homeless for a while, but then was taken in by a church group who managed to find her a job as a cashier in a grocery store."

"Sounds like a lot of links to connect, TJ. Did she tell you this in her usual rambling style?"

"Well, in a roundabout way. You must remember, she needs medicine for her mental difficulties regularly, but can't always afford it. On the other hand, she's very smart—and cunning. A great deal of this can be verified by various kinds of records, but some of it may be a product of her unmedicated mind."

Silence for a few moments. Then Grace furrowed her eyebrows. "Someone else was the real Ellen Terry? How did this Amy meet her?"

"That part of the story is pretty clear. They met in a drug dependency group. Ellen Terry was a drama teacher in a local private school who was making excellent progress getting off painkillers. She had been in the accident which killed her parents, and her injuries left her dependent on pain medicine. The real Ellen Terry was interested in murder mysteries and was writing a mystery herself, researching poisons. Again, from what we can check, the two of them moved in together in the fall of 2010, possibly to save money. Terry had no idea Amy Deffly had psychotic episodes, and they bonded through this drug group."

"So, let me get this straight. The real Ellen Terry was an orphan. She did get her teaching certification and was hired by the private school you've checked with in Nebraska."

"Right. We don't know what happened, but at some point, Amy began shadowing Ellen Terry, watching her, listening to her, fixated on her, often going to the school to help her with plays. Perhaps the real Ellen Terry began to be afraid of Deffly. We don't know the answer yet to that and maybe never will. The one thing Deffly couldn't do was go to Ellen Terry's classroom and observe her teaching."

"Oh," said Grace, thoughtfully. "That would explain why she had such strange questions about teaching."

"Correct," said TJ. "At the end of the school year, the real Ellen Terry disappeared."

Grace's face registered shock. "Did Amy Deffly tell you what happened to her?"

"Not yet. I imagine she's dead. She had no siblings or parents, so no one really missed her except the school. And since she resigned by mail, even the principal wasn't aware she had disappeared."

"How did Amy-slash-Ellen survive financially?"

"Before Terry's probable death, Amy Deffly had convinced her to sign for a joint savings and checking account. Ellen Terry's checks were automatically deposited through last August."

Grace sat back a moment, considering what she knew once the woman arrived in Endurance. "She must have received her last check in early August and looked for a school district that needed someone badly at the last minute. When Dawn Johnson asked for her credentials, she used the real Ellen Terry's references, but added her own photograph."

"If Johnson hadn't been so busy, she wouldn't have fallen through the cracks. The superintendent assumed her fingerprints were those of Ellen Terry. She forgot to have Terry re-printed."

Grace let out a deep sigh. "Oh, TJ. Two murders of good people because of carelessness. If only she'd remembered to have her finger-printed."

"The world is a huge place, the population only growing, and people fall through the cracks all the time. You must remember Amy Deffly, aka Ellen Terry, created this eccentric personality so people cut her some slack. They figured she was a character and put her weird teaching questions down to that. What I didn't tell you—because I've been too damn busy—is that Liz Hardy found a jump drive connected to her husband's electronic reader. It had the real teacher evaluations, which he must have worked on at home.

"Amy was going to lose her job. John Hardy couldn't tolerate her lapses in record keeping or grading. She missed deadlines continually for grading, and even when he got her grades they were so high parents weren't complaining. In fact, when we looked at her current grade book, she had no grades. Zero."

"Ginger Grant told me she hardly gave any grades, and she thought the test scores for the teacher evaluation were suspicious."

"She was right. Besides the records, she hadn't quite picked up on the knack of how to teach, so her instructional evaluation was negative. Hardy's recommendation was to fire her, and he went over the reasons with her the week before his death. According to his notes, he was also going to contact her former school. That must have made her desperate. After Amy killed him, she changed the evaluations for both her and Evan Harrington, hoping to have us focus on him as a suspect."

"Which would explain why Evan was shocked. It would be easy to get extra blank evaluation sheets. I saw a pile of them in the office."

TJ shifted her arm a little, a pillow under it. "Ouch. This is going to take a while. I hate having only one side that works."

"You'll get better, TJ. Take it from me. Now I can see why Deffly did the play. She'd watched the real Ellen Terry direct it, so she could fake the play-directing. What she couldn't fake was the teaching. When John Hardy decided to talk to her about it, she realized she would lose her job, and he'd alert her last school, possibly finding out she didn't even look like the real Ellen Terry, and then she'd be in serious trouble. This meant she had to kill poor John."

"That's it."

"But why Evan Harrington?"

"Now, he is a sad part of the story. She tried to blame him by putting the note on Hardy's desk about wanting to talk to him on Monday. She switched the recommendations in both Hardy's office and in Harrington's office, which he didn't keep locked. She used his key to get the poisons since he was often out of his room going various places, and gave the poisonous mixture to John in a cup of coffee she'd made for him with the excuse that she'd stopped in to talk with him about reconsidering her firing. She took away the poisoned canister and cup from his office."

"But I'm still not sure why she killed Evan too."

"He remembered."

"He remembered what?" Grace asked.

"A conversation in the teacher's lounge where Ellen Terry asked him about various kinds of poisons. At the time, everyone thought she was asking because of the play, but that conversation was where she found out Evan had poisons in his room. Evan remembered that conversation, but more than that, he noticed her hanging around in the science area on several occasions. Her actions were furtive, as if she were trying to hide her motives. One day she engaged him in conversation, but he found her reason for doing so rather strange. He mentioned it to Ginny Shadley, another science teacher Jake interviewed. What Evan didn't know was that Deffly still had the research Ellen Terry had done on poisons, so she picked the combination that was the most lethal and the quickest. She actually sat there and watched John Hardy die."

"Oh, TJ, how awful. How can a human being do such a horrible thing?" Grace shook her head. "I suppose then she had to kill Evan because he might remember her questions."

"Yes. He must have indicated he remembered something and she picked up on it. You know, Amy Deffly wasn't stupid. In fact, she was amazingly adept at reading people's body language. She heard his conversation about meeting you because she was in the building that night, listening outside his door. We found Evan's phone at her apartment. I have no idea why she kept it. Grace, your call was the last one on his phone. That was why, when the phone was missing, I was worried she'd come after you next."

Grace took a deep breath and looked down at her hands. "So sad. He was such a good man, as was John."

"True, Grace. Unfortunately, that's how these things happen. Dangerous people slip through the cracks."

"Did she explain how she got into the school when John . . . died?"

"Yes. It was quite premeditated. She took Evan's coffee cup from the teacher's lounge and Marilyn's lampshade from her closet, another unlocked area. Figuring Evan wouldn't check his poisons until spring, she stole those a week before she killed John Hardy. She had also sent an anonymous letter to Liz Hardy; she was covering her tracks, spreading blame among Evan, Liz, and Marilyn. She was particularly proud of the lampshade as a comic touch. The anonymous letter, of course, brought in Seth. She didn't even realize that. He told me the truth when he said he sat in the parking lot trying to get up the drunken courage to confront Hardy. Finally, he just left.

"The day she murdered John, she parked a block from the school and had everything she needed in a big bag she always carried. She put the poison in a coffee cup she put in her bag to take away after John died. She figured we might think it was done with Evan's cup. She came into the building through one of those doors without surveillance cameras, and threw the empty poison container and cup in a dumpster on the way home. She said it was easy."

Grace sat back on her sofa, crossing her arms.

"Yes?" TJ said, looking at Grace's face.

"Well, I find it strange that a series of events, such as you described, could work so well in her favor."

"Between planning and just blind luck, she made it all happen. She's amazingly bright, but her logic is twisted. I'd say Amy Deffly is one of thousands of people in this country who have mental health problems and won't get help or can't. Years ago, they could have been committed to a mental facility, but today it isn't easy to commit people. On the other hand, years ago, we had plenty of people incarcerated in mental wards who shouldn't have been."

"Oh, I don't know," said Grace. "I can't figure out how you do the job you do."

TJ used her good hand to move her shoulder slightly. "I'd say every so often a day comes along where all goes well, and I'm responsible for that. I'd like to think I could have saved John Hardy or Evan Harrington, but I couldn't. It's like you, Grace, when you talk about students you wanted to save, but it didn't work. You can't be responsible for the lives of others, just like I can't."

"But how do you sleep at nights, TJ?"

"Lots of nights I don't. But it doesn't keep me from getting up the next morning, starting all over again. It's good your job—teaching—allowed you to be optimistic about people. Most days I am too. That's what we try to do—protect the community. But then Jake and I have those days where this happens. One slip by the school superintendent on fingerprinting, and we couldn't stop two deaths. But I'd like to think we may have prevented more with Amy Deffly behind bars."

Grace sat quietly in thought. She blinked a few times and pursed her lips. "How sad that is."

"What?"

"Amy Deffly is nothing like Jeff. When her life fell apart, no one was there to help, and she ended up in foster homes with little support. What if someone had been there? Someone who loved her and gave her the help she needed?"

"Then the story might have been entirely different."

Grace was silent for a moment. "Look at Jeff Maitlin. I know, I know, he didn't have mental problems, but he could have. Both parents shot to death, no time to say good-bye, and a narrow escape himself. He was old enough to understand that. But he had grandparents who loved him, supported him, and helped him figure it out."

"You're right, Grace. The road was different for them both because of their circumstances. It's what you sometimes call 'falling through the cracks'—or in Jeff's case, not."

"What do you think will happen to Amy Deffly?"

TJ looked out the window for a moment where the sunshine was melting the icicles. "I expect she'll end up in some sort of mental facility, and with the horrendous crimes she's committed, she'll not get out."

They looked at each other bleakly, and before Grace could respond, they heard a voice coming around the corner and into the hospital room door. "Help has arrived! Time to feed the town hero!"

Lettie's body followed her voice, and in her hands was a huge blueberry pie. Behind her came Deb, Jill, and Jeff, carrying plates and forks.

Chapter Thirty

GRACE SPOKE TO Ginger Grant and her mother at the front door; they were the last of the neighbors and friends to leave after having Lettie's spice cake and ice cream. Everyone had gone to the Sunday matinee of *Arsenic and Old Lace* that afternoon. Now, Jill, Deb, and TJ had left Grace's house, Deb and Jill going to TJ's to settle her in for the night. Lettie had even given Eliot Ness, TJ's cat, back to the detective so she'd have some company while she recuperated. Grace promised to go over in the morning to help her since it wouldn't be easy to dress having only one workable arm.

"Thanks again for the flowers, Ms. Kimball," said Ginger. "I'm so glad you finally got to see the play after all you went through on Friday. It was nice of Ms. Atkins to step up, agreeing to be our temporary director so we could still go on."

"You are so welcome, Ginger. It went beautifully; your debut as Abby Brewster was spectacular, and I laughed so hard my ribs hurt even more. This time I was glad to see you actually had pie on the plate when you brought it out."

"Wasn't it amazingly cool that they gave Detective Sweeney a standing ovation when she came in with you? I could see it just around the edge of the curtain before it started. Maybe it will make her feel a little better since she still has to get over being shot."

Grace laughed at Ginger's serious expression. "I have a feeling Detective Sweeney will be fine, but it's going to take a lot of Lettie's pies to get her through rehab. That will be painful. Yes, people in town are so thankful she and Detective Williams found the culprit. They gave her a heartfelt tribute."

"To think the murderer was right there all along, our teacher! Really scary, Ms. Kimball. I knew she was strange, but I didn't realize she was scary violent," said Ginger. "We'll have to have a talk about that sometime. I'm not sure I understand the whole business. Makes me feel a little creepy."

"I'm available whenever you need me, right next door."

"Thank you, Grace," said Ginger's mom. "Now, young lady, you have an after-play party to go to at Ms. Atkins' house."

Grace closed the door behind them, wandering back into the living room, where Jeff was sitting in front of the fire. She still had a butterfly bandage closing the gash on her forehead, and one rib was bruised, so she'd just have to deal with the pain.

"More wine? I could go out to the kitchen for another bottle?"

"No," said Jeff, helping her gently down to the sofa. "I'm fine. Let's just be quiet here."

They sat a few moments in silence. The fire crackled and the room was invitingly warm. Only the two of them, thought Grace. How cozy.

"It was surprising to see that teacher, Marilyn Atkins, together with her husband tonight."

Grace nodded, taking a sip of wine. "After the play, she told me he was finally getting help with his alcohol problem. Contemplating murdering someone and trying to choke me were sobering wake-up calls. I'm glad she stepped up and helped with the play. The kids had worked so hard on it."

"I imagine the superintendent will need a new drama teacher and play director now."

Grace turned to him, a determined set to her chin. Lifting an eyebrow, she whispered, "Don't look at me. This is one time I will be saying no."

He chuckled and took her hand, holding it on his lap. "Do you think Johnson will be in trouble over that slip on her part to finger-print Amy Deffly?"

"Boy, good question. I don't know. Guess it depends on how the School Board feels. They're the ones who hire and fire. It did cost two lives. I can understand why it happened because school admin-istration isn't exactly what it used to be. I can remember when the superintendent was out in the buildings talking to people or discuss-ing policy. Now it appears to be a paperwork nightmare. I guess we'll see."

She moved herself slightly to get more comfortable with her sore rib.

"Lettie's cake was amazing tonight," he offered. "Boy, can she cook. You know, I had a thought. Maybe I should run it by you and see what you think."

"Sure," said Grace. "She's been putting weight on me for over twenty-five years."

"Well," he said, starting out slowly. "Here was my thought: down the road I'm going to turn Lockwood House into a bed and break-fast. You knew that, right?"

Grace nodded her head.

"Those are my plans; I think I may be on track to do the B & B in, say, three years. So, I have another idea for a project which will go with the B & B."

Grace squeezed his hand and said, "Really? Yet another project?"

"Absolutely. What would you think if I bought a little more of the lot on the north side of the house so Todd could rebuild the orig-inal carriage house? I'm sure we could design a very good-sized apartment in the upstairs. The first floor, of course, would be a garage for the visitors."

Grace leaned back, closing her eyes. "Sounds good to me. And who is going to live in this 'good-sized apartment' upstairs?"

"I thought I might ask Del Novak and, well, in three years he might even have a wife who would be willing to live there too. He could be the handyman/repair person, and she could be the cook for the B & B."

Grace suddenly opened her eyes. "What? Take Lettie away from me?"

"Well, not right away. In a few years. I would pay them, so they'd have a regular income to add to their pensions. Doesn't it seem like it would be a perfect situation for them?"

Grace frowned, taking in a semi-deep, painful breath. "You realize, of course, they'll be into their mid-seventies by then? How long do you think they want to work?"

"Those two? They'll be running rings around us when they're in their nineties."

Grace considered his plan. "Lettie is rather a good cook."

"Good? Are you kidding? She's spectacular."

"Does this mean I could keep her with me until you want to hire her?" asked Grace, trying to hide her apprehension.

"Of course. I had the thought that maybe by then we could be looking at you living in the house too. Well, officially, I mean. But, it's a bit early to think about 'officially.' At least, I figure that's what you're thinking . . . a bit early."

"You can read my mind, after all. But, alas, I can't read yours because you've only told me a little about what's happened to you. You have a lot of secrets, Jeff Maitlin."

He squeezed her hand and pursed his lips, thinking about what to say next. "Maybe we should fix the situation, especially since I want you to know I love you. I love you, Grace Kimball, and I would like you to marry me. There, I've said it for the first time in my life. I've lived in so many places since I left college, but never had anyone to care for me, nor anyone I've cared about like you. I think I must learn how to be together and not so alone, nor keep my own counsel. Was that what you had in mind?"

"It's a good start, Mr. Maitlin. So, how do you propose—oh, that's a scary word—to start fixing this situation? Do you have a plan?"

"I do. But, before I forget, I should mention I saw an article in a newspaper the other day at the office about a bed and breakfast that had a series of murders. It could be, I mean if you want to get involved in my B & B, you might still have to dodge a few bullets."

She looked up at the ceiling thoughtfully. "That sounds much more interesting than just fading quietly away."

He shook his head. "I'm beginning to understand TJ's concerns. I was afraid you'd say that."

"Your plan?"

"Oh, yes. I got sidetracked. I thought we might take a little trip—not a long one or the workers at the *Register* might mutiny. We could, say, go up to Chicago for a few days, and then go over to Indiana to visit the cemetery where my family is, and then spend some time in my small town. What do you think? Would it be enough of my past to give you some comfort instead of thinking I came out of nowhere?"

"Mmmmm—I think it sounds like a good start."

"Me too." He turned to Grace, giving her a long, lingering kiss.

"So where is this place—this small town where you grew up, which caused you to decide you wanted to live your later years in another small town? I don't believe we've ever talked about that, since someone wasn't actually talking." She looked at Jeff, watching his lips turn into a slow-moving smile.

"Grace, would you call me a superstitious person, someone who believes in signs?"

Grace thought for a moment. "Noooo . . . you seem like the hard-boiled, pragmatic city desk newspaper editor to me. You always have 'a plan.' Are you saying you have a side I don't know about?"

"Could be. I'd love to take you back home to all those places I told you about, and especially the small town in Indiana where I grew up." He turned to her, a real grin on his face.

"And what small town might that be?" she asked.

"It's a little town in Indiana called . . . Endurance."

Acknowledgments

I have grown to love these characters and the small town of Endurance over the past five years as I've been hearing their voices and setting their words on the page. It is with great reluctance that I bring their story to an end, trusting that Grace and TJ will remain close friends, Grace and Jeff will live their happily ever after plans, and Lettie and Del will be a part of that happily ever after too.

My deepest gratitude goes to two people who helped make this book, as well as the others, possible: my editor, Lourdes Venard, who offered guidance and advice throughout the editing process; and the best beta reader, proofreader, and friend an author could have, Hallie Lemon, retired English professor at Western Illinois University.

Readers may wonder about the creation of the school administrators and teachers in this book where Grace returns to Endurance High School. Despite teaching in a public high school for thirty-four years, I did not base any of my creations on colleagues I knew while I was teaching. They are all figments of my imagination. Grace's former students, however, have some semblance of reality in my past teaching life. That material was too good to pass up.

During the writing of this novel, I received expert advice from many people to whom I owe a debt of thanks. Detective Suzy Owens, of the Ames Police Department in Iowa, and Bruce Morath, chief deputy at the Warren County Sheriff's Department, gave me advice about police procedure.

Several administrators and teachers have helped along the way with information about recent changes in public schools and the operation of school boards. Jay Melton, principal of Monmouth-Roseville High School, District 238; and Galesburg District 205 teachers Jim Jacobs, Don Trinite, and Bobbi Uddin gave me valuable advice about changes in education laws.

When my laptop developed a serious dysfunction, Ben Bennett of Alpha Omega came to my rescue. He made sure my manuscript was backed up in case I experienced an unexpected computer death. Thank you, Ben. Whew!

And finally, I need to give a shout-out to the many residents, locations, and historical references in the small town of Monmouth, Illinois. They provide me daily with a rich trove of material on which to base my imaginary small town of Endurance.

Other Books Available by Susan Van Kirk

THE ENDURANCE MYSTERIES

Three May Keep a Secret
Endurance Mystery # 1

"Three may keep a secret, if two of them are dead."
—Benjamin Franklin

Grace Kimball, recently retired teacher in the small town of Endurance, is haunted by a dark, past event, an experience so terrifying she has never been able to put it behind her.

When shoddy journalist, Brenda Norris, is murdered in a suspicious fire, Grace is hired by the newspaper editor, Jeff Maitlin, to fill in for Brenda, researching the town's history. Unfortunately, that past hides dark secrets. When yet a second murder occurs, Grace's friend, TJ Sweeney, a homicide detective, races against time to find a killer. Even Grace's life will be threatened by her worst nightmare.

Against a backdrop of the town's 175th founder's celebration, Grace and Jeff find an undeniable attraction for each other. But can she trust this mystery man with no past?

Praise for *Three May Keep a Secret*

"Readers will love meeting the residents of Endurance, Illinois. Grace Kimball and her intrepid friends court disaster as they investigate who is keeping a dark secret."
—Terry Shames, National Bestselling author of the Samuel Craddock mysteries

"Van Kirk's appealing mystery debut . . . introduces recently retired Grace Kimball. Cozy fans will find a lot to like."

—Publishers Weekly Review

"Van Kirk's debut novel, following a memoir of her own days as a teacher, offers a promising new heroine who's clever, observant and smart enough to admit when she's been fooled."

—Kirkus Reviews

Available from Five Star Publishing (Cengage) in hard cover, soft cover/large print, and e-book. Find it online at Amazon, Barnes and Noble, or at your nearest library.

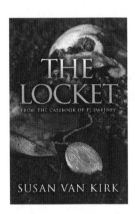

The Locket:
From the Casebook of TJ Sweeney
An Endurance Novella

The Big Band Era—Dancing on the Rooftop— Romance in the Air—And Murder in the Shadows.

". . . *the dispatcher called to tell her it was time to move the bones . . .*"

After solving a double homicide in the hot Midwest summer, Endurance police detective TJ Sweeney isn't given long to rest. A construction crew has found human bones while digging a building foundation on the outskirts of town.

Sweeney's investigation soon concludes this was a murder victim, but from many decades earlier. Trying to identify the remains and put a name to the killer takes the detective through a maze of dead ends and openings, twists, and turns.

And then it becomes personal . . .

The Locket: From the Casebook of TJ Sweeney is available as an e-book from Amazon.com and the Kindle Store at Amazon.com.

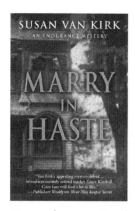

Marry in Haste
Endurance Mystery # 2

"Marry in Haste, Repent at Leisure"
—Benjamin Franklin

It is 2012 in the small town of Endurance, and wealthy banker, Conrad Folger, is murdered and his wife, Emily, arrested. Emily Folger was one of Grace Kimball's students in the past, and Grace knows Emily could never murder anyone. So, Grace joins Detective TJ Sweeney to investigate the murder, and they uncover a dark secret.

In 1893, Olivia Havelock, age seventeen, moves to Endurance to seek a husband. She finds one in Charles Lockwood, powerful and wealthy judge, but her diary reveals a terrifying story.

Two wives—two murders a century apart—and a shocking secret connects them. *Marry in Haste* is a story of the resilience of women, both in the past and the present.

Praise for *Marry in Haste*

"Her characters feel real, and her town of Endurance authentic and easily recognizable to those who have lived in small town America. Incisive and intriguing."
  —Anna Lee Huber, National Bestselling Author of the Lady Darby mysteries, the Gothic Myths series, and the Verity Kent Mysteries

"A retired teacher struggles to solve two murders committed decades apart. Van Kirk balances present and past crimes deftly in her second foray into detection."
                                                        —Kirkus Reviews 10/2016

Available from Five Star Publishing (Cengage) in hard cover and e-book. Find it online at Amazon, Barnes and Noble, or at your nearest library.

About the Author

Susan Van Kirk was educated at Knox College and the University of Illinois. After college, she taught high school English for thirty-four years in the small town of Monmouth, Illinois. Some of Grace's fictional memories are loosely based on that experience.

Van Kirk taught an additional ten years at Monmouth College. Her short story, "War and Remembrance," was published by *Teacher Magazine* and became one of the chapters in her popular creative nonfiction memoir, *The Education of a Teacher (Including Dirty Books and Pointed Looks)*.

Three May Keep a Secret was her first Endurance Mystery. An e-book novella about her detective followed, called *The Locket: From the Casebook of TJ Sweeney*. The second Endurance mystery, *Marry in Haste*, was published in 2016. The title for *Death Takes No Bribes*, like each novel in her series, is based on a proverb by Benjamin Franklin.

Van Kirk is a member of Sisters in Crime and Mystery Writers of America.

Visit her website at www.susanvankirk.com, or follow her on Facebook, Twitter @susan_vankirk, or Pinterest (The Endurance Mysteries)